About the Author

Martha Twine was born in London in 1948. She moved to Surrey in 1956. Educated at Guildford County School, she worked for over forty years in the public sector, mainly in London and the North East, during which time she gained an accountancy qualification, and worked in finance. She is now retired and lives in Haslemere, where she enjoys gardening and singing in local choirs.

Terror in Britain

Martha Twine

Terror in Britain

Olympia Publishers

London

www.olympiapublishers.com
OLYMPIA PAPERBACK EDITION

A CIP catalogue record for this title is
available from the British Library.

ISBN: 978-1-78830-166-4

This is a work of fiction.
Names, characters, places and incidents originate from the writer's imagination. Any
resemblance to actual persons, living or dead, is purely coincidental.

First Published in 2018

Olympia Publishers
60 Cannon Street
London
EC4N 6NP

Printed in Great Britain

TERROR IN BRITAIN

A British woman's ordeal at the hands of international terrorists,
inside the secret world of electromagnetic weapons.

INTRODUCTION

I worked for a public-sector organisation in the UK, and part of my work involved visiting countries outside the European Union. In 2010, I was working in Turkey. One warm night, I had just come back to my hotel from a meal in a local fish restaurant with my colleagues, when I noticed a black dot in front of my eyes, like an enormous floater, with white flashes when I moved my eyes in the dark.

When I got back to the UK, I went for an eye check-up as the black dot had become like a giant tadpole, constantly swimming in front of my right eye. I was told that there was nothing wrong with my vision, apart from a large floater.

'Is there anything you can do about that?' I asked.

'No,' I was told, 'there is nothing to worry about, and nothing you need to do. Just ignore it.'

Much later, I discovered that the black dot was in fact a Nano-camera and transmitter that had been inserted into the eye cavity through the nose, while I had been anaesthetised in my hotel room at night by those who wished me ill. They also inserted a microchip into the back of my head, so that they could locate me using wi-fi. The scale of these inserts was tiny.

But if the inserts were tiny, how did I know they were there? In the case of the microchip, I heard terrorist perpetrators describing to each other how it worked. I proved it to myself by using shielding materials which blocked the wi-fi transmitter, such as waterproof hoods and plastic hard hats. When I put on the shielding devices, the terrorists complained that they had lost track of me, and were unable to target me without sophisticated equipment.

It is hard to believe that an ordinary person like myself could be microchipped without realising it, but, as I discovered, criminals and terrorists today have copied advanced technologies from the military and science research organisations, and we need to get wise to that. The Nano-transmitter in my eye, when activated remotely by enemies of our country, could take and transmit photographs, using a method similar to email. When the camera was full, the floater in my eye was large, and when it had emailed its contents, it was noticeably smaller. The espionage applications were obvious. If there had been anything of interest to terrorists in my job, they would have seen it.

In 2013, I decided to have lenses put in my eyes, to block the signals being transmitted through the retina. The procedure worked. The terrorists could no longer send photographs to each other. But I still had a microchip in the back of my head, which enabled them to track my movements.

Other colleagues in my office who went on overseas business were also targeted. Looking back on it, I can understand what happened, but at the time, the main things I noticed in my colleagues were poor concentration, inability to work, bone problems and back pains. These symptoms all came on shortly after they attended a series of conferences in Eastern Europe.

I put it down to their age: they were all in their late fifties or early sixties. Perhaps lifestyle choices, not enough exercise, too much fried food, late nights or overwork had played a part in their apparent decline? Then one of my colleagues started talking to himself, as if having private conversations, and I began to wonder whether he might have mental health issues. He was off sick intermittently for six months, but it was not clear what was wrong with him.

It was about two years later when I found out, through talking to terrorists, that a group of London-based IRA activists, with connections to Al-Qaida in North Africa and the Mafia in Canada, thought that my office was involved in some kind of unofficial overseas diplomatic work, and had decided to spy on us. It appeared that the IRA had managed to penetrate a counter-terrorism office with connections to the London Metropolitan Police, and had

persuaded them to permit technical surveillance of my office. (I should add that they were removed by the Met Police, sometime in 2012).

Terrorists sometimes target charity workers, when they work in developing countries, mistakenly suspecting them of working as intelligence officers. This is similar to what happened to us. The difference, in our case, was that we were being targeted on our return home to our own country by IRA terrorists posing as British citizens.

The terrorists wanted to spy on my office through the camera in my eye, but I retired from my job shortly afterwards, and they lost interest in me. However, the technologies in my head made me a valuable investment. They sold access to me to some people-traffickers who worked closely with the IRA and Al-Qaida in the South of England, with instructions to assassinate me, once the traffickers had made as much money as they could from using me as a practice target for IRA training courses on the operation of laser guns and electromagnetic weapons.

These training courses were part of Al-Qaida's wider plan to take over Europe, and to put the population in prison camps. Al-Qaida organised large scale training for its adherents in how to run covert electronic prison camps, and how to control and terminate people in them systematically. I was used as a target for such activities in a series of training camps and courses over a period of four years.

This book is about what happened to me. Most of it happened in Britain. Incredibly, it all ended happily, thanks to: British Intelligence; our counter-terrorism people; Special Services; the RAF; and, in particular, Her Majesty's Prison Service. But there were many innocent victims, like myself, who suffered and died in their homes as a result of targeting by enemies of Britain, funded largely by Al-Qaida, with the objective of getting rid of Europeans covertly and replacing them with terrorists from North Africa, Asia and the Middle East.

The technologies used to make people fall ill are not new. Some of them involve microwave radiation beams, and others use sonic devices. There are precedents in the public domain. In the 1950s, it

was alleged, though not proved, that the US embassy in Moscow was being targeted with damaging microwaves. Three US Ambassadors to the USSR got sick and died of cancer. More recently, on 10 August 2017, it was announced that the US had expelled two Cuban diplomats after US embassy staff in Havana suffered 'mysterious physical symptoms'. *See the notes under the heading 'Introduction', at the back of this book, for references.*

The main targets in the UK were old people, because it is less suspicious when elderly folk get sick and die. The terrorists' UK work force was drawn from ex-convicts – particularly those convicted of child sex abuse, people in debt and drug addicts. Children were trafficked from France at an early age so that they would not be traced in the UK. They were put to work in child brothels and later trained as child soldiers under the Al-Qaida regime.

There was an extensive paedophile ring which had grown up around the IRA locally. People convicted of such offences were blackmailed into working against their country, and their perversions were tolerated by their IRA masters. I became conscious of this when paedophiles were given the job of monitoring what I was looking at through my eye camera.

When I went in the supermarket, the place was heaving with young kids; climbing in and out of the shopping trolleys, and running around in the shopping aisles. I noticed an intrusion on the direction of my gaze, as if someone was trying to 'drive' and change the direction of what I looked at. My gaze was being skewed towards toddlers. It turned out that the paedophiles were taking photos of the kids through my eyes, and then sending them to each other. I found this so distasteful that, whenever I saw a child, I averted my eyes.

THE ATTACKS BEGIN

I lived in a dull red-brick block of four flats, in a grimy part of Greater London. One day, when I went to collect my post from the communal post box area, I noticed that I, and my neighbour Francine, had both received letters in the same hand-writing. When I opened my letter, it was from a man with an Asian-sounding name, who was offering to buy my flat, quoting a rather unreasonable price. He said that he wanted to live near his relatives in the next block of flats. I wondered why the occupants of the other two flats in our block had not received similar letters. Then it occurred to me that they might be known to him already, and could even be relatives of his, as they belonged to the local Asian community, and were often seen coming and going with the occupants of the next block of flats. I thought nothing more of the letter, and put it in the bin.

A few weeks later, I had just come back from visiting a friend, when I began to feel incredibly sleepy. The next thing I remembered was waking up on my bed. It was two p.m., but a moment before, the clock had shown twelve noon.

'Why am I lying on my bed?' I wondered.

I could feel something like a staple under the skin behind my left ear. The back of my head felt tight. I glanced down at my right hand. There was a red mark like a recent shot from a hypodermic syringe. I knew that something was wrong. I decided to photograph the red mark on my hand. At that moment, I caught sight of a strange bruise below my left knee. I ran my hand over the area. I could feel two raised objects beneath the skin. I photographed the bruise.

'What is going on?' I thought.

For a moment, I felt strangely excited by the mystery of the situation. Then I realized that real life has no mysteries. I shrugged my shoulders and decided to go to the supermarket. It was a long time before I realised that local terrorists living in the flat above mine had been instrumental in putting more transmitters and tracking devices into my body, using local wave-lengths which their equipment was tuned to. The original chips in my body were linked by wi-fi to private commercial satellite, owned by Al-Qaida, with a global range, similar to a cellphone, but the local terrorists did not have access to them.

As I locked the door to my apartment I heard my neighbour Francine talking loudly on the staircase below.

'You can't do that to people. Stop it! Let me go!'

I watched her leave our apartment block. There was no one with her.

'Perhaps she is talking to someone on one of those earphone devices. Surely, she can't be talking to herself?' I thought.

As I followed her down the street I could still hear her voice…

'Oh, my God! Those poor people! They're cutting their arms off. I can't stand it. Help! Someone!'

Francine started waving and shouting, visibly distressed. Passers-by pointed and whispered to each other. I turned the corner to the supermarket, and she was gone from my view.

Later that evening, there was an ambulance outside where we lived. I heard men talking in low voices. A stretcher was being eased into the ambulance. It was Francine.

I learned that Francine had been sectioned with some mental illness. In the days that passed, her apartment was put up for sale, and quickly taken by someone related to people in the next housing block. I gathered that it had been bought by an Asian property developer, who was going to use it for rentals.

One night I had a strange dream, not like a normal dream. It was as if I was half asleep, passively watching a technicolor movie. There were a lot of young men and women being herded into what looked like an underground room. Then, unbelievably, as I watched in

horror, their arms were being removed with a chainsaw. There was blood everywhere. I woke in shock.

'This cannot happen,' I told myself.

I wondered if Francine had been exposed to a similarly disturbing visual display.

I made breakfast and listened to the radio, to take my mind off the dream. As I looked out of the window, to the house opposite, my heart missed a beat. I saw a young Asian woman leaving the building. I recognised her. She had been one of the perpetrators in my dream. But now she looked soberly dressed and composed. I began to wonder whether it was possible for visual images to be beamed across the street.

'But how could that happen?' I wondered, 'It just couldn't, that's all.'

Much later, it emerged that the Asians across the road were part of a drug-trafficking ring affiliated to Al-Qaida. The Asian family living in the flat above my own were of different ethnic origin, but belonged to the same group. Their flat was used to get access to me at close range, using light beam technologies. By now they had a CD of biodata about me, and wi-fi transmitter references to the chips in my body, which, with infrared scanners, enabled them to pinpoint the exact position of my body when lying in bed or sitting in my main room. They wanted to use our block of flats as a base for their illegal activities, and their job was to get me out.

I decided to find out more about what had happened to Francine. The mental institution that she had been consigned to was some way off. I established that she could be visited in the afternoons, and made an appointment to see her. Francine was looking most unsettled. Her hair was unkempt, and she appeared to have developed a tremor in her hands, something that I would have associated with a degenerative disease, rather than a mental health issue. She walked slowly and hesitantly, as if exhausted.

She smiled when I arrived.

'So good of you to come,' she whispered, and grabbed my hand, pressing it warmly.

'How are you?' I asked.

Francine's face clouded over. She looked around to make sure that no one could hear her.

'It's terrible here,' she said. 'They are forcing me to eat food when I don't want to, and drugs, nothing but drugs. I am a prisoner, and no one can help me.'

'Can you tell me a bit about what has happened?' I asked.

Francine began her story, in a low tentative voice, and I had to strain to hear some of her words. She had obviously been sedated, but still exhibited fear, as she recounted what, in her view, had happened.

'There are people talking in my ears,' she said. 'I know what you're thinking - *she's gone mad,* but they are not imaginary people. They are really there. They hate me, and they can hurt me with pinches and pricks. It is horrible. One day something happened. I don't know what it was, but I went out of my mind. I thought I was in a mortuary, with dead bodies everywhere. I really lost it, and I don't remember anything else in detail for some time. But now I am in this place.'

'Did you notice anything out of the ordinary before you got sick?' I asked.

'Not really,' said Francine, 'Except …. Well it's probably nothing, but I noticed a red mark on my hand that hadn't been there before, and it's still there: look!'

Francine pointed to her hand. There was a round indent, and a faint discoloration. I gasped. I had seen something similar on my own hand just a few days ago.

'That looks like a needle mark,' I said. 'You could have been drugged.' Francine nodded

'I know, I thought that too, but it doesn't make any sense. Who could have done it, and how? The psychiatrist says I have bipolar disorder and schizophrenia. If I mention anything more about what happened, they'll say I'm paranoid.' Francine sighed despairingly.

'I now wonder if I will ever get out of here. Those invisible people are still there hurting me during the day, but the terrible dreams I was having have gone. I'm on sleeping pills now, you see.' She smiled regretfully.

'Do you have any friends here?' I asked.

'Yes,' Francine nodded. 'There are some kind people here: the nurses, you know; and some of the patients, but it makes me sad to see their mental suffering.'

It was time to go, and I said goodbye. As I left, I had an image of Francine waving from the door, calling after me, 'Thank you, thank you!'

I wished that there was something I could do, but I felt helpless, knowing so little about Francine's life and current situation.

After three months, Francine came out of hospital and went to stay with her son and his wife. I was surprised to see that she was extremely calm and collected. A year later, her mental health was back to normal, but she had been forced out of her flat, and the terrorists had got what they wanted.

IT STARTS HAPPENING TO ME

I woke early one morning, and was drifting off to sleep again, when I heard two people, a man and a woman, talking quietly. It sounded some way off, and yet it seemed to be in my head.

'Do you want some coffee?'

'Mmm.'

'I'm going out tonight. How about you?'

'No, I've no time; too busy.'

'Shh, I think she is waking up, the green light is on.' Then I heard two other women's voices.

'Oh, is she? Well, I expect we'll have to watch her dress, then....'

'But perhaps she wants to run to the toilet first,' the voices mocked.

The two women burst into hostile laughter. It all sounded rather artificial. I switched the radio on, and they went away, but through the day, when there was silence, they came back. And then there were other voices of men and women, making derogatory comments intended to discomfort me.

Occasionally, when they thought that I was distracted with friends, I could hear them holding their own conversations. They were not happy people. They sounded afraid, as if a supervisor might catch them chatting. They had money worries. It sounded as if they were being paid to talk at me. Perhaps they were out-of-work actors. They certainly worked long hours.

It was about a week later that I noticed things happening in the house. When I sat in my favorite chair it would start to shake slightly, in the small of my back. At first, I thought that it was lorries

going by, but it became a regular effect. Then, one day, I went to the hairdresser, and the same thing happened there. When I was going to sleep, I noticed a tingling feeling start to flow over my legs and up my body. For the first few nights that was all it was, but then I began to feel sharp pricks in my legs and knees.

'Someone is definitely getting at me,' I thought, 'but why?'

It soon became clear that someone wanted me out of my apartment for good.

I began to hear scratching on my ceiling. It sounded like rats. It was rats. Now I am sure that the poor rats were there through no fault of their own, but there they were, and one day there was one in my kitchen. I called the pest inspector and he advised me to put down warfarin. That seemed to solve the problem.

Life went back to normal. I got used to the intrusive voices and ignored them. I went out with my friends, pursued my interest in photography, and spent long hours reading all the books that I never had time to read before my retirement. Not going to work anymore was so wonderful; every day I would float down the street, perfectly happy, without any particular reason, just because I didn't have to get up and hurry to work.

Then, one day I was skyping with a couple of my friends, Peter and Jan in North America, and they seemed distressed. They were trying to tell me that something bad had happened to them, but could not bring themselves to say exactly what it was.

'You tell her,' said Peter, 'I can't talk.' There were tears in his voice.

Jan began to talk about how they had been involved in some scam, in which two Asian men had offered a lot of money to help their charitable work to combat drugs dependence, but then the men had met them and something had happened to Jan. I could not gather what had happened, but I began to suspect that some kind of sexual assault was being described. Peter had been present, but had been prevented from acting to save her.

I became aware of a fine grid superimposed over the inside of my computer screen. It was as if my friends could not hear what I was saying. Talking very slowly, I said that there was interference on

the line, and suggested that we should try later. They got my message. We tried again later, and it was OK this time. They told me that they could no longer live in the States and were coming home as soon as possible. They had their flights booked for two weeks' time.

The day before they were due to fly home, I had a distraught email from Peter. Jan had been rushed to hospital with a heart attack. She had had a lifesaving operation, but could not travel for at least two weeks, and the couple had already vacated their apartment, so they had nowhere to stay. The same day, Peter had a phone call from England to tell him that his elderly mother had been admitted to a mental institution, with symptoms of psychosis, something that she had never suffered from before.

Peter and I worked together to make arrangements as best we could to find a place for him and Jan to stay, and, two weeks to the day after her heart operation, after being given the go-ahead by her doctor, Jan flew home with Peter. It wasn't easy, because of Jan's health, but they made it. Shortly afterwards, Peter visited his mother. As soon as she saw him, she was back to normal, and was released from the mental institution. Clinicians were at a loss to explain what had happened to her, as she had received a complete check-up just before the incident, and had been given a clean bill of health.

It was a year before I was able to make any sense of the disasters that had happened to Peter and Jan. They had a successful business helping people to come off drugs, and it turned out that the North American mafia, who ran drug trafficking as a core income activity, did not want people like that on their territory.

The next night I smelled a strange chemical smell in my apartment. I opened the windows, but it became stronger. In my bedroom, it became intolerable. I just could not breathe. I went for a walk. When I came back I could smell the chemicals coming down the hallway. I spent the night with my head stuck out of the window, and, in the morning, I packed my bags and left my apartment for good. Like Francine, I went home, back to my elderly father.

As I got on the train from London, I had the distinct feeling that 'they' were following me. The train was packed, and I had to walk through the aisles to find a seat. It felt as if someone was

'influencing' me remotely to sit in a particular place. Later I was to learn about the technology used to achieve this effect. I was determined to resist, and pressed on. Then I saw a woman vacate her seat, and I gratefully sat down in it.

What a lot I had to learn. Placeholders are people who occupy seats for specific purposes. Once you are aware of this, it is not so hard to detect them, but I had no idea of that then. Sitting opposite me were a very odd couple. Both in their early seventies, the gentleman was short and paunchy with a paper-white face, as if he was wearing make-up to cover some surgical scars.

He held a walking stick which had a strange horizontal handle, and every so often he bent down and appeared to be blowing or whispering into it. He did this particularly when attractive young women appeared, and I began to suspect that he was operating a covert photographic device for nefarious purposes. His female companion was exceptionally tall, with broad shoulders. Her silver hair brushed her collar, and she had a confident air.

At first, they did not seem aware of me. It sounded as if they might even be talking about me, as I caught the phrase 'working in Turkey'. All of a sudden, the woman looked up and met my eye. She clearly recognized me. She gave her companion's hand a squeeze and they both stared pointedly out of the window, as if trying not to laugh. They maintained an embarrassed silence until I left the carriage.

Who were they? Were they after me? These were questions which I tried to answer in the weeks ahead. But it was three years before I discovered that they were senior IRA officers, whose job included the management of attacks on victims like myself, as part of a wider remit to attack British citizens, funded by Al-Qaida. The man with the white face had survived a bomb blast while in service to the IRA. He had undergone extensive facial plastic surgery, and wore make-up to conceal the scars.

EARLY LIFE WITH THE TERRORISTS

One of the basic duties the terrorists had to fulfil was guard duty for prisoners. This meant watching me as far as possible 24 x 7, in every room of the house, subject to there being microdot cameras on the walls. A team of technicians had previously placed Nano-cameras around the house, while my father and I were out. This was not hard to do, as the locks on our doors were old fashioned and easy to copy.

The terrorists used wi-fi linked to private commercial satellite to watch me remotely, and communicate with each other about my doings via synthetic telepathy. Watching me pottering around the garden for hours made the terrorists irritable. An elderly man and woman, who had been blackmailed by the IRA into accepting their guard duty role, found it hard to sit there in observation mode, especially as they were experienced gardeners, and I was not. I was a beginner, getting excited by basic plant stuff, and making a lot of mistakes.

Every week, I raced to the supermarket to see if there were any cheap plants I could bring home. There often were. Then I would dig a small hole in the ground to put the plant in – or, as one Pakistani terrorist observed to his IRA colleagues, 'She seems to be burying things again.'

But quite often, the plant would not come out of the pot. The plant had been growing there so long that its roots had wound right round the inside of the pot several times, and it would not budge. I spent ages with a pair of secateurs trying to cut the plastic pot off the plant. This was not clever.

In desperation one day, after I had struggled for nearly forty minutes with a plastic pot, the elderly female terrorist broke her silence.

'Try filling the pot up with water and leaving it for a bit. Then turn the pot upside down and the plant will come out,' she said.

I tried this, and it worked. In fact, I have been doing it ever since, and it works every time.

Another time the terrorists came to my aid, not so much in my interests as in theirs. I got locked out of my Apple Mac computer, and could not remember the password. I contacted Apple, but they said that the only way they could help me was to write to some central office, where an envelope containing my overriding pass key was kept securely. This would take time and cost money. The password I had chosen was a word I'd heard used by the terrorists; I tried to remember it, but it escaped me.

Not being able to get into my computer meant that the terrorists could not earn extra money by trying to frustrate my attempts to write my blog. I was stuck, and so were the terrorists. I could not put photos of plants and flowers on my blog, and there was less for these virtual prison guards to do to enhance their earnings. Then, one night while I was lying in bed, the male terrorist just told me my password; straight out.

The word was 'cavitation.' When the male terrorist told me what my password was, I leaped out of bed and went to my laptop to try it out. It worked. I was so relieved. I went to update my blog immediately.

I first heard the word 'cavitation' used by terrorists in the context of some of their remote attacks. When I looked it up on the internet, I found that it meant: *'an ultrasonic cavitation device is a surgical device using low frequency ultrasound energy to dissect or fragment tissues with low fiber content. It is basically an ultrasound probe (acoustic vibrator) combined with an aspirator device (suction). It is mainly used for tissues with high water content and low fiber content, like noncirrhotic liver and pancreas'*

That sounded to me like an ultrasound laser, which could be used to carry out procedures on vital organs. I wondered if the terrorists used this technology for harmful purposes.

I enjoyed doing Sudoku, especially after a meal. I had books full of these number puzzles, and spent hours poring over them. I had my own method of working out where the missing numbers should go. I had never shared this with anyone else, but it worked for me.

After a while, I heard the elderly male terrorist telling his female companion that I had invented a foolproof method which would enable anyone to do Sudoku. He started teaching it to his colleagues, and even thought of bringing out a book about it.

Leaving aside the merits of my method of doing Sudoku, these minor incidents show how synthetic telepathy could be used to spy on the silent thoughts of another, and gain information from them.

The IRA ran training courses on how to hack into people's computers and smartphones. Being linked to a synthetic telepathy network meant that the terrorists would always hear me thinking my password, as I logged onto my iPad. When I bought things on Amazon, they knew my Amazon password. Terrorists started trying to hack into my Amazon account. But they were unaware that security was now a lot tighter. Unless the password you put in matched the IP address of the device you were hacking into, you could not fool the system into thinking that you were someone else.

Some female IRA trainees hacked into my Amazon account, and decided to buy something that I had ordered in the past, and send it to themselves. But because they were not using my iPad, Amazon would not authorise the payment from my credit card. Instead, it asked for a different card. The young terrorists used their manager's card. The only address that Amazon would deliver the goods to in these circumstances was mine. I was most surprised when Amazon informed me that my order for Guarana Jungle Elixir energy shots, at a price of £15, would be delivered in a few days' time. I knew I had not ordered it.

'Well, let's see if it's delivered,' I thought. 'And then let's see if I have to pay for it'.

Sure enough the goods arrived, and what a joy it was to discover that I had received a free gift from the IRA. Amazon was not so impressed with the transaction, however. Their security people picked up what had happened, and after that, whenever I logged in, it sent me an email with a secret code that I had to input, in order to proceed any further. So the terrorists were stuffed after that. A pity! I had a few expensive things on my wish list; but it was not to be.

About this time, I discovered another feature of being linked up to the terrorists' electromagnetic environment. Sometimes I woke up in the night and, with my eyes shut, found myself watching events that were not intended for my eyes, because IRA technicians forgot to disengage my access link. When a group of IRA terrorists from the UK attended a US mafia training course based in Los Angeles and Utah, I found myself watching events on the course. When an IRA terrorist fled to California to escape his debts, his enemies in the IRA were keeping tabs on him. I woke up to find myself looking at the inside of a hotel bedroom where he was staying. A porn movie was being filmed in the bedroom. The hotel looked out on the beach, and I recognised it as San Diego.

These experiences were more than just watching a movie screen. It felt as if I was there. On one occasion, I witnessed a terrorist training conference in the Czech Republic, where the IRA were demonstrating the use of electromagnetic weapons at night. I was walking along a corridor in a former Communist State building that had been turned into a conference centre. There was a carpet made from a strong rough weave in the middle of the floor, and as I walked, I could feel it under my feet.

There were a number of doors along the corridor, one of which was open. Terrorists from our local unit were giving lessons on how to attack victims using telemetry, infrared devices and electronic weapons. A group of people, including small children, were sitting around on chairs and window ledges. As I walked past a door, one of the children on the window ledge looked up and saw me. Our eyes met briefly, but I was actually at home in bed in the UK.

Early life with the IRA terrorists followed a fairly standard routine as follows:

- Waking triggered by microwave radiation beam to the head
- Aggressive synthetic telepathy attacks – voices of women and men, threatening various forms of violence
- Attempts to void my bladder or bowel involuntarily, using microwave radiation beams.

During all this, I would get up as normal and have breakfast. If I went to the toilet, the terrorists would turn on electromagnetic oscillators that alternately raised and lowered the gravity of parts of the body, slowing down my movements, like climbing a hill, while making comments about my removal of clothing, etc. When I got dressed, they would make comments about my physical appearance, and what I was doing. The verbal attacks via synthetic telepathy continued intermittently throughout the day, whenever I was not talking to people or listening to the radio or television. I bought a clip-on radio that I could wear when I went out, and this largely removed the problem.

If I went out in a car, they were left behind, but if I walked to the shops, they would track me via wi-fi with electromagnetic oscillators, operated by two terrorists, attempting to make each step I took very heavy, causing walking to be slow and difficult. After a couple of years, I learned that dragging a stick with a bit of rubber or plastic on the end, like a walking stick, prevented the attacks. Also, pushing a shopping trolley reduced the efficiency of the attacks.

If I went on a long car journey, the terrorists would practice tracking my car, using two cars of their own, one in front and one behind. The cars changed position from time to time, while their occupants tried to snipe at me with electronic weapons. The terrorists liked these outings, because they got extra money for them.

If I used my laptop, the perpetrators would hack into it via the house wiring, preventing access to the internet, and causing screen freezes. I had an internet blog, which I updated regularly. The terrorists would attempt to hack in, and alter what I wrote, making deliberate spelling mistakes, or altering the format. Eventually my laptop was completely broken. Then I bought a stronger one with an aluminum case, and better software security. I hardly used it on line, or connected it to house wiring. That stopped the attacks.

Sometimes, when I sat indoors, they would target my breathing through the nasal passages, seeking to replace oxygen in my lungs with carbon dioxide. This was only possible at close range. I discovered that they were operating from a window of the house next door. The asphyxiation process involved laser-beam delivery of carbon dioxide to the nostrils, in the form of a fine mist. I discovered that piglets are killed in abattoirs by replacing the oxygen in their lungs with carbon dioxide. I could combat this by opening the window and leaning out, or going outside. As I have asthma, these attacks posed a more serious threat than others, but my inhaler greatly reduced their impact.

Another asphyxiation technique used was to target the internal lining of my nose. This was done by delivering a plastic-like substance in a fine mist to the nostrils, using a carbon dioxide laser as a delivery agent, and then applying a microwave radiation beam to the area, which caused the plastic to expand inside the nasal cavity. Blowing the nose removed the plastic fairly quickly.

I could sometimes smell chemicals in the room, possibly delivered by the same method. Opening the window soon cleared the air, and I always slept with the window open. I found that drinking liquid oxygen drops helped to clear the brain of toxic gases or chemicals. But I wondered how elderly people in nursing homes or hospitals would fare, if subjected to similar attacks.

If I sat regularly in one place, the terrorists would target me with gravity-shifting oscillators. When I was in bed, they scanned the bed with a microwave radiation beam, which registered the silhouette of my body on a screen. They also used an infra-red device to establish my position on the bed. Then they targeted various parts of my body with close-range microwave laser beams, also known as maser beams, which caused varying degrees of pain.

A female terrorist of Pakistani extraction, known to associates as Esme, directed a microwave radiation beam at my hair. She succeeded in making it brittle, and bits broke off. One of the male terrorists set a microwave laser to target a point on my leg. I could move to avoid it, but if I was asleep, I sustained some minor burns, and one ulcer on my lower leg. The microwave weapon had a safety

device which meant that it switched off automatically after ten minutes, but that is still quite a long time to be exposed to microwave radiation, night after night.

Eventually I bought an EMF (electromagnetic field) shielding mosquito net, which blocked all further microwave radiation attacks. I had to order it from Germany, and it cost £800, but it solved the microwave problem. It did not prevent laser attacks, but I found that various plastics, plastic ground sheets and aluminum, including layers of folded aluminum foil also worked well as shielding devices. After that, the terrorists' attacks were reduced to a steady state, in which they sniped at me when they could, and attacked me with oscillators the rest of the time.

A friend of mine who lived in the North East was also being targeted by the IRA. She told me that she woke up one November morning with a horizontal break across one of her front teeth. A couple of weeks later the same thing happened to me. The break was horizontal and clean. I hurried to my dentist. He looked at me almost accusingly, as if I were hiding some domestic violence incident from him. I assured him that this was not the case. He seemed unconvinced.

'Come and look at this,' he said to his dental assistant, 'You're unlikely ever to see something like it again. The only time you might see it would be if a boxer got hit in the face, or perhaps as a result of a car crash'.

The dentist fixed my tooth expertly, and forgave me for presenting him with such trying symptoms.

Another form of attack carried out by the perpetrators caused sudden short-term loss of memory and concentration, either what you were about to say, or a particular word in your mind. The device, known to perpetrators as a 'faser', probably involved a kind of microwave laser beam device. I have seen it used on friends and family members when they were close to me. It can be particularly dangerous if targeted at motorists.

I was frequently targeted with sleep deprivation. In the morning, chemicals were sprayed from a gas canister into my bedroom, from a room in the house next door. The chemicals got into my system.

Then, in the evening, traces of the chemicals, which had got into the brain, were exposed to a microwave radiation beam, which expanded the chemicals, blocking normal sleep mechanisms. The objective of sleep deprivation was to make me available for targeting throughout the night, offering income-earning opportunities for terrorists. I tried to make up sleep during the day, spending more time in bed, which reduced my day-time activities.

I was targeted with painful laser beams on the hip joints. A number of my neighbors, those within range of the IRA safe houses, also reported similar symptoms. Of course, arthritis of the hip is widespread within the population, and it would be difficult to say whether criminal intervention had played a part in it. What I can say, was that I never had any pain before, and if I put gold nine-thousand-gauss-neodymium magnets on the pain spots, it went away, and my joints never troubled me again. The perpetrators tried moving the electronic weapon to a different spot, either the other hip, or a nearby body point; but when I applied more magnets, that was the end of the attacks.

On two occasions, I was attacked by North African Daesh extremists with a special kind of radiation beam which caused painful muscle contractions in the legs. Though intense, the attacks did not leave a mark on the body, so it could not have been a Taser. Luckily, I had a MEDICUR device to hand, which instantly switched off these attacks. The device describes itself as 'Pulsed Electromagnetic Field Therapy'. It operates within the range of 3-20 Hz. But if you didn't have something like that within reach – and who does, normally? - the results would have been agonizing.

This list of attacks sounds horrendous, and it is. But some of the methods used were not typical of the terrorist community. It turned out that I lived near a covert North American mafia research facility where these technologies were available to perpetrators. I managed to discover remedies and shielding devices, but I heard of other British citizens who were victims of these attacks, who did not know what was happening, and who had no defence.

Some of the technologies used by terrorists had valid clinical or industrial purposes. But terrorists and the North American mafia had

seen how they could be used covertly as harmful weapons. Apparently, electronic and electromagnetic weapons are commonplace within the criminal and terrorist communities of central Asia. Over the next three to four years, I met several unethical North American mafia scientists, working in research bases underneath large country houses owned by the IRA, who spent their time carrying out high technology attacks on local British citizens. These operations were funded by Al-Qaida. The point of these attacks was that they were invisible to the victims and could be carried out remotely by perpetrators without fear of detection.

Originally, the terrorists thought that they would make money by enrolling me in illegal human research trials, and offering me as a consensual human subject for legitimate research trials, forging all the paperwork. They entered me with several different made-up names and addresses at once, and facilitated several experimental remote procedures on me at the same time. But I found ways to shield myself and block their attacks, so they ended up out of pocket. Shortly afterwards, they were caught using multiple names and addresses on several human subjects, and lost their research sub-contract.

They then offered me as a human subject for North American mafia research on synthetic telepathy, because, unlike most of their victims, I didn't talk back at them with my voice, so I could not be made to look as if I was talking to myself, and therefore mentally unbalanced. Instead, I 'thought' my words back at the terrorists. This posed technical challenges to the terrorists, who had to adapt their Syntel (Synthetic Telepathy) system in order to capture my responses. North American mafia scientists were interested in how this worked.

When the terrorists spoke on the ultrasound system, which could not be heard by the human ear without technology, they spoke into a microphone. As I did not vocalise, they could not connect me to remote telecommunications links, as they did for each other. Through a research contract, they found a way to resolve this. They appointed someone to listen to my words and repeat them on to the telecoms link. It sounds crazy, but they were keen on this, as it

required little skill, and offered low-level operatives the chance to earn a little money. I called those people 'parrots'.

I know that the existence of synthetic telepathy sounds unlikely; but there is a quite funny scientific video demonstration of how it works, on YouTube and featuring Dr. Joe Pompei of Madlabs.

ATTACKS ON BIRDS AND ANIMALS

After the Afro-Asian Daesh terrorists next door started attacking me, we kept finding dead birds around the garden or in the road outside - a blackbird here, a robin there. The Daesh terrorists were torturing and killing birds for fun in their spare time, using close range laser beams from the top window of their house. I noticed a wood pigeon standing bolt upright with its eyes closed as if it had been electrocuted. In fact, it had been. The terrorists had developed a method of sending a muscle paralysing gas down a laser beam, in water droplets, so that the wood pigeon couldn't move. They then tortured it with electric shocks, and finally released it.

I saw a squirrel playing on our garden fence. Suddenly it froze for several minutes, as if it had been turned to stone. Then it leaped three feet in the air, after being electrocuted, and raced off. I looked up at the window where the terrorists often stood when they aimed at things in our garden. Sure enough, one of them was standing back from the window, and I saw him clearly.

The Daesh terrorists were paid on the basis of the amount of electricity they discharged from their battery packs. Over a twelve hour shift they were supposed to have found enough targets to run down the battery. So long as they presented their battery packs back empty they got their full wages. So they devised a method of doing this by discharging their electronic weapons into our compost heap. This was fairly harmless, although the top of the compost heap was sometimes boiling hot.

When the IRA wanted to harass me, they directed Daesh to empty the electrical charge from their battery packs on to our grass, which died, leaving a yellow mark. You could see that it was a man-

made event, because there was a straight line of yellow grass leading to a large yellow patch, indicating the direction from which the laser gun had been fired. The terrorists also targeted the roots of our hedge. Soon the hedge looked like a viaduct, with a strip at the top still growing, and a lot of gaps underneath.

When I bought new plants for the garden, the terrorists would try to laser the roots, causing them to wilt. They did this one time when my gardener was there, and he was astonished to see a good healthy plant wilt within two minutes. Luckily, I found that saturating the roots with water revived the plants, if you caught them in time.

I knew that, in North America, the mafia targeted domestic pets, but it was hard to believe that this would happen in the UK. In fact, the IRA did not target domestic pets, and cherished their own. Their staff never got time to take their dogs for walks. But the IRA arranged for a dog walker, who took five IRA dogs out altogether. I often saw them out in the road, and they were fit and well. So were the guard dogs at the IRA hideout at the top of our road. They were 'driven dogs', with electronic implants in their brains, that could be triggered to growl and attack, but, when not triggered, they were warm friendly creatures, with wagging tails.

The North American mafia and Daesh had no such finer feelings. One of our neighbours had three European mountain dogs. They were beautiful animals, but one of them got cancer and died, because the basket it slept in was within range of the Afro-Asian Daesh staff.

The same Daesh migrants had access to a house opposite where my father lived. He had two dogs. One of the dogs started screaming, and held up its leg, as if in pain. This went on for about twenty minutes. Several people tried to comfort it, but there was nothing they could do but hold its paw. If I had been there I would have tried shielding it with a plastic ground sheet, as that usually blocks laser attacks. During this attack, the Daesh migrants also transmitted a cancer-causing substance via the laser. Three weeks later, the dog developed a tumour, and eventually died.

One day, my father and I went out in his car, and when we got back, I noticed that the front door, which had been locked, was wide open. I went in and found the bathroom window on the first floor open as well.

'I must have done it by mistake,' said my father.

I started checking the house, in case anything was missing. I went up into the attic, and, to my horror, I saw a dead blue tit hanging upside down from flypaper. The terrorists had left their calling card.

The IRA had a contract with a North American mafia research laboratory on an island off the British Isles. The IRA paid to have cameras put in the eyes of birds. The birds had microchips attached to their backs, and some kind of skull pad, through which the terrorists were able to 'drive' them by wi-fi, remotely. They frequently used woodpigeons to keep watch on me from trees, when they had no other video access. They also trained terrorists to drive woodpigeons across the road; on to the windscreens of passing cars, to cause cars to crash.

I was sad to see birds and animals being tortured, so I decided to report it to MI5, via their website. It was the first time I had done this. I found a page where you could report suspicious activities and sent a brief email. Really, I did not think much would happen, and I did not know what to expect, but it was the beginning of an astonishing set of developments that culminated in the local terrorist unit being closed down by our security services. This goes to show that it is worth reporting things, and I will always be grateful to the heroes who work tirelessly day and night to keep us and our country safe from terrorism.

What happened next was really incredible. I was in the garden weeding, and I happened to look up for a moment at a point in the sky, at about forty-five degrees to the vertical. It was as if that tiny point had become a shiny dot, and then five glorious white birds burst from it in a star formation. They were a bit like giant seagulls, nearly as large as albatrosses. They were partly pure glistening white, and partly off-white. The off-white part looked soft, like mat fleece. I

did not see feathers, but the birds glowed in the light and had a proud demeanour.

These birds were clearly not real. They were some kind of manufactured, remote-controlled creation. They set about finding all the camera birds in the garden. They had swing-wing capability, and they dived into hedges and tree canopies. And here's the really amazing thing: they did not kill the camera birds, but cancelled the wi-fi transmitters in their bodies, so that the birds were freed from captivity.

'Let's hear it for our military!' I thought. They were showing that they knew about the illicit technologies used to enslave birds, and had technologies of their own, far in advance of anything the terrorists could dream of.

BILL TALKS

Sometimes I would hear my captors whispering about another prisoner they could target, if I was going to be out all day, to ensure that they got their full pay.

'He's available if we need someone,' I heard one of them say.

'Who is he?' I wondered. 'Where does he live? Perhaps he needs help'.

Then, one day, I heard them telling some visiting terrorists about him.

'He was one of us, you see, but he caught us breaking the rules, and reported us. But we had people at the top who saw to it, so that we could go on working here. Now he is in prison, as we call it.'

'What do you mean?' asked a visitor.

'Well, it's an old people's home, just outside the town, but he is always in there, so we can easily find him'.

I wasn't able to locate where the ex-IRA prisoner was located, but everything changed when I went carol singing that Christmas. We were going round some old people's homes, and after our singing, they very kindly offered us hot nibbles, mince pies and mulled wine, and a chance to get to know the residents.

I could hear two IRA women whispering on synthetic telepathy.

'Now we've got them both together, we can claim twice as much. You claim for him, and I'll claim for her'.

'Right,' I thought. 'He's got to be in here somewhere'.

I looked around at all the elderly gentlemen sitting in comfortable chairs with high backs, who were being brought mince pies. It could be any of them. But how to make contact?

Then I heard one of the IRA women saying, 'Pity we can't reach him, he's in the wrong place.'

'Surely you know you can never reach me in here,' said a man's voice.

He sounded irritated.

'Honestly,' he continued, 'They send these stupid fools round, without telling them anything. And, of course, they find out they can't get through the shielding, and then they start bewailing their fate.'

'That's exactly what happens to me, when I'm at home, too,' I thought.

'Who are you?' I heard the man say.

'I'm a carol singer, and I'm being targeted by the IRA,' I replied.

A grey-haired man of about seventy, sitting away from the window at the back, looked up and started staring round the room. I caught his eye and nodded at him.

'Is it you?' My lips moved silently.

He broke into a smile and beckoned me over.

'I'm Bill,' he said, extending his hand. 'Pleased to meet you'.

'Me too, I'm Martha,' I said. 'You're the first person I've met who is being targeted with synthetic telepathy.'

'I see,' he said. 'So you're starting to work things out. How long has this been going on for you?'

'Nearly a year,' I said. 'I've already heard about you. Would it be OK if I came to see you some time, as there are so many things I want to ask you?'

Bill burst out laughing.

'Well now, that's the first time in years that I've been propositioned by a woman, and I never expected it at my age.'

I laughed too. It was such a relief to find someone else who understood the same things that I was experiencing. I noticed that he had a slight Irish lilt to his voice, just occasionally.

Bill laughed again.

'Yes, I do still have a trace of my origins, though it's many years since I visited my old home'.

He had heard my unspoken thoughts. I was rather shocked for a moment.

'I know,' he said, smiling, 'It's hard at first, but you'll get used to it. There can be no secrets between you and me.'

'OK,' I said. 'So when can I come and see you? What's the best time?'

'Well', said Bill cautiously. 'I'd prefer it if you phoned first to ask if it's convenient. But assuming it is, about ten thirty in the morning would suit me best. Then, if the weather's fine, we could even take a turn around the garden here.'

I could see the other carol singers getting up to go.

'Would tomorrow be possible?' I asked.

'That would be great, Martha,' said Bill, smiling broadly. 'Oh, and by the way, if you could see your way to bringing me a small bottle of the hard stuff, that would be much appreciated.'

He gave me a wink, and a wave of his hand as I left.

Next day I turned up at Bill's place at the appointed time, with a bottle of Irish Whisky in a plastic bag. Bill accepted it graciously, and we strolled in the nursing home's well-kept gardens. It was warm and sunny, and eventually we settled on garden seats under a tree. Bill began talking, as if telling a story to a young child.

'You see, the IRA have been on the British mainland for a long time. I know you won't agree with attacking British citizens, but we do not recognise the laws of Britain. You see, there's a lot of history, and it goes back a long way. The English started it, in my view, so we feel we are not bound by their jurisdiction. We have a lot of sleepers – people who came to the UK deliberately to pose as British citizens, in order to avoid suspicion. We marry IRA sympathisers from Britain and other countries – mainly the US, Canada and France. Some of us have settled in the UK and brought up children with English accents.

'Officers are obliged to marry for business reasons. They have an official partner, with whom they carry out business and social duties. But often they are privately married to someone else in the IRA. Discretion is required when spending time with their real family. Most power emanates from the Irish Republic and is in the

hands of a few trusted families. They are the ones with direct access to funding from the North American mafia, and Al-Qaida. When the money's flowing, their families are the ones that get in on the act.'

'But where do you fit in to all this?' I asked. 'Do you still support the IRA?'

'Well, I do and I don't,' said Bill, shaking his head. 'I still believe we were right in what we did, but if you asked me now if I would do it again, well, no, I wouldn't. Because I've lived here in this town a long time, and local people have helped me when I needed it, and I don't forget that.'

'How did you end up in an IRA unit here?' I asked.

'Oh, I volunteered,' said Bill. 'You see, I was an engineer, and into IT and Telecommunications, and I felt I had something to offer the cause, after things died down on the British mainland'.

'But if things had died down, what was there to do?' I asked.

'Oh, quite a lot, Martha,' said Bill. 'You see, the IRA's policy, in sleeper mode, is to penetrate the society that they seek to undermine, placing children, family members and affiliates in positions within local authorities, as nurses, carers, clinicians, municipal staff, social services, and youth workers. We make a point of getting into the mental health professions as psychologists and psychotherapists, where we can facilitate the sectioning of whistle-blowers, trouble makers and targeted individuals under the mental health acts. That means that if anyone finds out about us, we can discredit them, if they report things to the Authorities.

'Once we can do that, we can easily recruit people to our cause. We look for character weaknesses – sexual indiscretions, alcohol abuse, gambling, and ways that we can get people bankrupted or in trouble with the police, and then we blackmail or harass suitable candidates into becoming unit members. We get best results from targeting small businesses which are in financial trouble; self-employed people who rely on the internet for their work – which we can easily take down - and single parent families'.

'It's funny you should say that, Bill', I said, 'My friend Dan once referred a man to me for advice, because he was being victimised in Manchester. He was self-employed, and ran his

39

internet-based business from his home. He told me that the IRA had identified him as someone they could entrap and employ, and they started with gang stalking. He had attended an evening talk about how to make money quickly; you know the sort of thing, you see them advertised everywhere. Well, he gave someone his contact details and thought no more about it. But soon afterwards his internet was disconnected, and he could not get it fixed. Having taken away his livelihood, the IRA parked a camper van in the road outside his house, from where they bombarded him with microwave radiation beams and laser pain attacks, designed to ruin his health and make him unemployed.

I urged him to get in touch with MI5, but he refused, because he did not trust the Authorities. Perhaps he had something to hide that he chose not to mention. He realised that the terrorists wanted him to work for them. He stopped contacting me, and I suspect that he was press-ganged into the service of the IRA and their subcontractors. But he did have a choice. Perhaps he went to the Authorities later on.

'Not very likely,' said Bill. 'IRA low-level operatives tend to become brainwashed and lose the will to seek help. Psychological intimidation is an important part of the process.'

'Well, the IRA's plans don't always work out as they intended,' I said. 'I knew another man who ran an internet support business and helped me to set up my first website. I ran a blog alerting people to the IRA's covert use of electromagnetic weapons and synthetic telepathy. In retaliation, the IRA decided to stop him working. They hired some villains to dig up and remove the British Telecom optical-fibre cables that supplied his local area with internet connections. No one in that area could go on-line for two weeks. The police never caught the criminals who did it. But the targeted man himself was not badly affected, because he was able to carry on his business via Blackberry, so the IRA's efforts came to nothing.'

'I'm beginning to understand why you get so much personal attention from our locals,' said Bill.

'Well, OK,' I said. 'But that kind of behaviour sounds more like hate crime to me than what I associate with IRA activities,' I said. 'I thought the IRA was all paramilitary stuff.'

'Oh, sure,' said Bill. 'It's all organised along military lines. You will find that all IRA people have military ranks, and require their soldiers to go through various types of organised training. Those working in civilian roles are exempt from most of it, and it's better for them not to know too much. But those required to bear weapons routinely, and work in military groups, must pass through recognised stages. After completing military training, they are given the rank of Lieutenant.'

'But do they do actual fighting still?' I asked.

'You told me that you've been targeted for a year,' said Bill. 'You shouldn't need to ask that. What do you think has been happening to you, and to people all around you? It's war, but not as you know it. The soldiers don't need to meet you face to face. They use remote electromagnetic weapons… and people get sick and die.'

Bill lowered his voice.

'I know this will sound harsh to you, Martha, but both male and female cadets are required to prove themselves by killing of a person regarded as 'the enemy', before acquiring Lieutenant rank. They typically select elderly people in nursing homes and people in hospices. They may operate from a car parked nearby, and they may send someone in to the building to point a device at the target at close range. The device will be controlled from the parked car by wi-fi, but it will be operated via a pointer device at close range.'

I felt pretty sick at that point. I did not ask Bill whether he had ever been involved in such things, in case he told me. But I suspected that with his technical background, he might have worked on support for technical weapons work.

Bill looked at me strangely for a moment. Then I remembered. Of course, he was on the same synthetic telepathy system as me, so he knew what I was thinking.

'Well, I'll be straight with you, Martha,' he said. 'I was never officer material, so I did not have to gain the rank of Lieutenant. But I worked in a special technical section and was classified as a Technician grade. There were about fifty of us in one Group, and twenty of us worked in the same building. It looked like a big private

house from the outside, tucked away in the countryside with its own grounds, so no one suspected.'

I needed time to come to terms with what Bill had just told me. I decided to encourage him to talk on. After all, it was better to find out as much as possible, because that way I could report it to the Authorities, and they could do something about it.

'Where would a Lieutenant fit into the wider scheme of things?' I asked.

After a moment's silence, in which I could tell Bill was weighing up the value of his continued contact with me, he continued.

'Well, it's like this, Martha. The IRA's military hierarchy includes regiments, units and groups. A unit might contain two hundred staff, made up of four groups of about fifty people. They have officer ranks, and a range of grades below officer rank, including technical staff, supervisors and foot soldiers, both men and women.'

'Their full-time staff are provided free board and lodging. Officers receive comfortable houses, but are expected to make these available to accommodate other staff at any time of the day or night. Officers who have seen active service in the past, are supported in retirement, if they have no personal income or pension. They live in communal houses, where board and lodging are provided - a cross between an officers' mess and an old people's home.'

'Ah, yes,' I said. 'I've noticed that the IRA have a strong preference for gracious Victorian country houses, set in their own grounds, well away from main roads, and shielded by woods. I've seen country residences with white pillars over the front door; others have mock-Tudor beams and ornate chimneys. There is always a large office, above ground floor level, for the chief executive, and an adjoining meeting room with an oval table capable of accommodating up to twenty-four people. The larger houses have smaller meeting rooms as well. These houses include a private suite for the ruling family, their wives and children, and lodgings for the "kitchen cabinet" and "household cavalry".'

Bill smiled.

'I see you've already visited some of our family residences,' he said. 'And we mustn't forget the social side. That's very important. There is usually a mezzanine floor, where the troops have a canteen and pub.'

'Another thing I've noticed,' I continued, 'is that your troops carry hand guns in holsters under their armpits, and some of them wear loose waistcoats to conceal the holsters. Those guns must be very hot and sweaty by the end of the day.'

Bill laughed.

'Well I hope you're not going to start lecturing an army of men about their personal freshness. This is war we are talking about. Those hand-guns are just for personal protection. Nowadays we tend to use electronic laser-powered rifles, as well as conventional semi-automatic rifles. But you won't see us carrying them. There is a strict rule that troops should be as invisible as possible to the outside world. Even those in civilian jobs must stay in their cars, and not be seen strolling about, unless they have an established local identity.'

'So when was the last time you carried a rifle, then Bill?' I asked.

'Oh, let's see, now,' said Bill, puckering his eyebrows. 'It would have been some time in the 1980s. And I was in Ireland then'.

'Did you ever go to prison, then?' I asked.

Bill studied the ground for a moment. Then he looked back at me.

'There's a lot of things you don't understand about our life. You think I should be ashamed about that, don't you? Well let me tell you, lots of our men went to prison then, and we took it as a badge of honour, to have spent some time inside.'

'But what about now, Bill?' I continued. 'Where are your friends now? They want to torture and kill you.'

Bill nodded.

'You see, everything changed when we got involved in North Africa. These people you see running around here in the electronic environment that we've created, they're not the same as we used to be. They are in Al-Qaida's pay. I'm not saying that we sold out to Al-Qaida, but... there are some who do say that. They also say that

Saudi money has turned us into mercenaries, and corrupt ones at that. And that's where I took issue with our local friends in their little electromagnetic world. They are a bunch of corrupt, undisciplined rabble. I tried to do something about that... which is why I'm here now.'

'But you're safe in here, aren't you, Bill?' I said. 'Didn't you say last night that they couldn't get at you in the building?'

'Yes,' said Bill. 'The IRA have placed reliance on electromagnetic and electronic weapons, as part of the covert war on Europe, but they get stuck when they come up against buildings designed to modern standards, with proper wall and roof insulation, and UPVC windows. That's why I bought myself into this place. It's brand new, and the shielding works. When I'm in the building, there's not much they can do, except witter on at me via the Syntel system, which means very little, when you get used to it.'

It felt as if we'd talked enough. I got up, and thanked Bill for his time.

'I wonder if you will come back again after this,' said Bill. 'We've only scratched the surface, and already I can tell that you're having second thoughts.'

I smiled.

'It's strange in war. There are enemies, and there are casualties, but if we stop talking, we can't go forward. If it's going to end, we have to start talking sometime.'

'Hope to see you again then,' said Bill, as I waved goodbye.

It was a week before I met up with Bill again. This time I was a bit more organised. There were two things that really bothered me – the people-trafficking that seemed to be endemic throughout the IRA subcontractors, and the way in which different international terrorist groups seemed to be affiliated to each other, and in each other's pockets. I thought that, if I concentrated on asking about those, things might become a lot clearer.

It was raining, so we could not walk in the garden. Bill suggested that we chat in the nursing home's small lending library room. There was a table and chairs, so that people could sit and read the daily newspapers, but hardly anyone went in there.

'How are you, Bill?' I asked. 'I wondered if I would find you with a knife in your back, after talking to me.'

'Oh, no,' said Bill. 'They won't want to kill the goose that lays the golden eggs. If it wasn't for you and me, lots of IRA subcontractors would be out of a job.'

'What's the difference between the IRA and their subcontractors?' I asked.

'These days, there's quite a lot of overlap between ourselves and organised crime,' said Bill. 'In this covert war, we use anyone who is working on the same side as us against the British, and that includes a lot of criminals. We use them to do our dirty work, things we wouldn't want traced back to us, if things went wrong. All the people we use have been in prison before, so if they are caught, no one will be particularly surprised.

Our relationship with Al-Qaida is a bit similar. They use us in places where they would look suspicious, but where we can pass unnoticed. We are Al-Qaida subcontractors. They give us money to carry out attacks on 'Christendom', which really means 'The West', and we give some of that money to criminals, who are subcontracted to us. There are very few actual IRA people involved.'

'But it looks to me as if most of the people working here are not being paid at all,' I said. 'They seem to be slaves. How did they get trapped like that?'

'Yes,' said Bill, 'I know what you're talking about. A lot of people who work for us have come to the UK illegally. They do not have the right to live or work here. We paid their travel costs, and gave them false EU identity papers. In return, they have to work for us, and pay back that initial debt. But there is high interest on the payments, and basically, however hard they work, those people will never get out of debt, and they end up as slaves.'

'What does that mean?' I asked.

'It means that they get food and shelter in order to complete their tasks, and that is it,' said Bill.

'But they can't leave?' I asked.

Bill looked at me as if I was an idiot.

'No one ever leaves,' he said. 'I don't leave. They don't leave, and you don't leave.'

'I'll see about that', I thought to myself, forgetting that, of course, he could hear my thoughts.

'Are you planning to kill all of us, then, Martha?' asked Bill, in a mocking voice.

'Seems reasonable to me,' I replied. 'But Bill, not changing the subject, can you explain to me about the children born into IRA subcontractors' families? They seem to be treated as slaves.'

Bill gave a sigh.

'This isn't really something I want to discuss', he said. 'But I can understand why you are asking. You see, once we start taking money from other organisations, we end up being run by people whose standards are different from ours, and I'm not just talking about Al-Qaida. A lot of our activities receive US mafia funding. The whole electromagnetic technology environment comes from them. Now the US mafia's attitude to kids is not that different from people-trafficking, and that goes for Al-Qaida as well. Child brothels, child labour, it is a different world. I don't like it, but these people have taken us over, and we are junior partners these days.'

'That's rather what I thought,' I said. 'I heard from some IRA women that there was an arrangement to for subcontractors to exchange their children with those of other parents in their unit, while still babes-in-arms, so that parents would not be too soft on the kids and would bring them up as child soldiers. The foster parents did not spend enough on food and clothes for the kids, and some made their kids work in child brothels. As a result, the physical and psychological development of the kids got stunted.'

'Well, that is not the IRA,' said Bill. 'We honestly do not do that. We arrange for our kids to be properly educated, which, I must admit, our gangland subcontractors do not. If they show aptitude, our kids go on to higher education, and they are prepared to take their place in society, so that they blend in with their community. But of course, they have to be prepared for their covert role as well. They regularly attend summer schools and outward-bound courses designed to wake them up slowly to their real identity as members of

a covert power, who do not recognise the laws of the land they live in.'

'I suppose it's a bit like being brought up in a remote religious sect,' I said.

'I disagree,' said Bill. 'You're not sufficiently aware of your own programming. All cultures have their own idiosyncrasies. It's just that your culture happens to be the prevailing one in the West. You accept lots of things without question. You pay your taxes and expect the Government to provide a range of services. We don't have a Government set-up. We have a parental hierarchy, so the patriarch and matriarch of each group take all the cash and see to the needs of their family. Your way is not necessarily better, it's just different.'

'In that case, there is more in common between the IRA and the mafia than I had realised,' I said. 'But can you tell me where the American cults fit into all this? Because I've met quite a few people from an American cult apparently working with the IRA.'

'Ah,' said Bill. 'That is another thing that has come to us from across the pond. They are a breakaway group, who specialise in psychological warfare, and covert use of chemical and biological agents, to counter those whom they perceive as their enemies. We frequently work with them as advisors. Say there is a local politician who is causing trouble for us on some project. There is more than one way to deal with that.'

'Oh, I know what you mean,' I said. 'I remember that there was a man who led a US charity in Africa, and he uncovered some kind of corruption, implicating people from the US. He got a lot of publicity for his cause. Then, one day, he was found wandering naked in the street, shouting at passers-by in a psychotic state, and it was said that he had been overworking, and would have to step back from his job for a while.'

'Yeah,' said Bill. 'I think you've got the general idea.'

'We seem to have covered a lot more ground than I was expecting today,' I said, trying to suppress a shudder of horror at the note on which our conversation had ended. 'It's been really helpful to have your take on things. Cleared up a lot of confusion. I guess I'd better be going now.'

'Before you go,' said Bill, 'Can you do something for me?'

'What is it?' I asked cautiously.

Bill drew a letter out of his pocket.

'Can you post this for me?' he said.

'Well I can,' I said, 'But is there a problem about your doing that?'

Bill shrugged his shoulders.

'Somehow, when I post letters, they don't seem to arrive. I'd be obliged if you could see to it yourself.'

'How would it be if I took it to the Post Office, and got it sent Special Delivery?' I said. 'That should do it.'

'Would you?' asked Bill.

He took my hand and pressed it warmly. I could see it meant a lot to him.

'See you around,' I said, waving goodbye.

When Bill said that his letters didn't seem to arrive, I could believe him, because I happened to know that one of the sons of a senior IRA manager worked in the back of our local Post Office. He was not a Post Office employee, but he had a job in security to do with the overall site in which the Post Office was located. I often saw his red Fiesta parked there.

Because of synthetic telepathy, the IRA would have known what Bill wrote in his letter and listened to him thinking while he was writing it. They would also have known that he was going to ask me to post the letter for him. The key to success was surprise. I did not stand around debating what I would do. I went straight out and did it, and the perpetrators were unable to influence the progress of Bill's letter.

I took a train to another town, and posted Bill's letter Special Delivery from there. Of course, the IRA subcontractors knew what was in my mind, and tried to attack me with electromagnetic oscillators, but I did not take much notice, as I had discovered that pushing a wheeled shopping trolley, wearing rubber boots and dragging a walking stick along the ground all earthed these attacks.

I never saw Bill again. The nursing home told me that his daughter from Ireland had come to visit him with her husband, and

had taken him back with them. He sent a nice postcard to the staff, with a picture of Ireland on it. The postmark on the card was probably nowhere near where he is living now. But did he shake off the IRA? I remembered what he had said.

'No one ever leaves'.

I Hope He Made it, Anyway.

IRA ELECTROMAGNETIC ENVIRONMENT

It is time to explain about the electromagnetic environment. The events I have been describing have an unbelievable quality about them. Things just don't happen like that in real life. But we have no problem with accepting all kinds of things as science fiction. In 2009 a well-known science-fiction movie called 'Avatar' came out. You may have seen it. According to Wikipedia, the film broke several box office records and became the highest-grossing film of all time for theatrical revenues, although when video and DVD sales and rental are included, 'Titanic' probably exceeded it.

In 'Avatar', it is possible to produce a genetically engineered body, with the mind of a remotely located human implanted in it, which can be used to interact within an alien environment. The avatar enables people to carry out potentially dangerous activities without putting their physical body at risk. 'Avatar' is set in the mid-twenty-second century. What I discovered is that advances in technology have made it possible to do something not that different, already, within a private world created using electromagnetic architecture.

One day, I found that, with my eyes shut, I could see my attackers, as well as hear them. I soon got used to this, and was able to observe the terrorists when they were not aware of it.

I watched six people in their twenties go into a work room that looked like a language laboratory. There were three men and three women. They wore unusual clothes made of a strong plastic material. The men wore black sports trousers and tops, and the women wore red dresses which came down below the knee. There was a long oblong table, separated into six wooden booths, three on each side, with six chairs around the table. Each booth had an electronic socket with earphones plugged in to it. The young people sat down at the

table, and put on the earphones. Then a technician came in with six brown metal helmets. The helmets looked like upturned soup plates.

The technician placed a helmet on the head of each of the six people, in turn, and went to a telecommunications consul to activate the equipment for each of them. As the equipment was activated, each of the six people DISAPPEARED. But they reappeared in an adjoining room, within the electromagnetic environment, one after another. They looked the same as before they had disappeared, except that their helmets were now invisible. The six people went up a staircase to another room. In that room, known as the 'police station', there were two men, referred to as 'police', operating electronic equipment.

The job of the police was to teleport people into specific artificially constructed areas made of plastic, within which they could carry out their terrorist tasks without being discovered. These artificially constructed areas looked like real houses, with real streets. The interiors of the houses were just like the real thing. There were gardens and roads outside, with trees and cars. The police could alter the size of people inside the area, to fit their environment.

The six people I had been watching were trainees. Once all the trainees had entered the electromagnetic environment it looked as if no one was sitting at the wooden booths, but, at some level, they were still there. It would have been dangerous to the trainees if someone had walked in and displaced the chairs. For that reason, the operating room was always kept locked by the 'police', whose job it was to keep an eye on what was going on within the electromagnetic environment, and to transfer operatives back to the real world, at the end of a twelve-hour shift, or if the situation required it.

I pulled back to get a higher view of what was going on. The entire environment was covered by a large green plastic shell, like the roofs of factories in an industrial site. The shell was the size of an aircraft hangar. Within the shell, but outside the electromagnetic environment, there were several men, overseeing the logistics, the lights, the power, and the interaction of the people within the electromagnetic environment. Everything within the electromagnetic environment was in miniature. But from that artificial electromagnetic environment, terrorists could target people all over the world via wi-fi and private satellite communications, without anyone finding out.

If the people were unexpectedly removed from their miniature world, they upsized as soon as they touched the ground. This temporarily winded them, as did unexpected teleportation events, but drinking a glass of water helped to ground them in the real world.

I was not living within this electromagnetic environment, but I could see and hear it, because of the microchip transmitter in the back of my head. What I saw and heard showed me that there were terrorists, concealed by technology, operating secretly in our country without restraint, and, because they were concealed, their intentions towards us were open and clear. They were here to hurt and kill, and they hated and despised us.

The electromagnetic environment offers opportunities for criminals and terrorists to do whatever they like without anyone spotting them, by entering into the electronic avatar, which becomes their alter ego. They learn to navigate in the electromagnetic environment, and they receive basic training in the use of electronic weapons and electromagnetic devices designed to cause pain and discomfort to targeted victims. Some of them specialise in the use of synthetic telepathy - Syntel, an ultrasound technology frequently used by gangsters to communicate secretly with each other when committing crimes. Synthetic telepathy can be used as a weapon in psychological warfare, for example, by using threatening language that only the victim can hear.

Working in the electromagnetic environment is different from anything else I have experienced. If the subcontractors are accepted for work, they queue up and are registered on the IRA's computer system. Then they are allocated a plastic uniform bearing a unique barcode number at the back, which is recorded on the computer, linked to the serial number of the microchip embedded in the head of each operator – or 'operative', as they are called by the US mafia. They are given to a boss, who is an IRA computer system IP address-holder. He or she allocates tasks for them to complete, either using electronic/electromagnetic weapons, or a synthetic telepathy microphone.

When the metallic helmets are activated, the participants are logged on to the computer system automatically. The helmet acts as an aerial and connects them by wi-fi to the police station. The avatars can only move within a designated area - for example, one floor of a

house. If a perpetrator wants to move to another area, he or she has to request the technicians in the 'police station' to re-locate them.

Sometimes operatives failed to achieve their set objectives, which meant that they lost money. When that happened, they demanded to be let out early. But the police would sternly tell them that they must wait till the end of the shift, like everyone else. But if there had been fighting going on, and people were in a wounded state, they might get 'airlifted' out early.

You can tell a lot about operatives just by looking at the uniforms they are wearing. The uniforms are there to let other operatives know the ranks of the people they are working with in the electromagnetic environment, while preserving their anonymity. Women operatives wear little girls' white party dresses, and women supervisors wear red frocks. Weapons operatives wear black sports gear and black helmets with visors. Weapons officer ranks wear black military uniforms. Officer rank Syntel operatives wear pale khaki military uniforms.

The IRA have their own avatar uniforms, graded by rank. Warrant Officers wear grey trousers and white shirts. Officer ranks wear dark grey suits. Senior management wear mid-brown suits – these are reserved for men who were operational in the 1970s and 1980s. It is these people who mastermind the IRA's covert electromagnetic projects in the European Theatre of War.

The North American mafia trained the original workforce for the IRA, to assist them in furthering Al-Qaida's war against the British Isles. They took teenage boys from middle-class IRA families, and offered them a secure future for life, as administrators and operators of 'police stations' within the electromagnetic environment. Their families had to agree that the boys should be castrated. The idea was that they would become docile, loyal servants, undistracted by sexual urges.

The clinical procedures were carried out in the North American mafia's secret underground bases. IRA families were proud to have their sons enrolled in this elite group, with good salaries, and access to senior people. The men held officer ranks. Their electromagnetic uniform was a long blue coat, like those of the US Army in the early days before American Independence. They kept their gelding status secret, some of them wearing artificial testicles. They were assumed

to be homosexuals, as they developed close relationships with others in their group.

The IRA do not trust their subcontractors and conceal most operational information from them. Subcontractors are locked in their work areas and are unable to leave the building until the end of the shift. Their activities are supervised by staff in the 'police station'. In many cases, the 'police' will watch proceedings from plasma television screens set out along one wall. They can supervise several rooms at once in this way, using CCTV or microdot cameras.

One Christmas, I got a shock when I watched the movie '*Polar Express*'. There is a scene in Santa Claus's workshop where the elves have wall-to wall screens showing each child in the world - on CCTV, so that the elves can tell which kids had been good enough to get a present that year. It was exactly like the large 'victim supervision' centres which I have seen in Los Angeles.

IRA non-commissioned officer ranks and IRA subcontractors represent the bulk of full-time employees. The background of these henchmen includes ex-convicts, career criminals, former security guards and vigilante group members from South Africa, Australia and Canada. Some were dishonourably discharged from the police force or Territorial Army in their home countries.

I am old enough to remember the IRA bombings on the British Mainland in the 1970s, and I was surprised to discover how different the IRA are in Britain nowadays. As Bill said, once the IRA started to get funding from Al-Qaida and the US mafia, their character began to change, and they became more like mercenaries. The people I met were not driven by a political cause. They were driven by the debts which they owed to their bosses, and the ambition to get rich quick by killing people and taking what they had got.

The IRA operatives I met were funded directly by Al-Qaida. They had their salaries paid in to overseas bank accounts. There was a specific account which held money for financing of activities that meet Al-Qaida objectives, such as:

-    Maintaining a group of people that could be mobilised as an army at short notice

-    Maintaining a group of people that could be mobilised as prison camp guards at short notice

-    Reducing the white Christian population of Europe

All subcontractors had to be sponsored by an IRA woman, who would be willing to buy an entrance ticket to the electronic environment from the police station on their behalf. The cash came from the Al-Qaida funding account, managed by the group of IRA women. These women delegated their sponsorship role to female criminals, whose day jobs involved child brothel running and drug trafficking. Known simply as 'Our Group', they paid money to the police station to organise covert terrorist activities targeting British citizens, such as:

- Hounding people out of houses needed for terrorist purposes;
- Hastening the demise of elderly white people;
- Entrapping people identified by the IRA as suitable employees.

After receiving cash sponsorship, subcontractors are given a card, completed by the IP address holder, specifying what tasks they must complete. If the tasks are competed successfully, participants get what to them is a significant amount of money. If the task is not completed successfully, participants are in debt to the IRA, but get another chance to wipe out that debt, if the women sponsors agree to come up with more cash. In practice, the outcome rarely depends on the activities of these guys. It usually depends on the skill or judgement of technical staff, operating remotely. The system is rarely supervised, and technical staff falsify results with impunity.

If the participant continues to fail, he becomes a debt-slave of the IRA. He has to stay with the unit, and carry out whatever tasks he is ordered to do, without pay; and if he fails to complete the tasks, he is tortured. But he gets free board and lodging, of a basic type. Lots of men who reach the end of the road are in this situation. They sit around waiting to be goaded into action with cattle prods, without knowing or asking what is wanted of them. They develop their own camaraderie, and, when they can, they indulge in any free alcohol or drugs that are going.

Down-and-out men make their way to our area from all over the South and West of England, in the hope of being sponsored. You can find pools of men living in camp sites, waiting around in case the IRA sponsors need someone. The tasks they are sponsored to carry out come under the heading of antisocial behaviour and include:

- Throwing rubbish in the gardens of targeted individuals
- Damaging their cars

-   Breaking and entering their gardens and properties to cause damage
-   Stealing from garages and outhouses
-   Rowdy street behaviour outside victims' houses
-   Broadcasting tapes of animal and bird noises to disturb victims.

IRA operatives with sufficient technical training are used to:
-   Hold electronic pointers at sufficiently close range to reach targeted victims, e.g. in parked cars, to enable technicians to:
-   Void the bladder and bowels of victims in or outside their houses
-   Create stomach cramps
-   Create pains in joints and other parts of the body
-   Operate electromagnetic oscillators, designed to manipulate the gravity of the victim's body, making walking feel like climbing a hill, putting people off-balance, and causing them to fall over. If victims wore a wrist-watch, it made it easy to track them.

IRA subcontractors have to learn a coded language, based on terminology used in the IRA's official manual. The code was developed for use when communicating by cell phone, in case they were listened in on. The manual is an Anglicised version of one used by the US Mafia. A woman who once worked for the BBC in the 1950s wrote it. Here are some examples of the coded language.

IRA code words	Meaning
Séance	Synthetic telepathy session (*'Say-ance'*)
Going into the garden	Signing on for a shift of synthetic telepathy
Daughter room	Torture room
They were talked to	They were tortured
Hacktivist	Hacker
Happy Birthday	The shift has finished early
Epoxy-resin; gorgonzola; fallopians; menstruals	Pejorative words for women
Toilet role, potty training, Virginia Bottomley	Euphemisms relating to pulsed laser beam attacks on bladder

	and bowel, to achieve voiding of contents and stimulation of lower intestine to cause diarrhea
Numbers:	
10, 100, 1000	1, 10, 100
Times of day:	
Dinner, lunch, breakfast	Breakfast, dinner, lunch
Upstairs	Above ground level
Downstairs	On or below ground level
Overseas	Outside the unit area
United States, France, Italy	Designated names of nearby villages.

Our local IRA unit was out of sync with the IRA headquarters in Ireland, and was looked down on by other IRA units on the British mainland, because they had lowered themselves to the level of bandits, willing to defraud Al-Qaida if they could get away with it. They came from two notorious IRA families, who were hopeless at management, and who lapsed into bankruptcy periodically.

One of the IRA families was related to the North American mafia. The other family had worked extensively in Africa, in collaboration with the African National Congress in South Africa, and with Al-Qaida in Algeria. Al-Qaida gave that family blood-brother status, and continued to fund them, no matter what they did.

It was not that easy to carry out most terrorist tasks successfully. As a result, an ever-increasing number of unemployed men were living as debt-slaves under the IRA. The IRA could not dismiss them, as they might talk about their work. The only option was to do away with them, but the IRA held back from that, afraid of being discovered by the Authorities.

The conditions these men lived in could be terrible. I saw one encampment with a large waterproof canopy, like a circus tent. Inside, there were no toilet or washing facilities. Men urinated and defecated on the ground, and lived on wooden slats above. Food was brought in to them, and they threw rubbish and containers onto the floor below. Periodically, lorries would arrive and cleaners would

come in and pile whatever was on the ground into trucks and remove it. The place stank, but it was home to the men.

Women subcontractors rarely used electronic weapons, but they had a role in attacks on victims, as synthetic telepathy operators, reporting back to technicians what the victims were doing, and whether they had been targeted successfully. There was a strict rule that you should never name the victim or say what she is doing, e.g.: 'She just rolled over in bed to avoid the laser beam attack'. You have to say, 'I just rolled over, etc.', as if talking about yourself, so that no one listening in will guess what is going on.

The position of women at the lower end of the IRA subcontractors' hierarchy is tragic. They come from disadvantaged backgrounds, and some of them have been slaves from birth, with no official identity and no possessions. They are trafficked from place to place and treated like some lower form of life. They are the kind of people that the Modern Slavery Act of 2015 was meant to help, but there is no one to tell them that, and many of them are unable to read or write. A proportion of them are illegal immigrants from Asia and Eastern Europe.

One day, I was coming back from the supermarket, when I passed a municipal children's playground. Inside the enclosure there were four women in their twenties, dressed in the kind of clothes that can be obtained from stores which accept welfare coupons. They were overweight, owing to poor diet. They sat together on the ground, whispering confidences to each other, heads bowed, as if they feared the critical gaze of ordinary people.

There was a deep sadness about the little group, which caused me to stop for a moment. As I looked at the women, I noticed a space behind them. It was not an empty space, it was as if the space was invisibly occupied. The scene looked familiar. Then I gasped with shock. The hairs stood up on the back of my neck. I recognised what the scene reminded me of. It was a painting of women sitting at the foot of the cross, and the space behind them was the space that the cross occupied.

THE NORTH AMERICAN MAFIA's CO-OPERATION WITH THE IRA

It is well-known that the IRA have received financial and technical support from Republican sympathisers in the US. On closer inspection, these Republican sympathisers turned out to be members of the North American mafia. By September 2011, there was a tripartite agreement between the IRA, the North American mafia and Al-Qaida, based on mutual cooperation over many decades in Africa. The IRA received training in the use of electromagnetic weapons from the US mafia in Los Angles and Utah, and, in return, opened the door to the British Isles for North American terrorists to participate in the electromagnetic aspect of Al-Qaida's European theatre of war.

The North American mafia used to have a significant presence in the UK. Their staff attended language labs on a regular basis, to ensure that they sounded convincingly British. One young man I met told me that there was no work for him in the States, and that he had been offered good prospects to work for the mafia in London, provided that he could cultivate a good English accent. His accent would have fooled me into thinking he was British, as he had acclimatised since moving to London, but his cultural background gave him away. He was too overtly ambitious. His aspiration was to make a lot of money as quickly as possible, no questions asked, which came over as somewhat un-British.

Many of the North American mafia types whom I met had seen better days. They were crack cocaine addicts, and some of them did heroin as well. They hid it well, but it affected their performance. They were not firing on all four cylinders. Their management made

sure that they were adequately supplied with drugs, and they were allowed comfort breaks if they needed a fix. I found this strange, as addicts are likely to be poor workers with frequent absences. But the North American mafia preferred addicts, as they could be easily compelled to carry out any task, however repugnant, rather than risk losing their regular drug supply.

All the mafia types I met said the same thing. They could no longer make a decent living in North America, because the US military and the FBI were cracking down on them. They'd been told that life was easier in Europe, and were encouraged to go there. But perhaps their managers were keen to be rid of them anyway, as the North American mafia have always been notoriously over-resourced; hence the term 'mob-handed'. If a management meeting was required, at least twenty of them would always turn up, and their office furniture reflected this – huge oval tables on every floor.

North American mafia offices were based in inner cities like London, Manchester, Milton Keynes and parts of the North East of England. Their buildings tended to be utilitarian sixties red brick, with cement water towers on the top. I saw four identical buildings of this type positioned around the M24. Each building had four floors with a boss's office and meeting room on the second floor. The rest of the staff sat round large tables with laptops in front of them, in communal rooms, operating electronic weapons remotely. They worked with the blinds drawn, whether it was day or night. Their underlying purpose was to be ready for mobilisation as a military force, waiting for the call to rise up and take over the Western World. Al-Qaida had paid for them to go to the UK and prepare for that event.

I knew of three large buildings in central London operated by the North American mafia, specifically to hold soldiers in readiness for the call to action. They occupied their time by targeting British citizens within range with electronic and electromagnetic weapons. They also took commissions to target victims in other parts of the world, via private commercial satellite, in collaboration with technicians local to those countries. The idea was to avoid living in the location where attacks took place, in order to avoid discovery.

The US mafia activities were similar to those undertaken covertly by the IRA. There was also a Canadian mafia branch, which was much in evidence where I lived. I met a couple who had come from Vancouver to work in England. The wife had a young baby, and she said that her reason for coming was to avoid having to donate her baby to the cause. In the case of the North American mafia, this meant handing it over to a child manager at about the age of four.

The child managers brought up the children of other parents under a strict military regime. The children had to undergo IQ tests. If they passed, they were put on a mind-control course which involved brutal brainwashing, to produce an alternative personality as a slave or 'child soldier', willing to obey orders without question. The method used to achieve this was electric shock torture. Similar methods of brainwashing have been described in books such as George Orwell's *Nineteen Eighty-Four* and have been attributed to the Soviet Communist approach to treating dissidents as mentally ill, using electroshock treatment, amongst other methods, to bring about a different state of mind in human subjects.

Tragically, the young woman found that a similar regime was operated by the North American mafia where I lived. She was again under pressure from unethical US scientists to have her child put on the child soldier programme. In the end, she returned to Canada.

The term 'Faeces Group' was coined by the North American mafia to describe harassment that involves remote voiding of the bladders and colons of victims, using electromagnetic devices that originally had a clinical purpose to assist with constipation and bladder problems. Telemetry technology was normally used to achieve results. The telemetry operative used infra-red and sonar scanning devices, which helped to identify the contents of the lower bowel and bladder.

It was claimed that the North American mafia had illicitly acquired a space station technology which they adapted to their own nefarious purposes. I do not pretend to understand how it works, but apparently it could transform a liquid into a gas, or a gas into a liquid. It could also dry out liquids so that all that was left was hard

matter. This process could be directed, via laser technology and telemetry, to within the human body. So, for example, the terrorists could cause gas to accumulate within a person's intestine. It was said that technicians made a tiny hole in the intestine with a laser in order to do this. They could also turn solids into liquids, causing diarrhea. Another thing they could do was to create gas pressure to force faecal matter down the intestine, thus triggering an involuntary bowel movement.

The intention of the Faeces Group was to coerce people into becoming prisoners in their own homes, afraid to go out because they might be attacked with severe stomach cramps, somewhere where there was no toilet. The Faeces Group aimed to be self-financing by carrying out attacks to order. North American financiers put up the money for these activities, and expected a good return on their investment. In practice, anyone attacked in that way would go to a pharmacist, and get some stomach medicine, and use incontinence products, so I do not see why the terrorists set such store by this device.

The terrorists mainly targeted elderly people in nursing homes, and got money from Al-Qaida for doing it, as part of that organisation's objective to kill white people living in 'Christendom'. Bladder and colon attacks do not kill people, but they counted for remuneration purposes.

The IRA and their subcontractors used the same methods to punish their employees, making them wet and dirty themselves in public. But the equipment had crueller uses. It could induce agonising stomach cramps, and even shred the bowel and bladder wall. In the hands of a group of drunken Birmingham ex-convicts, working under contract to the IRA, these devices were deadly torture weapons with which they terrorized their female staff, typically single mothers with no family to support them.

The female faeces group staff had the job of targeting the genitals of close-range victims with electric shocks, to harass them. I heard a female terrorist shouting, at a male colleague, 'Don't bother me now! I've got twelve women's genitals to target!'

Timing was everything in such cases, because the victims were only guaranteed to be sitting in their armchair or lying in bed at certain times. Failure to carry out these attacks at the right time could result in brutal punishment. I saw one of the drunken Birmingham louts direct an electromagnetic weapon at one of his staff. The woman, in her thirties, was lying on the floor, writhing, with blood and faeces spewing from her colon. Her three-year old daughter stood there watching. She was one of the kids who was used in the Al-Qaida child brothel.

The US mafia had a spin-off from their Faeces Group work. They trained their operatives to position themselves within range of where toilets were being flushed, and activated a remote device which freeze-dried and extracted human waste – a process a bit like freeze-drying coffee grains, transporting the product to a silo nearby.

Sounds crazy? Sure. But the reason they did it was that human waste contains minute particles of precious metals such as gold, silver, platinum, and rare elements such as palladium and vanadium. The waste was later re-hydrated and transported by tanker to a plant where the precious metal extraction process takes place.

Low-level Daesh staff from Algeria were used for these tasks. They had no idea what they were doing, or why, but they got extra bonuses, which were enough to motivate them. The human waste was stored below ground in the local secret research centre. A tanker was hired to transport the waste to the processing plant. When the tanker arrived, it was filled with water, and freeze-dried waste was mixed in, prior to transportation. The tankers arrived every two months.

One morning I saw three large water utility vans parked outside the gate of the US mafia underground research centre. The driver of one of them was talking on his cell phone.

'He's refusing to come out,' he said.

The vans stayed there for some hours, while men in yellow flak jackets negotiated with someone on the other side of the gate. My gardening friend and I watched from across the road, while we ate our sandwiches. Then a police motorbike arrived. Agreement had been reached, and the tanker was escorted out of the research centre

by the three vans and the motorbike, and taken to an undisclosed destination.

Later on, we heard that the North American mafia had been stealing water from the utility company to fill the tanker and had been caught doing it. They were fined over £100,000, which they paid immediately, and the case was closed. After that, the North American mafia gave up on the idea of human waste extraction.

I first became aware of North American mafia underground bases by following staff back to their place of work. Some of them were going down flights of stairs into what looked like a cellar. Others were entering what appeared to be garages but were entry points. In some cases, there were buildings owned by the North American mafia above ground, with lifts that went first to an underground car park, and then several levels lower. It must have taken time to dig and build these underground sites. I wondered how they could do it in secret, without having to transport enormous amounts of earth and rock, which would have been noticed by the local council.

Eventually I learned the secret of the underground excavations. They do not use conventional technologies. With the right industrial technologies, it is possible to produce lasers that can burn out earth and rock. There is no residue left except gases, which can be removed through underground air conditioning systems. It would not be cost-effective to do this, normally, but with Al-Qaida funding, that was not a problem.

Another use for high-powered lasers was the disposal of bodies. When I learned how to defend myself against electronic weapons attacks, by killing my attackers outright, the terrorists had a lot of bodies to dispose of. The underground research facilities had their own laser-powered cremation service, which did the job effectively.

The underground research bases were staffed with North American scientists, clinicians and technicians – electrical engineers, radio engineers, IT specialists, security guards, armed paramilitary groups and many others. There were job opportunities for UK staff, but few applied, except as security guards.

The research clinicians spent much of their time carrying out 'unnecessary operations' to meet the requirements of the IRA and their subcontractors. These included:

- Routine castration of ex-convicts, paedophiles and other staff on their payroll with a history of crimes of violence
- Insertion of Nano-transmitters into the heads of all employees
- Insertion of eye cameras linked to the retinal nerves of some staff
- Insertion of inner-ear implants into the heads of some synthetic telepathy operatives
- Insertion of metal plates into the heads of child 'super soldiers'. The plates had electrodes extending into the brain, through which a manager could influence the children remotely via wi-fi.

The scientists were responsible for obtaining and supplying viruses and bacteria for close range remote applications, using carbon-dioxide lasers or water droplet sprays as delivery agents. There was a section specialising in psychological warfare, including use of psychosis-inducing drugs, and virtual reality displays, projected into the brains of victims, using lasers to beam light through their skulls. The clinicians worked with scientists and radio engineers to develop remote assassination methods.

The underground bases had many levels; access to which was strictly limited, so that operatives could not go into areas other their own. Entrances to the base were guarded, and no one without a security pass could enter.

Milton Keynes is a town in the East Midlands. It was also the location of the North American's mafia's science and technology research headquarters in the British Isles. The technology was secret and involved unethical people - doctors who didn't mind doing evil things to human beings, scientists who happily played around with genetically modified foetuses, creating Frankenstein monsters. Staffed almost exclusively by people from North America, these scientists had their own subculture.

Spying was high on their agenda – attempting to spy on NATO, space stations, and Western defence mechanisms in Europe, North

America, or wherever. Private commercial satellite, wi-fi, and infra-red are used by all terrorists these days, but the Milton Keynes mob used laser mirror technologies and heated plasma, combined with infrasound and ultrasound. They were linked to other underground facilities, mainly below large country houses located across the British Isles.

Could that happen without the British military's knowing about it? I think not. But it is well understood that there will be foreign nationals acting as covert spies around military bases, and the host country will know about them, and monitor their activities without overt intervention. After all, if they removed the spies, others would replace them, so better the devil you know.

I got to know about these technologies by observation and personal experience. There was a US mobster who lived nearby. He let the Milton Keynes lot use his premises. One day I was walking down the road, when I caught sight of someone standing behind their hedge, pointing a very long telescope at me. It was at least five feet long, large, heavy and the end of it curved to touch the ground. It had to be supported by a kind of tripod. It looked like those long Swiss horns that you see in the Alps. I stared at the man and his implement. He shimmered a bit. He was there, definitely, but no, he wasn't. Was it a hologram? I wasn't sure. I was reminded of the poem by William Hughes Mearns:

> 'Yesterday, upon the stair,
> I met a man who wasn't there.
> He wasn't there again today,
> I wish, I wish he'd go away.'

A few days later, I was looking out of the kitchen window into our rhododendron hedge; in the middle, there was a shimmery spot. The next day, the shimmery spot had grown to twice its width, and there were no rhododendrons in the shimmery bit. Within a week, it was a massive archway. Then, one evening, I was lying in bed when I saw a light in my work room. I watched in astonishment as people entered through the archway. There were three figures crouched

around a TV screen. They were all a bit shimmery in the dark, but I could see that there were two middle-aged men and a woman, in her thirties, with shortish blonde hair. They had a conspiratorial manner and were giggling audibly, their shoulders shaking with laughter.

I looked at the TV screen they were watching. A senior man from the North American mafia office up the road, in his sixties, with silver hair, was standing in the nude, proudly displaying himself, while other males in their fifties and sixties, equally unclad, disported themselves. It was a homosexual porn movie, starring a group of local terrorists. What gave it an interesting edge was that several of the participants were stoma patients, wearing their prostheses.

Why did some of the men have stoma bags? Because they belonged to a culture of abuse in which, from their earliest years, children were the target for indecent assaults. Electronic and ultrasound devices were used in attacks on their colons and lower intestines. In later life, these guys all had intestinal problems that had to be treated by surgical removal of tracts in the intestine.

It turned out that the blonde woman I saw in my work room was a professional IRA photographer, here on official business, reporting an IRA conference. She was co-opted to provide special services for the terrorists' gay group. She was sworn to secrecy, and this was why she and her mates had chosen my work room for a private viewing. But it showed that somebody knew my workroom fairly well, and had, no doubt, visited it in the past.

After the air tunnel incident, I noticed similar shimmering air tunneling linking different terrorist safe houses. There were two that crossed roads. There was also one from an IRA-US mafia hideout to the bedroom of an attractive female IRA employee. I saw it developing, but I doubt that it got to its final destination, as later that week, there was a big wooden stick laid across the gap in the hedge where it had emerged. Somebody decided to put an end to that plan.

The Milton Keynes mob were developing infrasound technologies locally. I do not understand why they chose to do this, because infrasound technologies are easy to detect. The terrorists built a large operations hall, two roads down from us, with a grand

façade, like a private clinic, to house their infrasound equipment. One night, at three o'clock in the morning, there was the most awful noise. It was like a machine that had gone wrong, groaning and shrieking. At first, I thought it might be some kind of burglar alarm malfunctioning, but the tone was much too low, more like a terribly loud lawnmower. It went on for an hour.

I gathered from IRA gossip on the synthetic telepathy chat-line that the Milton Keynes mob had left suddenly, because of the activities of the British Military, and that local IRA technicians were trying to make the infrasound device work, without success. No doubt the neighbours had something to say about that. The IRA didn't try it again for six months. When they did, it made the same horrible noise. They switched it off immediately, and that was the end of their infrasound operations. Once the advanced technicians had left our area, the local scientists just couldn't figure out how to make the technology work.

Spying was an integral part of the North American mafia's business, and the IRA also took a strong interest in military industrial espionage. One of the IRA groups attached to our local terrorist unit had a family member who worked as a secure government courier at the European Space Centre. He had an Irish passport, and, as a member of the European Union, had gone through whatever security procedures he needed to, in order to become a courier. These posts are carefully checked, but evidently there was nothing to link his background to anything suspicious. His job meant that he carried sensitive documents from place to place. It would not be easy for anyone to access documents unofficially, but I guess they tried.

Another IRA family with members living in the East Coast of the United States wanted their son to get a job in the US National Security Agency. Their son kept applying and going for interviews. He had to sit all kinds of tests in order to qualify for consideration. Each time, he was rejected, and then he was 'timed out' and wasn't able to apply anymore. His family blamed him for being a failure. But I wonder whether the National Security Agency had asked their British counterparts if they had anything on this guy. You would expect them to, and if they did, my guess is that the British gave him

the thumbs down. But that didn't seem to have occurred to his family, who were not the brightest of the bright.

At an early stage in my kidnap, I woke one night and found myself within the electromagnetic environment, in a military office. The staff had Irish accents and wore greenish uniforms. A grey-haired man in his fifties, dressed in civilian clothes, was ushering in a man of about thirty. He had dark hair and brown-rimmed glasses, and looked studious, with a long fringe, flopping over his face. The room contained videoconference equipment. On the video screen were two people I recognised as IRA staff from where I used to live in Greater London. At one time, they had infiltrated a counterterrorism unit, and had operated in the same building as the local police station – the Metropolitan Police had later kicked them out. They wore synthetic telepathy headphones. The grey-haired man greeted them as old friends.

The young Irishman was helped to put on headphones by the older man. They all tried to communicate with each other via synthetic telepathy. The young man could not get the hang of it, and everyone was laughing at him. Then a young woman in green military uniform brought the two Irish men cups of tea. From their conversation, I gathered that the young Irishman was applying for a post at a North American military base in Yorkshire, for which competence in synthetic telepathy was required.

I don't know if he got the job, but I suspect not. Six months later, I was an involuntary witness at a North American Mafia training course on synthetic telepathy in Los Angeles. The room was divided into two parts. There was an inner glass area, where only participants could operate. Then there was an outer area, with wooden benches for people to sit on and watch participants through the glass. I saw the young Irishman with the long fringe sitting on the wooden benches, taking notes and asking questions.

It looked to me as if the IRA had tried to get one of their people into a US NATO post in the UK, via the Irish Republic, but had failed to do so. But it is possible that he was successful and managed to get a transfer to a military post in California, where he made contact with US mafia operations.

The North American mafia had an entire wing of their operations devoted to drama and acting ability. They needed actors who could pretend to be other people in a lot of different situations. They also needed people who could pretend not to be themselves in order to stay covert. These actors did not necessarily have North American or Irish accents. They had to be able to blend into their surroundings easily, sometimes at short notice.

The US mafia used gang-stalking a lot in the States. This involved a troupe of actors hounding a victim in the street without doing actual violence. They would harass them at traffic lights, giving them knowing looks, sidling up to them, brushing against them, laughing loudly at them, as if sharing a joke at the victim's expense. Then there was open tailing of the victim *en masse*. Wherever the victim went, these guys would appear to be busily doing something nearby; often on their smartphone at street corners.

Victims might find their cars scratched unattributably, rubbish thrown into their gardens, petty break-ins into garages. There might be nuisance phone calls where the caller could not be traced. These actions were designed to unnerve the victim and to affect the balance of their minds, particularly if the US mafia wanted the victim to become paranoid and registered for mental health purposes, as an unreliable witness.

A more sinister application of the acting groups was 'rent-a-mob'. Political demonstrations against a democratically elected government would be infiltrated by these people, suitably disguised. These guys were often the first to smash shop windows, or start a fight with other demonstrators, after which they faded out of the picture. The actors went through a lot of training for these roles, including practising throwing bottles and stones at the police. Some of them were not just actors and threw fire bombs in bottles, designed to cause maximum trouble and confusion. Ambitious young Western terrorists vied for these roles, as they were seen as a fast-track to promotion into the smoke-filled rooms of the North American mafia.

In September 2016, a local conference was held on how to harmonise terrorist practices between the North American mafia/IRA

and European Terrorist organisations. Apparently, a terrorist working party had reviewed differences in approach between the two groups and was proposing that the North American mafia/IRA should alter their practices, to fall in line with Al-Qaida/ Islamic State practices for the European Theatre of War.

A woman terrorist speaker arrived, to set out the revised procedures. She was a representative of a Pan-North American-European working group, funded by Al-Qaida. Al-Qaida do not normally interfere with the operations of their terrorist partners, except to give feedback on an annual basis, when they renew funding contracts. Informal interactions are not encouraged. However there had been areas of contention, hence the harmonisation conference.

The main area of contention was the North American mafia's habit of arriving on the 'battlefield' without checking out the terrain in detail, and charging in, all guns blazing. Their European counterparts said that, in future, the Yanks should sit down and wait for specialist advisors to carry out an overview of the terrain and hold meetings with leaders of the terrorist cells to decide which terrorist groups were best suited to which tasks.

That seems fairly straightforward as far as strategy goes, but in what circumstances would the North American mafia/IRA be working with their European counterparts? It sounded as if there were going to be joint operations across several European countries, involving representatives of different terrorist groups. The Islamic State movement had claimed responsibility for terrorist attacks in France and Belgium in 2016, but there was no evidence that the North American mafia/IRA had participated.

Another area of contention raised more recently by Al-Qaida was the use of slave soldiers. Al-Qaida deplored this practice, not so much on ethical grounds, but because it produced poor quality soldiers. They have always stressed the importance of using volunteers, citing the good performance of their volunteer soldiers in Iraq and Afghanistan. By contrast, the IRA and North American mafia relied increasingly on blackmail victims, drug addicts and soldiers enslaved from childhood, who were easily press-ganged.

However, as detailed later in this book, Islamic State rely heavily on ordinary cocaine to enhance their soldiers' endurance,

hence the correlation between drug trafficking and terrorism from central Asia.

AL-QAIDA'S ELECTROMAGNETIC OPERATIONS

Al-Qaida is one of the main sources of funding of terrorist activities, and they commissioned North American mafia technology specialists to develop their electromagnetic operations. I have met a few Al-Qaida staff via Al-Qaida's electromagnetic communications system, mainly in France, Algeria and Tunisia, and I have observed the terrorist training which they sponsor in Algeria. It looks to me as if, somewhere, there is an inner ring of Al-Qaida potentates who wish to re-open the Ottoman war, conquer the Western World and turn it into an Islamic Caliphate. Their religion happens to be Islam, but their interests are the ancient ones of empire building by invading other countries, conquering them, and demanding tribute.

The Al-Qaida inner ring may not be the smartest people, but historically they have commanded a large reliable flow of funds from Saudi Arabia. This has enabled them to buy in high-quality staff from the US mafia - scientists, technology experts, and specialists in conventional types of warfare. They have also invested in covert technologies, chemical and biological weapons, electronic, electromagnetic and other types of radiation weapons. They commission the training of terrorist groups to use these technologies, and have a large training contract with the IRA.

Their strategy is to start their wars in secret, with covert technologies such as electromagnetic weapons, infiltrating and destroying populations silently, reverting to overt technologies only when there is military opposition. Like all terrorist groups they target the poor, vulnerable and dispossessed members of society first.

In Europe Al-Qaida require their staff to have a legitimate interface with the outside world, such as a local part time job, to enable them to blend into the population without arousing suspicion. Typically, they may appear as office cleaners, carers of elderly or disabled people, nursery nurses, shop assistants, taxi drivers, or courier van drivers. Their earnings from these types of employment are usually low enough to qualify them for welfare benefits, and some of them are registered with the UK Department of Work and Pensions. But that is just their part-time work. The rest of the time they are employed on better-paid work for their terrorist cause.

Al-Qaida's funding relationships with terrorist groups are always governed by a contract, which sets out the objectives that Al-Qaida wishes to achieve, and broad guidelines about how the recipients of funding are required to carry out tasks in support of these objectives.

One of Al-Qaida's main investments is in training of children and young people. They have infiltrated many countries, not only in the West, but in Eastern Asia as well. They require all the terrorist groups that they fund to carry out training of batches of young children 'outside of Christendom', and to train them up as child soldiers. This is easy to achieve in Asia and Africa, but not so easy in Europe or North America.

Al-Qaida have made a special effort to recruit and retain black people, particularly in Western countries. Al-Qaida-funded terrorist groups are ordered not to attack black people unless specifically required to do so. By contrast, whites are never off-limits.

I met a teenage girl called Katherine, an Al-Qaida 'batch kid', who had attended a summer training camp in the Irish Republic in 2015. Run by the IRA, it was funded by Al-Qaida, and there were lectures and pep talks given by Al-Qaida representatives. The batch kids were being taught a new motto to chant:

'WHITES OUT! BLACKS IN! WHITES OUT! BLACKS IN!'

'But you're a white yourself, Katherine,' I said.

'I know', she replied, 'But Al-Qaida says that we must now think of ourselves as being black. We will be treated as though we are black, and we must work with our black brothers and sisters.'

When this message was relayed to the IRA in the UK, there was some dismay. At the next Al-Qaida conference in the North West, senior IRA figures questioned the Al-Qaida representative about it and received confirmation that this new approach would not affect the standing of the IRA, who were regarded as 'honorary blacks'.

Further talks which I had with Algerian Daesh illegal immigrants, working in the terrorist unit where I lived, confirmed Al-Qaida's racist intentions. The Algerians were very clear that their purpose was to come to Britain, kill all the white people, starting with the women, and to take their possessions. I spoke to one Algerian who stated he had been promised that he and his family could live in our house, but he had to kill all the white people living in it first. He wasn't very keen to do this, as it seemed a bit risky, so he kept trying to subcontract the work to other Algerian Daesh immigrants who were less aware of the activities of our Counter Terrorism people, and our British Military.

There is ethnic discrimination against black people within the US mafia. In the British Isles, North American mafia blacks work in separate buildings, in low-quality jobs. This is not in line with Al-Qaida's guidance, but Al-Qaida cannot enforce its guidance, although it raises such issues at funding meetings with terrorist groups. The IRA's London Metropolitan Regiment does not segregate blacks by building, but it only offers them limited promotion opportunities.

Within Al-Qaida's ranks, there are some sincere Muslims who believe in the teachings of the Quran, and say that everyone should protect women, widows, and respect the elderly, irrespective of race or ethnicity. These people do what they can within Al-Qaida to practice their principles. But they are not the ones with greatest influence.

Al-Qaida provides funds for the training of Islamic State and Daesh soldiers. They are not the only organisation to fund these activities, and they do not fund all terrorist activities, but there is a formal hierarchical Al-Qaida training wing dedicated to this work.

Al-Qaida has bases in many countries. Some of these are fairly well-known, such as those in Afghanistan and the Philippines. There

is a large Al-Qaida base in Algeria, and a smaller one in Tunisia. I have spoken to Al-Qaida employees from Tunisia and Algeria. Some of them were nationals of those countries, seeking to migrate to Britain. Others were US, Canadian and French nationals, based in North Africa, drawn from the North American mafia or similar groups. The North Americans were responsible for setting up the large underground science research base in Algeria.

Al-Qaida used to have bases in the British Isles, but in 2014, owing to the increased surveillance activities of the security services and the British military, they found it safer to withdraw the management of their UK operations to the Irish Republic and France. They still visit the UK, and their training wing hold conferences once a quarter, in different parts of the UK or the Irish Republic. On one occasion, the conference was held in the North West, near Birmingham.

During conferences, an official Al-Qaida representative makes an appearance at some point and gives an update on Al-Qaida's strategy or tactics, followed by discussion about how this should be translated into action in the UK.

Our local IRA terrorist unit's Al-Qaida representative lives in France. He facilitates the illegal importation of terrorists from Alegria and Tunisia to IRA units in the UK. The IRA are responsible for meeting them at sea ports and transporting them to IRA registration points, where they are enrolled on the international computer system, and provided with false identity documents for themselves, and any family members they wish to follow them.

A Tunisian terrorist affiliated to Islamic State, whom I met locally, told me that he and his colleagues crossed from Morocco to Spain, where they took a coach to Paris. In Paris, they were met by French Al-Qaida supporters, who provided them with vehicles. They boarded the ferry to a British port and made their way from there to whichever IRA unit they had been allocated.

After our Al-Qaida representative left the UK for good, he recorded CDs with messages for different IRA units in Britain. On 1 November 2014, at three a.m., someone broadcast the message to our local IRA unit on the synthetic telepathy system, and I heard it. I

assume that the message was in English, but, as it is possible to bypass language differences and relate at a pre-verbal stage via the electromagnetic environment, I could never be sure. The message was delivered in a grave, serious tone. The main points were as follows:

Strategic Issues:

- It was not possible for Al-Qaida staff to carry on their work in the UK as before. Staff should not worry about this. Al-Qaida would arrange for them to be moved to places where their good work could continue.

- The raising of batches of children 'outside of Christendom' had proved non-viable in a Western context and would be dropped from Al-Qaida contract objectives. (That meant Al-Qaida would no longer fund these activities).

Local Issues:

- There was praise for several women's groups, who were singled out for their sterling service.

- The contribution of local [IRA] management in the past had been good, but motivation appeared to have declined. Nevertheless, in recognition of past services, their work would continue to be supported by Al-Qaida.

- The behaviour of some men had not been in line with Islamic principles. These men had been spoken to in the past and repented, but they had slipped back.

- As for the 'four thieves', suffice to say that if Al-Qaida were operating under their own jurisdiction, they would know how to deal with them.

- Al-Qaida had received representation from a number of women's groups, about the continued uses of an elderly woman (me) over some years as a target for training of warriors. Al-Qaida deplored this practice and begged that it should cease.

The local IRA and their subcontractors took no notice of this, as attacking me on training courses had become one of their main income sources. In 2016, I decided to make contact with Al-Qaida in France. By then I had learned much more about how to travel using the terrorists' multinational electromagnetic operating system. I

recalled the sound of the voice of the person who delivered the message on the CD and tuned-in to the frequency. I found myself in the French countryside, in a modest cottage, more like a barn. It was night. A man dressed in a long black robe and hood was talking to some Asian soldiers, wearing military camouflage uniforms. The man hurried to a large wooden trunk, and drew out several rifles, which he gave to the soldiers.

The robed man did not have the frequency of the person who delivered the message on the CD (who, it turned out, had died a year before). I greeted his replacement. He cried out in shock and fell on the ground. I decided to withdraw and try again when he had recovered. The next night, I returned. The man was lying on a bed, still in a nervous state. An Asian soldier was looking after him. When I appeared, the man moaned.

'The ghost is over there! Look!' he cried, pointing at me.

The Asian could see me clearly, probably because he was fully logged on to the multinational computer system, using either an inner ear implant or an external earpiece. He saw a figure clad in a long black down coat and hood, - my default outer clothing in winter, but in keeping with Muslim women's dress.

'What is it, sister?' he asked.

'I have come about the warrior training courses in Exton,' I said.

The man went to a table, where there was a bound volume of training courses for 2016.

'Ah yes', he said. 'I see we have three courses currently operating at that location this month.'

'I want you to stop treating me as a target for your training courses,' I said.

'That is not something that I can authorise,' said the man. 'You will have to speak to my boss'.

'Where is he?' I asked.

'He lives in the big house up the road,' said the man. 'But I suggest that you visit him tomorrow afternoon.' I agreed and withdrew.

The next day, I looked for the big house up the road. It was not hard to find – a gracious nineteenth century building, with a pleasant

back garden sloping down a hill. There was a wall with a wrought iron gate, leading to what looked like the vegetable garden. The house was on a high hill, with a panoramic view, overlooking a grass plain, dotted with trees, in a remote part of the French countryside.

I went to the front door. I saw a man of mixed Arab-French descent, clean shaven and in his late fifties, wearing an old chunky-knit grey crew-necked jumper and grey jeans. When I arrived, he beckoned me into the patio at the top of the garden, and three of his henchmen showed up. They were Asians with dark hair and beards, wearing layers of dark clothes, reflecting an Arab-French fusion chic.

'I know why you are here,' he said, politely. 'And I understand that things are not being done as they should be in your area.' Then he lowered his voice, so that his braves could not hear what he said.

'It is difficult for me. You see these things are decided at a higher level, and I am not able to change the way things are.'

'Then I will leave', I said.

There was no point in further discussion. After that, I made a point of 'dragging and dropping' the bodies of Al-Qaida training course students *en-masse* into Al-Qaida's back garden from a height of 300 feet. There were so many, particularly at weekends, that all the braves could do was to cover them with tarpaulins and wait for lorries to come and take them away.

ISLAMIC STATE ELECTROMAGNETIC OPERATIONS

Islamic State soldiers did not appear in my area until 2015. They first appeared in buildings owned by the North American mafia's underground research base. The North American mafia had not wanted to house them but, having been in receipt of Al-Qaida funds for years, they found it hard to refuse.

When terrorists talked to each other on synthetic telepathy, they used avatars so that they could recognise each other without revealing their real identity. Not all participants had the viewing equipment needed to see each other. When Islamic State officers first arrived in the area they could not see me, and they sometimes joined in conversations I could hear. They made the assumption that they were among friends, and that I was a female IRA manager.

I was out gardening one afternoon, when I heard a voice say,
'Sorry for the delay in arriving; we had to stay, as we had missed a plane crash.'

I made further enquiries about this, and it emerged that the voice belonged to an Islamic State officer, who was one of a group of six from Libya where they had had a schedule of training which had included how to initiate a plane crash. The group had missed their training on plane crashes and had to wait for the next course. It sounded as if ground to air missiles were involved.

The Islamic State officers said that they arrived by freight transport. The following week, I saw a huge lorry attempting to come up our road. It was heading for the secret underground research base. On the side of the lorry were the words 'freight liner'. Operating in electromagnetic environment mode, via the Al-Qaida

telecommunications system, I looked into the secret research base garden, and saw a reception party. There was a bearded religious leader, wearing a kind of black headdress, and another man, both in long black robes. Six tall strong men of Pakistani ethnicity were standing in a line, dressed in khaki uniforms, being greeted. They were escorted to a house within the perimeter of the research base, which was set aside for the use of Islamic State.

The Islamic State group soon made themselves at home. The freightliner lorries arrived twice a week; on Wednesdays and Saturdays, at about lunchtime. I looked inside their house, and saw a Muslim lady housekeeper, wearing a long black robe and headscarf. There was a bookcase in the property, containing Islamic books. I watched as she pushed the bookcase aside, revealing a cache of rifles hidden inside the wall.

An IRA employee came out of the building and walked across to the front of the research centre, where there were some charming Victorian cottages. A high wall concealed a stone staircase going down about twenty feet into an underground area below. My eyes followed him down. He went into a hallway, where there was a door and a doormat outside it. He took off his shoes and placed them in a nearby niche in the wall. Then he entered the room.

I saw a long, low, living room, with white walls. Twelve men of Middle Eastern ethnicity, wearing long black robes, were sitting in a circle on the carpet. An older man with a long grey beard and a black headdress appeared to be leading the group. He held a large parchment-type book in his hands. The other men showed him great respect, but the IRA man did not.

'You've got to get out of here,' he said, addressing the elderly teacher. 'She knows where you are. It's not safe now.'

'Why should I?' said the teacher. 'I've told you before, you've nothing to fear from her if you just leave her alone. I haven't attacked her, and she hasn't attacked me.'

'But she's written to the British Military about you,' said the IRA man. (This was true.)

'I've nothing to fear from the British Military, either,' said the teacher. 'I've done nothing wrong.' And he continued his teaching, ignoring the intruder.

The next day, I was looking inside an underground walkway that connected the Islamic State hideout to a larger IRA safe house. Outside the kitchen of the IRA building there was a tall man of Middle Eastern appearance, wearing a long cream robe and a red hat like a fez. He was in charge of a group of small boys about five years old. They had been trafficked there for the Islamic State soldiers' 'refreshment'. They were kept separate from other brothel kids, to ensure that they did not pick up any diseases. They flocked around their handler, hugging his legs. They had no one else in the world.

Later on, I saw one of the Islamic State soldiers mistreating a small boy. I attacked the soldier and he fell, dead. Another Islamic State officer took up the fight. He died as well. Then one of them threatened me with a gun, saying he knew where I lived. In the end, I had to dispatch four of the six.

The last two Islamic State soldiers went into their safe house on the perimeter of the research base and descended into the basement. There was a lift there that went down to the underground living space that I saw before.

By now I figured that it was time to send a short report to the British Military. I emailed MI5 about the Islamic State developments. Two days later, an unusual craft that looked a bit like a flying cigar case with black things suspended from it flew over the research facility. Then some small aircraft flew round the perimeter of the base. The next day, I heard my favourite aircraft, the Chinook, approaching really low. It went to where I had seen the Islamic State soldiers. I was pleased that our Military were on the case.

Things went quiet on the Islamic State front for a while, and then, one day, I heard an Islamic State officer on synthetic telepathy, saying that he had just arrived in Britain, from a sea port, where he had been met by the IRA. They took him to a railway station and put him on a train to a large town, about half an hour from London. He had been told to get out and wait on the station platform. A Muslim cleric met him and directed him to a different platform, where he

took a different train, emerging at Exford. The local IRA picked him up there and drove him to our local area.

'That was quite a journey,' I commented.

'Yes,' said the officer. 'And I was accompanied by fourteen others, though I left them when I changed trains. My work here is to start up a cell, planning attacks on the European mainland from Britain.'

'Oh, I see,' I said, in a neutral tone of voice.

'Honestly!' I thought to myself. 'They just do not understand the meaning of the word "covert". They must blurt everything out the moment they arrive.'

This was the second time that an Islamic State officer had mistaken me for a female IRA manager. He naturally assumed that anyone talking on Syntel would be a terrorist too.

In 2016, Al-Qaida held a week-end conference, hosted by our local underground US mafia base. One of the Al-Qaida teenage 'super soldiers' told me that she and a friend had been admitted to the conference. Al-Qaida had given a talk about their work on the 'European Theatre of War', and described planned Islamic State planned attacks on the European mainland. The conference delegates were then invited to go to another room upstairs, where they could meet Islamic State officers actively engaged in this work and watch them demonstrating how they carried out various tasks.

It never occurred to these people that British military aircraft seemed to be permanently nesting over the area, and that the conference could have been live-streamed straight to the Authorities. Al-Qaida and the North American mafia had access to fairly advanced technology themselves, but they never gave a thought to the technologies that our military might employ.

Some time after this, there were a number of terrorist attacks in Europe, including the one in Nice, where a lorry deliberately drove into crowds of people celebrating Bastille Day in July 2016, and the lorry attack on a Berlin Christmas market in December 2016, for which Islamic State claimed responsibility. I do not think our local Islamic State cell had anything to do with these. However, on 3 February 2017, when an Egyptian man attacked a soldier with a

machete outside the Louvre in Paris, all our local terrorists were on the alert.

When news of the attack was announced on the radio, some IRA terrorists went scurrying to check on the internet. Then I heard them whispering that they had been told to expect a terrorist attack that day. That does not necessarily mean that the local Islamic State cell was involved in it; but they were at least aware of it.

It seemed to me that the unsuccessful Louvre attack indicated some lack of preparation and lack of knowledge about security arrangements at the French museum. An Islamic State officer from the local terrorist cell must have heard my thought, as he came on Syntel to say that the terrorist who carried out the Louvre attack did not understand what he had to do and got confused. He added that our local Islamic State cell had carried off some successful projects, but they had to be discreet, and did not need to show off about their achievements.

He also said that their plans included the British mainland as well as the European continent. I responded that, in that case, the British military must have blocked their plans, as there had been no recorded successful Islamic State terrorist attacks on the British mainland in the last three years. The terrorist confirmed that the British military had indeed blocked their plans regarding the British mainland.

It was a month later that we learned of the murder of a policeman outside the Palace of Westminster, and the deaths and injuries of pedestrians on Westminster Bridge. I did not get any insights into that attack. By now the IRA had ordered their staff and subcontractors not to discuss anything about Islamic State on Syntel ever again.

The British military's interest in Islamic State activities locally became so obvious that in the end, the terrorists moved their cell to a site about a mile away. We could tell where it was, because the military helicopters kept going there. The military always let us know when Islamic State officers arrived on Wednesdays and Saturdays, because we could hear the aircraft escorting them up the road. I hope that British citizens will be reassured by this. Our military and security services are second to none.

BOATS, DRONES AND UNDERGROUND TUNNELS

The IRA, Al-Qaida and Islamic State work co-operatively, running a complex import-export business involving people and drug trafficking. Terrorists from Asia, Africa and the Middle East are trafficked into Europe, and drug consignments run in parallel. The IRA are active at ports across Europe, running a tracking service to ensure that people and drugs can be followed at every stage of their journey. The goods are mainly transported by sea to European ports. Their time of arrival has to be known exactly, so that IRA units can organise unmarked vans to pick up and drop off their cargoes. One of the main drug routes from Kabul goes across Turkey to the Mediterranean Sea, from where cargoes travel by boat to various ports in the UK and Europe.

The IRA's operations sometimes started in distant places, but I had recently learned a new method to travel the world. It works a bit like cell-phone roving, because you need to be connected by wi-fi and satellite connections to achieve it, and I was permanently connected to Al-Qaida's satellite system, so I could do it.

I would find a photograph of the place or person I wanted to visit and attune my frequency too the frequency of the photograph, and then suddenly, in my mind's eye, I would be there! I hope this is the travel method of the future, as it is a lot quicker than present arrangements. I also found that if I 'took a picture' of someone in my mind, I could go back to that picture and make contact with the person concerned. This was useful if terrorists were running away, and I wanted to get at them. I would just snap their picture, and then pull them out of the ether. A similar method worked for sounds. If

someone was talking on their mobile, I could tune into the sound of the other person's voice, and either be in their location, or pull them out of the ether.

After I learnt how to manipulate the terrorists' electromagnetic computer system architecture and found I could travel anywhere in the terrorist world, I decided to carry out a fact-finding exercise. A good deal of the IRA's business seemed to be transporting people from place to place. I wanted to understand more about this.

I saw an IRA port office outside Calais. It was in a light airy white building with three floors. The boss sat in a penthouse, with soft filtered light coming in through opaque glass roof windows. He was at the hub of a business that hummed with activity, but his office was always quiet. On the next floor down, there were three offices, in which IRA staff sat at white tables, with large daily work sheets, plotting imports and exports through the day. The chart required constant updates, as arrival times changed, with additions and cancellations. In the next room, telephones rang with updated information on the actual position of cargoes. Another room dealt with interaction between exporting and importing terrorists to and from IRA units across the British Isles and parts of Europe. On the floor below, there was a room with less natural light, where finances were managed.

I watched as two external consultants were ushered into the top office to meet the boss. He was an elderly man with greying hair, and a grey suit. He greeted the visitors and wasted no time in getting to the point.

'Can you provide us with a sufficiently high view to survey all our sea transport across the Mediterranean? I want minimum visibility for your device: just a speck in the sky'.

The two entrepreneurs nodded. They were an 'Own Drone' business, and there was nothing illegal in the services they were offering.

'We can do all that. Whatever your requirement, we can meet it. But costs will vary depending on specifications.'

'We need clear, accurate, timely information,' the boss continued.

He regularly imported drugs, arms and Islamic State terrorists from the Near East, by boat. He looked cautiously at the two men, wondering if they were up to the job. I left them haggling over prices and went to visit the 'downstream activities'.

It was somewhere in Northern France, on the border with Belgium. A French couple were eating a meal in a modest Victorian cottage. Their parlour was dimly lit, with dusty curtains, and the view of their back garden was a patchwork of dark and light greens – all foliage, and no flowers. In the living room across the hall, two Frenchmen and a uniformed Islamic State Officer were working on projections of business for the coming week. They were expecting several consignments of Islamic State soldiers, to be dropped off at various points across Europe. They also had to co-ordinate Islamic State soldiers needing to join the delivery vans on various points along the route, for onward delivery to a range of destinations.

The details of these pick-ups and drop-offs were being plotted on a large chart in a room in the cellar. Four men were sitting round a table under a naked electric light, working out every point of the complex delivery system. There was a plasma screen against one of the walls. It was linked to a camera outside the house. A man wearing long white robes could be seen peering into the camera, waving. He was requesting permission to enter. One of the terrorists at the table operated an automatic door lock, and the robed man appeared in the front hall. There was a large trap door in the hall, which lead to a brightly lit underground corridor. I followed it for what seemed about half an hour. It stretched about three kilometres, with rooms leading off along the way. It would be possible for a large number of men to live down there without difficulty, provided provisions were brought in regularly.

A sturdily built Asian man with a black beard emerged from the trap door and went into the living room. He reported that a convoy of five lorries was due, and that preparations were now ready to receive several groups of Islamic State soldiers, who were to be dropped off at various points above ground. The robed man in the hallway bowed and waved to the group in the living room, to indicate that he was the

driver of the first lorry and wanted to know where to park his vehicle.

Two French men got up from the table and went out to guide the first lorry to the side of the road. As they did so, two Islamic State soldiers jumped out of the back of the lorry, and one jumped in. One of the French men climbed into the cab of the lorry alongside the robed driver and guided him out into the main road. Looking back along the road, I could see four identical lorries, waiting behind. The convoy proceeded in a North Easterly direction towards a roundabout. I was watching from the first lorry, and, not being used to driving on the other side of the road, got a shock, as a car overtook the entire convoy from the left side and turned into the roundabout.

The first lorry stopped at the junction, its parking lights flashing. Two men leaped from the back and brought out a step ladder. Five Islamic State soldiers emerged from a culvert below the side of the road and climbed into the lorry. Then all five lorries took off towards Belgium.

I decided to go 'upstream' to places from which Islamic State soldiers and drug consignments originated. The first place I visited was in Saudi Arabia, in Riyadh. I was inside a marble building. It looked like a bank. The boss had an imposing office. His desk was on a raised step, so that he looked down on those arriving, putting them immediately at a psychological disadvantage. He wore Arab dress, a long white robe and head-covering.

As I crossed the spacious cool entry hall, I could see women and children running in all directions.

'She is here, we must get out now,' a woman shouted.

The boss's wife came running from a side-door into the top office.

'Get out now, come on', she cried, tugging at his arm. There was obviously some kind of radio wave detector warning them of my presence.

'It's my duty to stay here,' said the boss; and he stayed at his post.

He was one of those responsible for routing funds for Al-Qaida out of Saudi Arabia. I wondered where the funds were destined for next.

Looking across the Saudi Arabian desert, I searched with my inner ear, like a bird listening for worms. I picked up a frequency transmission coming from way down underground. I tried to find the source, but it was so far down underground that I almost gave up.

'I must have made a mistake,' I thought.

Then, suddenly, I saw light. It was a corridor, with arched ceilings, leading into a wide hall, with ornate marble columns, and marble tiles on the floor. There was cool fresh air pumping through the place, and a fountain playing in the centre courtyard. It felt pleasant and relaxing. I entered a very ornate dining room, with alcoves, and a raised floor level at one end, reached by marble stairs, with doors leading to adjoining rooms. The high ceiling was domed. Underneath it was a marble table, laid for a delicious meal, with fresh fruit and fruit juices, to accompany it.

Two men in white robes and turban headdresses were sitting eating. They appeared to be enjoying a happy time, laughing and joking. They were warned of my arrival by Al-Qaida's efficient communications system. They both scrutinised their smartphones and seemed to be receiving information from them. As I appeared, in my long black down coat and hood, they greeted me respectfully. They explained that they were the recipients of Al-Qaida funding, engaging in drug and arms trafficking in support of Al-Qaida objectives.

'I am just a humble drug-trafficker,' said one of the men.

'Business is obviously doing well,' I replied. But I knew that their business covered a good deal more than drugs.

I did not see any soldiers in this subterranean place, but I was aware that Al-Qaida had troops to call on in neighbouring Yemen, and many parts of Africa and Asia. I looked across to Afghanistan, and found two sites, both underground, with long tunnels and rooms. I remembered the complex underground dwellings in Cappadocia in Turkey, carved out of the lava of extinct volcanoes. The Afghan tunnels were dustier, and the rooms more basic. The soldiers,

variously clad in dark robes or loose-fitting jackets and trousers, were at home in their environment, negotiating their networked pathways like mountain goats. They did not look like Islamic State soldiers, but Al-Qaida was funding them just as generously as those we were used to seeing in Syria and Iraq from our television screens.

It was not just Al-Qaida we had to deal with. I had become aware from IRA funding meetings that, somewhere in the Far East, there was a rival group of terrorists that also funded the IRA. I tuned into the frequency that seemed to go with this group and found myself in a part of the world that I did not recognise. The scenery was lush and tropical, with jungle and mountains emerging out of it. There were beautiful empty beaches – empty until you looked out to sea. There were large ocean-going liners, similar to, but smaller than the Queen Elizabeth II, parked out there, and a small frigate.

Inland, there were domed palaces. The buildings were not ostentatious. They blended into the background, and some of the architecture looked ultra-modern American in style. I visited one palace. It was located entirely on the ground floor, or on floors below ground level. An obese, elderly man was swimming in a pool with colourful mosaics on the walls. There was also a rather unappealing casino, with a rich red carpet and red furnishings. Hardly anyone was in there, except a man and a woman drinking coffee. They seemed to be staff. A little way back from the beach there was an outdoor pool. A tall glamorous young woman with long dark hair and tanned skin was strolling by the pool. She wore a black swimsuit, and over it a long black robe with slits around the bottom, which blew this way and that in the breeze as she walked.

I boarded the liner in the bay. The top floor was occupied by a portly elderly man dressed like a sultan. His family of wives and children were also living there, and his two eldest sons were in attendance, in his private office, assisting with day-to-day business. The floors below were more familiar to me, being occupied by the usual terrorist staff, sitting at laptops with headsets, connected via private satellite to units in different parts of the world, intent on carrying out remote electromagnetic attacks on those whom they chose to target, assisted by local operatives in the targeted locations.

This was part of the other group that was funding the IRA. I tried to place the location in the atlas. It looked as if it could be somewhere in Malaysia.

Something had to be done about these sea-going terrorists. It seemed a good idea to take them out of circulation, so I lifted them into dry dock, hundreds of feet above the sea, and surrounded them by a strong electromagnetic field that concealed them from view.

I paused in my travels, to take stock of what I had learned. All the people I had seen or met were well organised and hard at work. They made our local terrorists look like lazy couch potatoes by comparison.

'If they and their like could see how our local terrorists wasted their funding, perhaps they would put pressure on those responsible for allocating funds to the British Isles to reallocate their investments elsewhere,' I reasoned, somewhat unrealistically.

I decided to carry out a propaganda exercise, to try and discourage further funding to terrorist operations in our area. I went back to all the places I had visited and transported the people I had met into large cage-like living spaces, suspended from tall wooden structures about forty feet above our garden. The structures and their contents were invisible unless you had a computer-brain interface connecting you to the terrorists' computer system networks. I constructed an opulent dwelling for the Saudi potentates and merchants, and an exclusive domed dwelling for the Malaysian sultan. A more modest construction with white carpets and self-assembly furniture housed the IRA and their French counterparts from the Calais office.

The constructions I built were at a higher frequency level than those normally experienced by the terrorists. When contained in them, the terrorists stopped experiencing fear, pain, cold, heat, hunger, thirst and fatigue. Those on drugs came off immediately. You could say their environment was a half-way house to the after-life, because once people entered the electromagnetic architecture, there was no return to the everyday world. Within a few days, they all disappeared, moving on to whatever their future destination might be.

These visitors attracted considerable attention across the Al-Qaida networks. Terrorists watched via satellite, from their smartphones, and several sent large baskets of flowers to the Saudi potentates. I brought out groups of our local terrorists to explain themselves to the Al-Qaida visitors. The sorry crowd of criminals, drug addicts and traffickers who made up the IRA subcontractors locally, shocked the visitors considerably. The locals shouted obscenities at the Malaysians and the Al-Qaida guests, and picked fights with each other. Women from the child brothel brought out children as young as a year old and held them up for sale.

'Look Sir, here is a very nice young boy, see, he has all his male parts fully developed', shouted one of the gross women.

The Saudi potentates shuddered, but one of the Middle Eastern drug traffickers asked for the child to brought nearer.

'Just give us your credit card details', continued the woman, and we can do things to the child while you watch.

That was her last word on the subject. I removed her at once, and put the poor little boy in a large cot with a safety net round it, suspended from the construction that I had created.

The propaganda exercise did have some effect. Al-Qaida instructed the IRA to stop funding one of its subcontractors, but overall, not much changed. Well, it was worth a try.

I decided to return to France, to the start of the long underground corridor. In a room underneath the terrorist safehouse, there was a meeting in progress. Two men in Arab dress, with white robes and black headbands around their head-coverings, sat on one side of the table. On the other side were two Asian men in battle fatigues, that I took to be Islamic State soldiers. Chairing the meeting was a European man in his late thirties. He spoke in French, but it was not his first language. I suspected he was IRA, because I had seen Islamic State soldiers from the IRA's Calais office dropped off at the safe house. I listened for a moment. They were discussing timing of the next consignment of Islamic State soldiers later that night. Another European man was busy in the next room. He was surrounded by filing cabinets, and sat at a table, examining papers, matching delivery notes to invoices.

'What happens at the other end of the corridor?' I wondered. I made myself transparent to avoid detection, and floated along the top of the corridor, looking at side roads that led off in different directions. As I got towards the end of the corridor, I saw three Arabs in white robes like the ones in the safe house, lounging against the walls, as if they had nothing to do. Then I saw a patch of daylight. The corridor was coming to an end.

There was a short flight of steps. I went up them and found myself in a large formal garden, with well-cut lawns and trees. On the other side of the garden was an enormous red-brick building that looked like a palace. It was oblong, and instead of a roof there was an enormous red-brick dome. A fountain was playing outside the building, and the side of the building was decorated with thick white ropes, hanging in curved loops, about four feet above the ground.

I looked up at the red-brick dome. There were round windows like portholes running along the sides. I went in through one, and found an enormous dormitory, with fifty camp beds in it. Each bed was neatly covered with white linen, as if waiting for a specific occasion. But the place was deserted.

I went down some stairs on to the first floor. There was a private area, with an enormous bedroom, and a bed with a canopy and red velvet curtains, and a door leading to a sunken bathroom, with what might have been a jacuzzi in it. I followed the corridor into a large reception room, with ornate chairs around the walls, and several three-piece suites, with elaborate coverings, on thick-pile red carpet. The design of the carpet looked Chinese. Then I went through a door into the next room. It was similar to the first room, but at the other end, on a raised dais, was a large desk and chair, with curtains on each side. A man dressed like a Sultan wearing a large turban was sitting at the desk. His feet rested on a footstool which protruded from underneath the desk. The reason for this became apparent, when a man wearing white robes, like the ones I had seen earlier, entered, and prostrated himself, before reaching to kiss the feet that protruded from under the desk.

At that moment, a liveried servant appeared, announcing the arrival of two honoured guests. The first guest, a man of South

American ethnicity, dressed in the uniform of a General, strode into the room. The Sultan came down from the dais and took him by the hand, greeting him warmly. The General was accompanied by an entourage of twelve soldiers, wearing green, red and white uniforms, who lined the walls of the reception room outside.

Then the second guest arrived. He was an emaciated man in his eighties in a wheelchair, wearing a light brown suit, accompanied by one attendant, who withdrew to the reception room. His face was drawn and grey, and I guessed immediately that he was an IRA senior officer. He held the rank of Brigadier.

Drinks and aperitifs were served. The General drank whisky with obvious appreciation. The IRA Brigadier had a gin and tonic, and the Sultan sipped a glass of what looked like red wine.

'What a strange combination!' I thought, not sure whether I was referring to the drinks or to the meeting participants.

'I am grateful that you were able to come at such short notice,' said the Sultan.

'Always a pleasure to see you again,' replied the General.

'Perhaps we could get straight down to business,' said the IRA Brigadier. 'I have to be somewhere else within an hour'.

'Of course, of course,' said the General, lighting a cigar. 'Come on then, what's this all about?'

The Sultan lowered his voice.

'You know we have had trouble in the Far East, losing several yachts, and some of our staff are on display in aerial cages over the South of England.'

'I did hear something about that,' smiled the General.

'What is your point, Sultan?' asked the IRA Brigadier.

'She has been seen in this area,' said the Sultan.

'How could she find out?' asked the General. 'No one knows about this place. What's your view, Brigadier?'

The Brigadier looked uncomfortable.

'We will need to review the situation and come back to you. You must understand that this is the first I have heard of these developments.'

'Well, all right,' said the Sultan. 'But don't be too long about it. Can I suggest that we meet again tomorrow morning? We really cannot leave it any later.'

'Tomorrow morning is fine,' said the Brigadier. 'By then I hope to have better news for you.'

'Great! That's what we like to hear,' laughed the General.

The three men stood up and took leave of each other, the General again escorted by his twelve henchmen.

'I wonder what the French Government would make of all this?' I thought to myself. 'These people should not be at large.'

I looked up French prisons on the internet. I found one in the centre of Paris. It looked like a walled fortress and was described as a high security prison. Returning to the French safe house, I scooped up all the people in the underground meeting, and the man in the adjoining room, together with all their filing cabinets. Then I called up a picture of the prison in my mind and tuned in to its frequency. I found myself in a large hall, leading to other buildings. People were walking through large archway doors on either side, leading to courtyards outside.

'If I dump all these people and their furniture on the ground,' they might get hurt,' I thought.

So I created some large mattresses to form a cushion on which to place things.

As soon as I threw down the mattresses, there was a commotion. Prison officers blew whistles, and iron curtains were drawn across the archway doors, sealing the hall off completely. I carefully deposited the men and the office furniture on separate mattresses. The prison security must have involved some advanced technology, because the prison officers could see me.

'Who are these men?' asked a prison officer.

'They are Islamic State, Al-Qaida and IRA terrorists,' I replied. 'I found them plotting terrorist activities in a safe house leading to an underground tunnel three kilometres long. At the end of the tunnel is a foreign palace where a terrorist potentate from the Far East is living.'

The Prison officer interrogated the men I had brought in.

'Who are you?' he asked one of the robed Arabs.

'My master lives in the palace at the end of the underground corridor. It is to the North of Paris. My house can also be reached from the underground corridor,' he added.

'Can you take us to this place?' asked the prison officer.

'Yes sir, of course,' said the Arab, politely.

French prison officers had already lined up the Islamic Soldiers against the wall and disarmed them. The prison officer then turned to the two Europeans.

'So, are you the IRA?' he asked. One of them nodded. But the other one looked towards the filing cabinets, table and chair that had once been his office. Two gendarmes were loading them on to wheeled pallets to take them away.

'Stop!' he cried, 'That's my furniture. Don't you touch it. You've no right. It's mine!'

He ran and sat in the chair with his elbows on the table.

'Alright, here you are then,' said one of the gendarmes, in a good-natured fashion.

He and his mate lifted the table and chair, with the IRA clerical worker still sitting there, and moved them to one side. Meanwhile, another gendarme was reading papers he had taken from the filing cabinet.

'And you, Madame,' said the prison officer, looking at me. 'What is your name, please?'

I told him my name, but it was unfamiliar to him, and he asked me to spell it. At this point the other IRA man decided to step in, and wrote down my name for the prison officer. It seems that he had been well briefed by his English colleagues.

'Well, then,' said the French prison officer, smiling at me, 'Thank you for your help.'

I was rather taken aback by that, as no one had ever thanked me like that before.

'Oh, my pleasure,' I stammered. 'I will leave you to your work. Goodbye.'

And I left.

A couple of hours later, I checked in on the French safe house. There were gendarmes everywhere. I went down in the underground corridor. There were some Arabs in handcuffs up one end, but I could hear the sound of shouting and fighting up the other end. An Arab was driving a kind of wheeled vehicle along the corridor, while another was firing a semi-automatic weapon at some gendarmes, and other Arabs were throwing missiles. There was smoke everywhere, and some of the corridor lights had gone out. I could just see three gendarmes pointing handguns. One of the gendarmes was hit in the arm.

Luckily, several more gendarmes came running from the other end of the corridor. The Arab who had been driving the vehicle produced an incendiary device and was shot dead. Then the other Arabs surrendered. I went outside into the palace garden. There were some police vehicles parked in the entrance to the drive, and a number of Islamic State soldiers in handcuffs. They had been picked up at various points from houses that led to the underground corridor. I searched the palace for the Sultan, but he was not there.

Next day I recalled an image of the Sultan from my mind and tuned into the frequency of it, in an effort to find out what had happened to him. I found him in a cage with bars round it, watched by prison officers. No longer wearing a turban, or rich clothes, he was lying on a wooden bunk bed. His cage included a table and chair. A prison officer brought him a plate of chips, and he got up and sat at the table, eating them, while he and the prison officer chatted. He seemed hardly troubled by his sudden reversal of fortune.

I was glad to see that he was behind bars, and impressed with the speed and bravery with which the gendarmes had acted to protect the public from the threat of terrorism. There was no mention of these events in the French newspapers, and people went about their business as usual, unaware of what had taken place the night before.

ILLEGAL RESEARCH ACTIVITIES

Over the five years that I spent in close company with the IRA and North American mafia, it seemed to me that about thirty per cent of their operations related to illegal, non-consensual, human clinical research carried out on white people.

The principle of consensual human subject research on volunteers is perfectly legitimate. Say that your country has funded research into certain types of cancer. There will be dedicated research facilities, some attached to hospitals and universities, authorised to carry out properly regulated tests on cancer suffers. These cancer patients will have consented to take part in trials on new drugs that offer hope of a better quality of life for longer.

Private clinical research companies also carry out similar research as part of large multinational research projects. Finding enough patients with the right medical conditions is not always that easy, particularly if the sample specifications require them to be in a particular age range, gender or ethnicity.

Private sector multinational research organisations are highly regulated, but I learned from IRA terrorist discussions that a few, based outside the UK, used subcontractors who were willing to pay unethical companies to go touting for sample cases. This might simply mean scanning government health computer records for people recorded with medical conditions that fit the sample profile, and approaching their doctors to ask their patients if they would be willing to participate in the trials. I met an IRA operative who worked as a local council health worker. She had access to the government NHS computer which lists all UK patients' records. The health worker had been bribed to obtain details of patients living in

her locality for a fee. I heard that this arrangement applied in other parts of the UK as well.

The North American mafia employ unethical scientists who will do anything for money. They are willing to target people in the right demographic groups, using remote technologies, and to give them artificially created symptoms of diseases, such as accelerated or irregular heartbeat. The victims then visit their doctors because of their symptoms, get accepted by a consultant, and may be invited to participate in research trials.

Simply getting the victim to visit their doctor gets the perpetrator a cash bonus under Al-Qaida's funding arrangements. Getting the victim to see specific unethical consultants gains another bonus. In the UK, if the victim ends up having an artificial hip or knee replacement, the perpetrator gains a large bonus. In some cases, apparently, the supplier of the prostheses offers the inducements. It sounds unbelievable, but it has happened. It is hard to spot this type of urban terrorism. Some of the terrorists I met used to be involved in such crimes, but they got caught by various governments, struck off approved lists of health research subcontractors, and some served prison sentences in the US.

I found out that the US mafia, in collaboration with the IRA, had registered me as a consensual human subject involved in a number of different clinical trials, using different names and addresses, but always using my body. The trials were registered in the United States. All the tests were performed on the one person at the same time, which would never happen with legitimate research, and the perpetrators tried to falsify the test results to conceal these irregularities. After a while the research companies got wise to this and prevented further falsification of evidence. But that did not stop the non-consensual research altogether. The perpetrators just moved to another country.

The fact that there was nothing wrong with my health made me an attractive subject for illegal research, as human guinea-pigs must not be receiving any medication prior to starting trials. If I so much as took a hay-fever tablet, that stopped the terrorists' research attacks for twenty-four hours, as it showed up on their telemetry print-outs.

The terrorists tried, unsuccessfully, to give me the symptoms of arthritis in hip and knee joints and diabetes. They also operated as subcontractors for an illegal research organisation using me for non-consensual trials on a remedy which enabled people to work normally despite extensive sleep deprivation, and tests on long-term effects of exposure to ultrasound synthetic telepathy.

How did they do it? There was an IRA house about twenty yards away from my bedroom window. They occupied that house, and had their own clinical facilities, using wi-fi telemetry to target specific parts of my body. The terrorists had created a CD containing my biodata and a record of the wi-fi frequency required to locate the microchip at the back of my head, from which to calculate the placement of my body.

There was a full time female doctor who supervised a number of IRA research laboratories, and she lived at the safe house, with a qualified nurse who was supposedly her daughter. They subsequently transferred to more lucrative posts in central London, but were replaced by other qualified clinicians.

I bought a 'smog meter' which measures microwave radiation. I can remember reading articles about the environmental dangers of microwave radiation form cell-phone towers. Using the smog meter, I found out that radiation from our local cell phone tower was minimal in comparison to almost every piece of kit used by the IRA terrorists to target my apartment, my father's house, and the houses of other British citizens living in our area. It was easy to find where the terrorists were operating, by walking up and down the roads where I lived with my smog meter.

Terrorists delivered various chemicals to my skin and respiratory tract using a carbon dioxide laser. They had gas canisters and loaded the contents into some kind of laser gun. Occasionally, I saw these laser shots firing through thin walls outside my apartment. They looked like tiny fleeting lights that disappeared immediately. The range for these devices could only be about twenty to thirty yards.

The terrorists also tried to create stomach lesions, by inducing a raised acid balance in the stomach. I am not sure exactly how they

did this, but it resulted in a burning sensation in the stomach, which I neutralised by taking a sip of cider vinegar.

I could hear the perpetrators discussing remote scans using diagnostic equipment to assess my ph. level. From then on, I always put several slices of fresh lemon in any drink I had. That made me unsuitable for various illegal research trials, and stopped the attacks.

The terrorists prided themselves on their targeting of hip and knee joints, which brought them a steady income from new cases referred to clinical consultants, requiring hip and knee replacements. Attacks on joints were initiated by a skilled telemetry operative, who directed a laser to crack the outer casing, after which less skilled perpetrators went in and spent some time creating pain and swelling in the victim's joints.

A lady in our road was targeted in this way, and in two months she went from never having had any pain in her joints to having evidence of severe damage in one hip. She was immediately referred for a private hip replacement operation. While she was still in hospital, the perpetrators started targeting her other hip. Several people in my road, and people known to me, developed these sudden acute symptoms.

In one particularly tragic case, a poor gentleman whose hip had been targeted, delayed his hip operation because the perpetrators had also targeted his daughter with cancer, and he wanted to be sure that he could be at his daughter's bedside when she passed away. The daughter left three children without a mother.

The lowest of the criminal fraternity were being employed by the IRA to carry out prison guarding, to guarantee that victims were in the right place at the right time for whatever clinical interventions were required. They did this by making sure their victims became tired at certain times of the day, delivering sedative gases via carbon dioxide lasers.

They discouraged their victims from walking too far, by the use of a 'drag-net' which projects a magnetic force field over the victim's own magnetic field, altering the gravity of the person, so that they feel heavy and pulled down when they try to walk. Most of

the IRA's targets were elderly people, because so much of the illegal research required their human subjects to be over fifty.

There was a lot of initial investment for illegal research activities, before any money came in for the terrorists. The perpetrators had to be fairly close, in order to provide this twenty-four-hours-a-day supervision. The target's regular activities had to be recorded, and a CD of biodata had to be developed. It could take up to six months to set up a case, involving renting of rooms on the top floor, which enabled perpetrators to direct laser beams downwards. Rooms had to be visible to other perpetrators working in cars nearby, so that they could triangulate against a naked light bulb and refine their targeting, using Global Positioning Satellite calculations.

There was another IRA terrorist unit in the next town, which targeted their own victims; and woe betide the terrorists in our area if they tried to poach them! Our area got increasingly over-targeted.

Some of the IRA terrorists had particular religious sensitivities. They would not target people who attended the local Catholic church. On one occasion, they were giving people broken right forearms, as part of a research programme. They induced falls by projecting an electromagnetic field over victims, unbalancing them and making them fall over, particularly when they were coming down stairs. But Catholics were exempt from these attacks.

I was in my living room reading at about ten thirty p.m. An apartment in the house opposite had been let to a couple of Afro-Asians. They described themselves as 'Daesh'. Through my connection to the Al-Qaida electromagnetic environment, I found myself looking into the apartment opposite. I heard a strange laughing sound, and I saw a young white woman with shortish fair hair, lying face down on the ground.

She was wearing a T shirt and a pair of panties. At one side, sitting in a low chair, was one of the Afro-Asians. He was making the laughing sound, because he had just taken a canister of laughing gas. A third man was sitting in the position from which I was viewing the scene, but I could not identify him, as I was looking through a camera in his eye. It appears that some internal

105

switchboard operator had failed to disconnect me from the circuit, enabling me to see what was happening.

I took in the entire scene in one moment. In the background, I saw a Caucasian man disappearing through a doorway. His face had been intentionally obscured by whoever was cam-cording the event. I was concerned about the health of the female. I heard a woman whispering behind a door leading to the room.

'What shall I do?' she said.

'Call for a doctor,' I said. 'Put a blanket over that girl. She may be losing heat.'

'I can't,' said the woman. 'Nobody can. Only the boss is allowed to go in there.'

'Well call up the boss and tell him what's happened,' I said.

'OK,' she agreed.

She got on her mobile and talked to someone. My vision was partly obscured at this point but I could still hear. About five minutes later, a medic arrived. I heard footsteps coming up the stairs. Then I heard steps in the room opposite, and whispered comments.

'Can you walk?' the medic was asking the Afro-Asian.

'No,' he said.

The medic tried to lift him, but he was too heavy. The medic helped him into a better sitting position. The medic beckoned the woman who had called for help. She came in timidly. He examined the prone female.

'We'll have to move her,' he said.

Together, he and the woman carried the woman's body out of the room. That was the last I saw or heard of them, as the scene went completely dark at that moment. It later emerged, from whispered discussions that I heard on the Syntel system, that some kind of secret research experiment was being conducted. The experiment involved paralysis of human subject's bodies, so that they could not move or make a sound. Each subject was connected via wi-fi to telemetry diagnostic equipment that measured heart, blood pressure and other bio indicators. Electronic equipment of some sort was used to induce extreme pain, and to measure what that did to the woman's body, until she died. Finding out at what point she died was key to the experiment.

A lucrative private contract had been agreed with an electronic weapons manufacturer who needed experiments of this sort to be carried out on white people. A similar experiment was carried out once a month, for several months, on unwanted women members of the terrorists' staff. Women were getting nervous that it might be their turn next.

I heard that the girl I saw lying face down had committed the sin of standing under the boss's window talking to a man friend, after 'lights out'. These employees all lived a slave's existence.

Events of this kind were unusual, and had a bad effect on staff morale. Those involved had to keep a low profile. I found out that the death experiment involved the participation of the two other perpetrators in the room, a telemetry operative - whose eyes I looked through - and a 'pointer' to direct the equipment at the victim. The 'pointer' was the Afro-Asian who had been unable to walk. He had requested to be given some minor wounding to make it look as if he was a victim. He inhaled the laughing gas as an anesthetic. It was well worth his while financially.

The man I saw disappearing through a door at the back of the room was one of the IRA general managers. He was known to associates as Michael – but they never used their real names. He was present to supervise the killing operation, because it represented an important, lucrative, contract for the IRA.

GENETICALLY MODIFIED HUMAN SLAVES

The Al-Qaida research facility in Algeria, staffed mainly by North American and French mafia scientists, specialised in human genetic modifications. There are strict laws governing human genetic modification, but in Algeria the North American mafia operated without any restrictions. They produced several types of sub-human slave species useful for their terrorist requirements.

Their main slave product was a black genetically modified male sub-human. The genetically modified foetuses were delivered by caesarean section. There were different batches of these guys. Within each batch, they all looked the same. They were no taller than five feet high, and clinically obese in Western terms. They did not look quite normal, having large round heads, and their IQ was definitely lower than normal. But they felt human emotions and suffered fear and pain.

They aged fast, and looked elderly by the age of thirty. Their life expectancy was only forty years. They were designed to eat a simple vegetarian diet of gruel, to be taken in liquid form. But once in the West, they gravitated to fast food, which created health problems including diabetes and constipation.

They had no concept of 'mother', and no previous interaction with women at all, which was what first led me to suspect that they had been produced by some laboratory process. With no family, they exhibited hive-mind traits, preferring to do everything in a large group. Their lack of basic education left them in a primitive condition. They were sensitive about their physical appearance, and used to get together to practice 'standing tall', and measuring each other to convince themselves that they were still growing.

The Algerian sub-humans were designed as spies and prison camp guards. As spies, they were positioned to keep watch on people and places, without moving for long periods of time. They were not proficient in reading or writing, learning mainly by ear, but they had a special gift in being able to replicate any sound they heard, repeating conversations verbatim in any language – whether they understood it or not, sotto voce, into concealed microphones attached to their clothes. Some were fluent in English, French and Creole.

The spies were 'cyborgs', with cameras attached to the retinal nerve of one eye and inner ear implants. They were linked by wi-fi to underground processing centres, which recorded what they saw and heard, and analysed it. I was told by an Islamic State soldier that such spies were used in Syria, to good effect.

Production of these sub-humans exceeded demand. Some of the batches were trafficked as slaves, offering sexual services and house cleaning to Islamic State terrorists. Others were given training in the use of electronic weapons and synthetic telepathy. They lived in cellars and underground shelters, in insanitary conditions. Those brought to the UK had to acclimatise to daylight, as they had spent much of their time lying in the dark on their bellies staring through a tiny hole in the wall, just wide enough for their weapons.

The dwarves referred to themselves as 'Daesh warriors'. They were taught that they were here to fight Al-Qaida's war against white people, and that, when the war was over, they would be given white people's houses and property for their personal use, in whichever country they were located.

Al-Qaida had planned to use them as prison camp guards, for the repression of white women, in the European theatre of war. In the UK, the IRA trained the dwarves to attack white women covertly, focusing particularly on older women in restricted environments such as nursing homes. The attacks were carried out from cars and buildings close to where the women lived, using infra-red to locate their targets through walls, and working with technical specialists to deliver laser and electromagnetic attacks. The objective was to erode the health of victims through the infliction of pain, confusion of mind and externally-induced malfunction of vital organs.

Al-Qaida had a contract with the IRA to import to a significant number of Daesh dwarves from North Africa to Britain. Every week, sixteen of them arrived in my local area. They came from France by boat to minor UK ports, where they were collected and taken to reception centres. There they were given forged identity papers of citizenship of an EU member country, giving them the right to live and work in the UK. After Britain leaves the EU, the status of these illegal immigrants will be untenable, and they will be taken to French-speaking countries instead.

I met some of the Daesh dwarves. It was difficult to tell them apart. Because of this, they were desperate to make a personal impression. Wanting to be seen as special, they cultivated an air of self-importance and a swaggering walk, boasting to each other about how they had tortured big tall women. Despite this, they were uncomfortable except in the company of their own sort. Their behaviour was acutely dysfunctional. If intimidated, they had a tendency to crawl under a table, blanket or tarpaulin.

These Daesh dwarfs had evolved their own subculture. They motivated themselves to carry out attacks on people by getting together, all facing into the centre of a ring, and masturbating, making loud growling noises. After this, they believed a spirit had entered into them, which enabled them to carry out warlike activities. Although malefic and prone to kill anything smaller than them, they developed deep attachments to members of their own group.

They were frequently employed to spy on me when I was outside gardening. They listened in to my thoughts, repeating them loudly into a microphone, which broadcast on an ultrasound frequency clearly audible to anyone with the right receiver. These activities gained them a small cash payment, which they gleefully lost on one-armed bandits in the IRA canteen. Regrettably, their main interest, apart from gambling, appeared to be visiting the Al-Qaida child brothel, which was open to Islamic State, Daesh and IRA employees from one p.m. until three p.m. every day.

Despite their less than appealing habits, the Daesh black dwarves had an air of innocence. They had all been schooled in a Daesh version of Islam, and could refer to texts that they knew by

heart. On one occasion, when they had been parroting at me while I was gardening, I decided to give them a dose of their own medicine.

'Right,' I said. 'We are now going to have a reading from the Quran. Let's hear you parrot that for a change.'

There was a copy of the Quran in my bookshelf, and I selected a section which describes how people should be kind to elderly widows, and show them respect.

As I began my recitation, I was surprised to see all the Daesh dwarves get out small prayer mats, and sit in a devout pose. Later I learned that, after my reading, they had clustered together, questioning about the text they had just heard. It was new to them, because they only knew texts written by their own religious teachers.

The Daesh dwarves preserved their own military dignity. On one occasion, during the wars that were to come over our terrorist area, several Daesh dwarves had been fatally wounded, and men from the local research centre had to humanely terminate the lives of any still breathing, using lethal injection. The one dwarf still unharmed stood to attention throughout the process, a lone figure with no one else to mourn their passing.

'I had to do it, it was my duty. Now I want to join my dead colleagues. Life has no meaning for me,' he said.

The most genetically modified human species produced with Al-Qaida funding were a group of white research centre technicians. They were less than five feet in height, with large bellies, and thin arms and legs. Their faces were round and strangely child-like, although they looked old. Their appearance was so un-human that they always wore masks with inane smiles on them.

As described earlier, North American mafia research staff conducted non-consensual experiments on humans. Once the research experiments were completed, they terminated the people they had experimented on, in order to prevent evidence of their activities being discovered. The genetically modified white sub-humans were bred to carry out this gruesome work.

The job of these sub-humans was to carry out whatever tasks needed to be done at close range, in order to terminate human research subjects. This might involve climbing up to the third-floor

111

windows of buildings, where victims were located, and pointing electronic devices at them, which were operated remotely, from a safe distance, by IRA henchmen. The IRA would not take the risk of carrying out these tasks, for fear of discovery, but the white sub-humans were like monkeys, hopping on roofs at night, and lurking in the shadows. It was hard to see them.

'Where have you come from? How were you constructed?' I asked one of them.

'I came from the United States,' he said. 'I was first created as an embryo, and put in the fallopian tubes of a female. Then, at a later stage, I was removed and put in the womb of another female. Later, they cut open the side of her body and took me out'.

These sub-humans were sharp mentally, and could run rings around lower-level IRA operatives. I suspected that they had probably spent their entire life in underground research bases belonging to the North American mafia. The only time they left the terrorist compound was in cars driven by others. They had no personal rights, no registers of births and no legal possessions, but they had a family feeling for each other, doing everything in their power to protect their clan.

They wanted to be mistaken for normal humans, and copied the mannerisms and expressions of the North American mafia and IRA staff with whom they worked. On Syntel, they sounded like IRA supervisors. You would never guess that they had lacked a normal childhood or education, to hear them talking. They had a good sense of humour, and could be heard cracking jokes, in low whispers, at the expense of their colleagues.

On the electromagnetic computer system, they used avatars that looked like old-style gangsters, with hats that concealed their features. Within the terrorist compound they went around with an ageing group of paedophiles, male prostitutes and child traffickers, forming a kind of risqué gentleman's club. They cultivated English public-school accents. No one ever saw them without their disguises, and few realised that they were not human.

AL-QAIDA'S SECRET ALGERIAN BASE

A number of IRA terrorists who acted as virtual prison guards for me told me that they had worked at the Al-Qaida research facility in Algeria. They were posted there by the North American mafia, who brought Western expertise to the large encampment, as part of wider financial deals between the two terrorist groups.

Originally the Algerian stronghold was an old-style Al-Qaida base, with limited infrastructure, and a large number of North African tribespeople, armed with rifles, wearing dark robes and long head gear. They kidnapped people and held them to ransom. They operated a large training programme in the use of firearms, guerilla warfare and prison camp management. The IRA people I met were not trained as warriors. They went to learn prison camp techniques. Some of these, such as the faeces group controls described in chapter seven, were brought in by the North American mafia. In Algeria, brutal torture and execution methods were taught as standard to prison camp guards. Prisoners did not live long, and were given hardly any food or water.

The concentration camp was divided along gender lines, in accordance with Islamic principles. Women jailors guarded, punished and executed women prisoners, and men did it to men. But the women prison guards were supervised by men. It was an excessively repressive regime. The women who tortured and executed women victims would end up as victims themselves if they failed to obey orders with great enthusiasm, to the letter.

I spoke to a female IRA-Daesh terrorist, an Anglo-Pakistani known as 'Esme', whose family used to live in South Africa. Esme spent some time working in Al-Qaida's Algerian Centre. She could

barely read or write, having been brought up outside the normal education framework, like so many terrorist kids. She had been trained first by the North American mafia in Los Angeles, and then by Al-Qaida in Algeria. She was the leader of a North American 'Faeces Group'. Her victims tended to come from poorer groups within society, and those least able to protect themselves.

In Al-Qaida's concentration camps, Esme's job was the control of women prisoners. As part of this, she regularly tortured a woman to death, pretty much every day.

'Torture and death were a daily routine for us, really,' she told me, calmly.

She recounted how women prisoners, completely covered with black robes and headscarves, were tied down on the ground, and how she was given a whip with several metal barbs on it, and ordered to beat the women. This she did with such determination that her male supervisors had to order her to stop, eventually, as she had cut a hole through the now-dead body of the woman, and was ploughing into the earth.

Most of Esme's victims were white North American women who had been kidnapped by the mafia, or by unwanted mafia employees.

'Did any of them talk to you?' I asked.

'One woman laughed at me, and said - you can do what you like, but you cannot change me,' said Esme.

'What happened then?' I asked.

'Oh, she didn't speak again,' Esme replied.

Esme was praised for her diligence by the Algerian Al-Qaida organisation, and promoted to a leadership role in the IRA-Al-Qaida cooperative arrangements in the UK. That meant that Al-Qaida's funds for Faeces Group work were channelled through her. She was given *carte blanche* to start up similar groups across the British Isles. She began her work in IRA units in the South of England, The IRA were embarrassed at having to work with her, as she was fairly uncouth, and lacked the judgement required for a management post, but they did not wish to upset Al-Qaida.

Back in the UK, the IRA had to find places where Esme could be given a suitable role that did not involve torturing women to death too obviously, as she would have attracted the attention of the British Authorities. She was allocated a commanding role in 'Our Group'. She took part in the training of female terrorists, and managed some of the genetically modified sub-humans whose job was to terminate non-consensual human research subjects targeted within the North American mafia's research programmes. She brought in henchmen from the IRA to carry out covert telemetry and electromagnetic technology attacks on British citizens, using a dedicated account sourced by Al-Qaida. The IRA welcomed this, as it brought in new business opportunities for their staff.

As Esme aged, she began to suffer from dementia. She was given less responsible roles, such as bringing up Al-Qaida batch kids. She ended her life running a child brothel for Al-Qaida employees. She left a dreadful legacy. Such was the harshness of her regime; that children entrusted to her care became programmed carbon copies of herself, with the same behaviour patterns.

The first time I visited Al-Qaida's Algerian research base in the desert, my intention was to 'return to sender' some Algerian terrorists who were attacking me in the UK. I saw the prison camp area, and the kidnap victims who had just arrived. Two old-style Al-Qaida prison camp guards wearing long black robes and hoods rushed out and dragged the new prisoners to a fence, where they tied them up, and proceeded to hit them with sticks, before dumping them in wooden prison huts. I looked into one of the more distant huts and found a poor woman in her fifties. She had been terribly beaten. As the Algerian base was an electromagnetic environment, I was able to take away the pain, and make her feel better, but there was a limit to what I could do. She had internal bleeding, and, unfortunately, she died the next day.

On one occasion, I dropped some terrorists in the Algerian base from a great height. They fell dead in what must have been the old punishment blocks, where the earth covered mass graves, before the North American mafia introduced laser-powered cremation services.

As the terrorists' bodies came raining down, the prison camp guards thought that they must have been thrown from a plane, despite the clear blue sky above them. Whenever a body fell to the ground, they would grab their rifles and fire determinedly into the air, even though they couldn't see anything up there.

I watched as the Al-Qaida representative in France, with authority over training and operations in France and the UK, suddenly came into focus on my inner view. He got on his mobile directly to the Algerian guards.

'Stop that, you stupid idiots,' he shouted in irritation. 'There's nothing up there.'

The guards put down their rifles, looking a bit shamefaced.

That incident showed me how effective Al-Qaida's control of its technology freeways was. The Al-Qaida manager was watching me in the UK, could also see what was happening in the Algerian base at the same time, and could communicate with his staff there instantly.

When Al-Qaida signed a contract with the North American mafia to develop their Algerian site, everything changed. Al-Qaida employed North American mafia technology experts to build their world-wide electromagnetic architecture, using private commercial satellite to provide wi-fi links with 'roving' coverage, similar to what you would expect for mobile phones. Al-Qaida owned the infrastructure, and had executive over-ride on all systems.

The North Americans built a vast underground research base in the Algerian desert. They brought in modern technologies and equipment, as well as highly skilled North American scientists. Their front was that they were part of a large multinational conglomerate, carrying out work that would help humanity to conquer diseases, and participating in charitable projects in Africa.

Al-Qaida's research centre covered medical research, genetic engineering, biological warfare weapons, chemical weapons, electronic and electromagnetic weapons. Back in the UK, there were several smaller North American mafia underground research bases, which got supplies of biological agents from the Algerian Al-Qaida base. These agents included common and rare viruses, bacteria and their antidotes. They were used in the non-consensual human subject

research carried out locally. The North American mafia used Algerian Daesh dwarves as couriers to bring products to the UK. The couriers had to be given the antidotes to the biological agents before transporting them, in order to prevent the possibility of infection.

One autumn, an Algerian Daesh employee, who lived in a house opposite ours, brought in a rare type of influenza that featured ear-ache. I heard that he had gone sick with these symptoms himself. Then I got it. Luckily no one else got, it as far as I was aware, but it was a worrying development. What if he had given it to lot of people? I heard that he had stored the products in his home fridge before handing them over to the North Americans.

Another Algerian Daesh employee approached me on synthetic telepathy, mistakenly thinking that I was an IRA woman manager. He offered to get me a range of bacterial agents, at a price of £150 each, plus opportunities to access the child brothel. The man told me that the bacterial agents were kept in a refrigerated area shared with an American charity working in Africa. He had a pass, courtesy of Al-Qaida's Algerian research base, which gave him the identity of a charity worker, and access to the refrigerated area, from where he proposed to steal the products.

On another occasion, I noticed something wrong with a few plants in our garden. Bits of them were going brown and dying, and it looked like an environmental problem; but I could not work out what it was. I made an enquiry to our county Environment Agency representative, and she kindly came round to have a look. She was very knowledgeable about bugs, fungal attacks and other plant hazards. She surveyed the garden, and immediately focused on a hawthorn bush with browning bits.

'Oh, that looks interesting,' she said. 'I'll just take a few samples.'

She took out a knife and sliced bits off into a large plastic tube.

'I'll send these for analysis and let you know the outcome in a week', she explained.

A week later she telephoned me, quite excitedly.

'We've found what it is,' she said. 'It's a rare foreign virus, and yours is the only case in the UK. There is one other case already

recorded in Europe, so no further action is required. If yours had been the only case in Europe, your house would have had to be quarantined.'

'Oh, thank you for letting me know,' I said, wondering what quarantine would have involved. I also wondered how the virus could have got onto our bush. I suspected that it might be something to do with the activities of the local North American mafia research base, but I had no evidence to support my suspicions.

In recent years, Al-Qaida's influence across North Africa has expanded greatly. Al-Qaida representatives operate openly in Algeria and Tunisia. I visited the Algerian underground base, and found a large number of soldiers sleeping on camp beds in a hospital hall. They were waiting their turn to undergo minor clinical procedures to insert microchips into their heads, and nano-cameras behind the retinas of their eyes. Across the wide corridor were four blocks of operating theatres, where surgeons and doctors worked round the clock to complete this work.

Al-Qaida have exported trained soldiers to the Middle East, Central Asia and Europe in large numbers, some of whom arrive in the UK. I found underground tunnels underneath the cities of Algiers and Tunis, leading to Al-Qaida centres, where soldiers in their early twenties, trained at the Al-Qaida desert base, were awaiting transport to Syria and Iraq. The soldiers were all volunteers, keen to fight for their cause. Morale in the Al-Qaida training camps was high. Some of the more experienced soldiers running the military training had started their career in Libya, when Colonel Gaddafi offered nine months' basic weapons training to men from across North Africa. But the Al-Qaida soldiers being turned out now had more of a Western approach. At the Al-Qaida Algerian base, the IRA were under contract to provide 'British style' army techniques, claiming to employ mercenaries who had been trained in Britain. The training included proficiency in electronic and electromagnetic weapons, as well as mainstream fire-arms.

When I became more proficient in navigation of the electromagnetic environment, I used to pick up groups of these illegal immigrants, and teleport them straight into Algerian and Tunisian prisons. I thought this was working well, until I dropped off twelve Algerian Daesh couriers in an Algerian jail. At first, they

were put in the cells, but, as I watched, one of them bribed a guard to let them make a phone call. Half an hour later, the Al-Qaida representative was in the prison complex, smiling and waving at the couriers, who were let out, and escorted to a coach provided by Al-Qaida, to take them straight back to a seaport, from where they travelled directly to a port in the South of England.

IRA YOUTH TRAINING GROUPS

The IRA spend significant resources on recruiting young people in the British Isles into their ranks. They do this covertly. They are a proscribed organisation – it is against the law to belong to the IRA, so they cannot advertise themselves. Their activists infiltrate charitable organisations involved with youth, for example offering inner-city slum kids holidays in the country, or outward-bound courses for boys who have been in trouble with the law. The young are befriended and then incriminated in such a way that they become collaborators in some illegal act, after which they are controlled by threats of disclosure. Initially the incrimination is very minor, but it teaches kids that there are people who believe it is OK to be above the law. The next step is for the kids to be made to carry out illegal acts, such as shop-lifting and under-age car theft, for which they are likely to get caught by the Authorities. Once the kids have a criminal record, the IRA use them to carry out illicit activities, as and when it suits them.

The IRA ran a junior students' weekend course, which included woodcraft, cross-country running, and a night exercise in which the students had to make their way, one by one, from behind a local petrol station, over a stream, up a hill, and through several private gardens, collecting a large stone along the way, which they had to throw over the fence into my garden. The last stretch of this exercise was videoed from a neighbouring house rented out by the terrorists.

The youths knew they were trespassing and carrying out minor damage to someone's garden. They were urged on by IRA youth trainers, men in their thirties, who acted as role models for young boys in their early teens.

I was not aware that my garden was being used for the youth training course, at first, but one day I noticed a pile of stones behind a wall. A few days later, the pile of stones had grown. Then one night, at one thirty a.m., when I was out catching slugs (this will seem a pointless exercise unless you are a gardener), I heard two boys crawling through the undergrowth of my neighbour's garden. One was close to the pile of stones. I was suspicious, and next night I waited to see what was happening. Sure enough, I heard what sounded like kids crawling through the undergrowth at the back of my neighbour's garden. I could dimly glimpse one of them. He looked about fourteen.

I ordered them to stop, and they froze. Then I told them to turn round and go back the way they had come. But they did not leave. They just stayed there. So I got the hosepipe and soused them heavily. They did not break cover, but stood there getting wet. I gathered from other IRA operatives on Syntel that the kids had been praised for their endurance, and given a certificate of achievement. However, the youth midnight field courses stopped. I used the pile of stones to reinforce a bank in my garden. The stones were large and specially cut. I suspected they had been stolen from another neighbour's dry stone wall, further down the road.

It was three a.m. I woke up, and with my eyes still closed, my interior vision via the electromagnetic computer system showed an unfamiliar scene. It was an attic room, and a young woman in her underwear was being threatened by a young man. His arm was raised as if to hit her, and her arm was raised to shield herself. Instinctively, I brushed him out of the room with my hand, and he fell back against the opposite wall in the room next door. Another young man entered the room, and, putting his arm on the roof beam above his head, began to do acrobatics. I dismissed him as well. As I did so, a third young man, whom I hadn't seen, gave out a screech, and started hopping about on one foot.

'Augh, she's got me,' he cried.

I saw that the young woman had fired an electronic laser handgun at him.

'Fine,' I thought, 'She can look after herself'.

There was a noise coming from the floor below. I went downstairs. It was dark. Men and boys were milling about, but it was hard to see what was happening. I could just make out a large plasma screen TV, showing a grainy skin flick, and some men masturbating in front of it.

'Open a window, someone,' I heard an older say.

A tall black guy got up.

'Why do you need to watch a movie?' I asked, somewhat pointlessly, since the reason was obvious. 'Can't you manage without it?'

'I need help to get through the night,' said the black guy.

'For God's sake, open the window, someone,' repeated the older white male.

I smashed the window, thinking that it was an emergency.

'Don't smash it open like that, boys,' said the older man, who could not see me.

I smashed the plasma screen that was showing the porno movie.

'Now boys, that's very naughty of you,' said the white male.

Another young woman suddenly came into view in the shadows. The tall black guy made a lunge at her. She spat at him. A young white boy rushed to her aid. The black guy punched him in the face. I hit the black guy in the groin, and he fell to the floor.

The older man got up in a hurry and ran down stairs into the back garden. He took a large whistle out of his pocket and blew it loudly.

'Everybody out! Everybody out now!' he shouted.

Eight teenage boys, another black guy and two young women ran out.

They looked a ragged bunch, standing there in the early morning. Guessing them to be one of the IRA's youth summer camp courses, I had a go at them.

'Call yourselves Irish Republican Army, do you?' I shouted. 'That's no way to behave. Let's see a bit of discipline here.'

The boys stiffened up and got into a line.

'That's better,' I said. At this point, one of the boys put up his hand.

'Please, Miss,' he said. 'I'm not a member of the IRA, where do I sign up?'

An older IRA woman, who, unbeknownst to me, had been on duty, came forward, and said, 'That will be taken care of, don't worry.'

'I didn't know we were with the IRA,' said another boy, more politely now. 'Not that I've any objection, I wouldn't mind joining up either, but no one told us about it.'

'Honestly,' said the IRA woman to another female standing next to her. 'I don't know why we go through the charade of bringing them on an outward-bound course; they're all quite OK with the truth anyway.'

The older man decided to assert his authority, as he was supposed to be the responsible adult with the boys.

'Now then boys, all go into the house,' he said.

No one moved.

'What's your problem?' he asked.

'There's a man in a black coat and hood in there, and he's dangerous,' said one, referring to me. 'He's punched several of us, and they're lying upstairs.'

'And now he's standing right next to you,' I said.

The boys and girls all screamed, and ran into the house.

The elder man went in, to inspect the casualties. He came out and reported to the IRA women:

'There's one black guy down, who can't walk. Says he's been hit in the bottle-brush area.'

He stared at a boy in front of him.

'Sonny, where's your front teeth?' he asked.

'The black guy punched me,' said the boy.

There was another black adult male, still standing.

'You'll have to carry the injured boys downstairs,' I said to him.

'No way,' he said, 'It's not my job. I don't work here. Me and my mate just snuck in here for a laugh tonight.'

The two boys I had brushed aside came down the stairs by themselves. They were winded by my impact, but otherwise OK. The boy who had been shot in the foot couldn't walk down the stairs.

'You've got to go and get him,' I told the other black guy.

'OK,' he said, sullenly.

He marched up the stairs and started dragging the boy towards the stairwell, like a sack of potatoes.

'Ouch! Mind what you're doing!' cried the boy.

The black guy had clearly lost patience, and he chucked the boy down the stairwell.

I jumped up, and caught him high up in the well. To prevent hurting him, I very slowly and cautiously supported him down the space of the stairwell, and gradually laid him on the ground.

'Wow! I'm floating!' said the boy.

The others gasped, and ran off in a fright. Everybody made their way towards the breakfast room, to receive hot drinks and reassurance.

'What was all that about?' I asked the IRA woman.

'These are slum kids from London, on one of our charity outings,' she said. 'They are good recruiting grounds for us. The old man shouldn't have put on the porn movie. All those lively youngsters running around, and only two girls in the group, it was bound to give them ideas.'

Postscripts

The brave boy who came to the aid of the young girl was taken to a dental surgery later that week, and a few weeks afterwards he was given replacement front teeth. He was quite pleased with the result.

'They're better than my original ones,' he said, grinning proudly.

I discovered that the two black guys who 'snuck in for a laugh' had just come out of prison. There was no proper supervision of the kids, and the man and woman supposed to be in charge of them were totally unsuitable. If I had not been there, the two girls, and probably some of the younger boys, would have been abused by the older boys and the adults. They would never have realised that the IRA was behind their holiday, but the kids would have been contacted later, and drawn into a life of crime, in preparation for terrorist service.

THE TERRORIST TRAINING CAMP

In the second year of my virtual captivity by the IRA, they hit on the idea of making money from selling me as a human subject for their terrorist training camps. The microchip transmitter in my head offered them rare opportunities for practising tracking and targeting a 'British citizen. They set up the training camp with the cooperation of the North American mafia, who set up the technical infrastructure required to support this.

Up till then, most of the terrorist training was carried out on old people in nursing homes and hospices, or on vulnerable people, mentally or physically disabled, unemployed and single parent families. The terrorists did not have many opportunities to train on someone fit and well, who had worked in the outside world.

It looked like a real money-spinner to those claiming ownership of me. Soon all the IRA and North American mafia units in the area had signed a contract agreeing to send their junior staff to be trained, for a fee. In return, they would receive a certificate of attendance, which stated that they had successfully completed certain types of attacks on me.

In practice, the course was a rip-off. The students received very little training of any sort, and the tasks they were set were impossible to complete. They were either sent home without a certificate, necessitating further training courses, or they bribed a low-level operative £10 to be given the authorised certificate.

The content of the course was the same in all cases. The students arrived at night and were made to stay on duty outside in the countryside, irrespective of weather or temperature, often with no outer clothing, food or water. They were allowed to go to a canteen

for breakfast at six o-clock, but before they got there, perverted operatives would target laser beams at the bladders and bowels of all the female students, causing them to void the contents, after which they were made to stand in line with the rest, being jeered at by males.

Some of the units complained about the treatment of their female students, but the complaints fell on deaf ears. Having set up the course, there was nothing that the IRA were prepared to do to introduce supervision or quality standards, because it would affect profit margins. The course was in fact little more than a job creation exercise for aging under-employed terrorists, of which there were many.

Most of the male teachers on the course preyed on younger males, treating them to the same tortures as they meted out to female students, if they did not participate in sexual acts. There was also a 'Thursday night initiation' event for young males. The male students were encouraged to drink a fair bit, and then their brains were exposed to microwave beams, which expanded the alcohol content in the brain. They were then facilitated to carry out an atrocity, for example, the brutal gang-rape of a young male or female student, aided and abetted by their repellent teachers. The incident was videoed and played back to the hung-over lads the next day. The teachers then blackmailed the boys into carrying out unpaid services at future training courses.

Relatives of senior IRA families were not treated like that on training courses. They did not have to stand out in the cold and wet all night, nor were they attacked by their tutors, and they were given prime opportunities to complete their tasks, which were signed off as achieved, irrespective of performance.

The tasks the IRA students had to complete consisted of the following:

-    Spend one shift, lasting eight hours, in 'conversation' with me via synthetic telepathy. They were to say abusive things, and make malicious comments about whatever activities I was engaged in. This proved difficult, as I drowned them out with a radio – talking rather than music being the more effective, as the IRA technicians

could modulate their microphones to reduce the volume of music in the students' headphones, and in my audio-receptors.

- Sit in their 'police station' watching plasma screens displaying me getting undressed, bathed or on the toilet. The female students were to say rude things at me, while the male students were to aim electronic close-range laser beams causing pinches or pricks, or to try to knock me over with their gravity oscillators. I did not intend to put up with this, and I deployed a range of shielding devices, including waterproof fabrics, plastics, aluminum, sun block blinds and the like. I could subvert their objectives at night simply by keeping lights switched off, as most of their facilities lacked night-vision cameras.

- Aim 'masers' - a type of microwave laser beam - at my head, in an attempt to wipe words and thoughts out of my mind. They tried to make me forget the names of things, by focusing these beams intensively at me. The beams only had a short-term effect, and wearing a waterproof rain hood tended to prevent them, because they were unable to find where I was, as it blocked the microchip transmitter in my head.

- Watch my mental pictures from a kind of MRI viewer that was linked by wi-fi to the microchip in my head. * The IRA had an arrangement with the nearby North American mafia underground research base, to use their technical facilities, connected by wi-fi.

- Operate an infra-red device to find out where I was sitting or lying through the walls of my house.

- Discover what I was looking at, by monitoring a webcam receiver linked by wi-fi to the transmitter attached to my eye camera.

- Direct a harmless type of microwave beam at me, which would reflect the outline of my body, showing how I was sitting, standing or lying in more detail.

- Direct a laser gun to attack my genitals, arms, legs or other body parts via wi-fi, using coordinates set up beforehand by the IRA technicians. The students used a kind of smartphone screen known as a 'voodoo doll' screen, which showed a stereotyped human form, with different parts of the body highlighted, and buttons to press to emit different types of painful sensations. This method requires a CD

of biodata to be inserted into a laptop, in order to establish the exact position of the victim, after which the coordinates are entered onto the voodoo doll screen. *

*For more on this, see the book '*Project Soulcatcher*' by Robert Duncan, Higher Order Thinkers Publishing, 2010, ISBN 1452804087. Robert Duncan notes that there is a unique body resonance signature, heart beat signature and brain wave print for every individual.

- Male students were required to operate a small electromagnetic oscillator device, working in couples, where each student targeted one of my feet, attempting to raise and reduce the gravity on each foot, as I walked along. This was supposed to demonstrate ability to restrain a victim within a virtual prison camp environment.

- Operate the oscillator device in a public place, in an attempt to make walking difficult, and deter me from leaving the house. I stopped this by dragging a walking stick with a plastic cap on the base, or by pushing a wheeled shopping trolley, both of which prevented the attacks.

- Use a tracking device to pick up the wi-fi transmissions from the microchip in my head, and follow me via satellite, when I went out. There was a short-range device, and a long-range wi-fi satellite device which could follow me if I went on longer journeys.

Once the British military came on the scene, much of this stopped. I remember watching at night, when IRA students were due to carry out a night field exercise. This involved night orienteering and tracking a human quarry, trespassing in people's grounds, wading through streams, and getting completely lost. When these events occurred, military aircraft or helicopters would appear, shining search lights down onto the students, and herding the young criminals back into the vehicles that had brought them.

Over time, my use of shielding devices meant that the IRA were no longer able to offer me as a human subject for terrorist training apart from training in synthetic telepathy, but they lied to their clients that I was available, took the money up front, and then blamed their clients for their lack of skill in being able to find me. For an extra

fee, they would alter their telemetry print-outs to show that they had carried out all kind of attacks on me as well. Eventually, their management got wise to this, and stopped money changing hands.

After the first year, the IRA management began to think that the training course had the potential to be an accredited course for their officer cadre. In the weeks after the decision was taken, specialist teachers were brought in, and eventually some skills transfer was achieved. So what did the trainees finally get taught?

- Martial arts
- Making fire grenades in bottles, and throwing them
- How to stall a car at close range, by means of electromagnetic intervention
- How to 'guide' birds into car windscreens, and create potential accidents
- The correct way to carry out an assassination attack, using electronic weapons. This involved a hit man, two female navigators to plot the victim's position; GPS coordinates; and a telemetry operative, to get an accurate fix on the victim's body.
- How to harass a victim using synthetic telepathy
- How to mob a victim wherever they went, using 'gang stalking' techniques
- Following a victim's car using wi-fi tracking
- Release of chemical agents from gas canisters, at close range, via a laser delivery agent.

Not all the trainees got the chance to learn all these skills, but opportunities were provided, particularly to young members of established IRA families. At the end of three years, the IRA decided to have a passing-out ceremony for their graduates. This took place in July, with a garden party, presenting of certificates, and posing for photographs.

The graduates now had to earn their new rank of Lieutenant, by proving themselves capable of carrying out a killing. For members of IRA families, this was organised for them, so that all they had to do was point a device at someone and the deed was done. The real work of carrying out the killing was undertaken by technicians, but the young cadets were able to demonstrate that they had won their spurs.

In one case, a female student who belonged to an important IRA family was taken to a hospice, where she had to kill a child. I heard that she wept when she was obliged to carry out the killing. Old people's homes were used selectively in a similar way, so that students from influential IRA families could get their Lieutenant's rank.

The IRA training unit had a tradition of holding alumni events on Bank Holiday weekends. These events were not strictly related to training courses, but they benefited from running in parallel with them, because big events with a host of activities created a sense of occasion. Known as 'hunting parties', they offered senior veterans from the local IRA aristocracy a chance to get together in a relaxed environment, to enjoy good food and drink in convivial male company, and to relive the 'glory days' when they once killed British citizens or fought in campaigns overseas.

These ancient 'hunters' were no longer capable of doing much, so there were 'gamekeepers' on hand to ensure that they all bagged a few 'pheasants' when they went out with the boys on Saturday and Sunday night field exercises. The 'pheasants' were usually vulnerable British citizens, mainly elderly, who lived on their own, or in sheltered accommodation. IRA technicians had done the field work, setting up the viewing sites, ensuring the quarries were in range and immobilised at the right time, through the use of sedative gases, administered in advance. All the 'hunters' had to do was to fire their weapons, to be ensured of a kill.

The weapons were remote electromagnetic devices that left no mark, but which could cause heart failure and strokes. As always, hospices, hospitals, and nursing homes were the easy options. There was an element of risk in these hunting parties, and as the British Military began to increase surveillance over the area, these types of killings stopped. Instead, the IRA identified those within their employment who were not worth keeping on, who could be offered as substitute targets. The targets were often people who had not appeared in the outside world for some time, ex-convicts - both male and female, people with behavioural problems, the criminally insane or mentally retarded.

Towards the end of the IRA's three-year training course, a technical specialist was brought in to conduct formal training in electronic heart attack techniques. There was much interest in this course, and several IRA units signed up to attend it. The assassination techniques involved:

- Locating the heart, using the victim's existing biodata – conducted by a telemetry operative
- Imposing a small electromagnetic field over the location of the heart – conducted by the telemetry operative
- Calculation of the GPS coordinates for the heart area, and identification of the exact hit point within the heart – conducted by two individuals referred to as the 'navigation team'
- Setting up of the electronic weapons to carry out the hit – conducted by the hit man
- Activating the electronic weapons to complete the hit – conducted by the hit man.

Several trainees at a time participated in the preparation of each stage. I would be lying in bed in the early morning, when I became aware of an area around my heart, being tested, tentatively, by the trainees, using electromagnetic devices. They all had a go. Then, individually, they aimed small lasers at my left chest, in the general area of the heart. This was not going to achieve much, but it gave them the general idea of how it would feel to trigger an attack, if they had been given the powerful electronic weapons required.

The training course management offered a modest prize of £100 as an incentive to any operative able to finish me off. In the meantime, one of the Afro-Asians was commissioned to work with the assassination team to prepare and carry out a serious assassination attack. I was dozing in my greenhouse, listening to music in the early evening, when I became aware of an electromagnetic field superimposed on my heart area.

I thought nothing more of this, as it happened regularly during the training course, when, suddenly, I heard a helicopter swoop down really close. There was a bang. I heard some screaming, and saw two women running away from a car in the road below, their long brown hair streaming behind them, and their eyes wide with horror. I looked

at the small car. Both the back passenger-doors were open, and so was the front passenger door. Lying on the pavement outside the front passenger door, I could see a pair of feet. One of the Afro-Asians had been hit.

A few minutes later I heard the sound of an ambulance siren racing to the scene. I learned later that the would-be assassin had had a heart attack, but had recovered later in hospital. He was given a week off work. The British military helicopter hit the weapon he was holding in his hand, as he was getting ready to shoot at me. To make sure his weapon was extra powerful, he had added further electronic boosters under his armpit, which he could activate by squeezing his arm against his side at the critical moment. When our military hit the weapon he was holding, the charge ran up the wires along his arm and blew the armpit booster. This was what had caused the heart attack.

On another occasion, I was sitting in my father's garden on a sunny afternoon. It was still and peaceful. Again, I felt an electromagnetic field superimposed on my heart area. Suddenly I heard a helicopter coming in fast and low towards the house next door, at the level of the third floor. There was a bang, and I heard what sounded like three people screaming. It turned out that the hit man and his two navigators were leaning out of the window, looking into our garden, all holding electronic equipment, and the military helicopter targeted the equipment they were holding before they could trigger it. They all sustained skin burns, and the skin on the top of their hands was pulled towards their weapons, tearing, as it was vacuumed up by the electric charge. They had plastic surgery to put the skin back. Those involved were the female IRA-Al-Qaida officer known as Esme, her male business partner, and the assassination specialist brought in to conduct the training.

After that, the trainees wore plastic gloves to protect their hands when they carried out attempted attacks on other British citizens in our area. I heard that when the British military hit their weapons, the electric charge pulled the gloves off their hands, and some of the skin on their hands went with it. After that, the assassination attempts stopped.

Assassinating people by electromagnetic weapons might be hard to detect, but it was not easy to achieve, except by professional specialist hit-men. Our Pakistani neighbours, who were affiliated to ISIS and Al-Qaida, had a much simpler approach to getting rid of people. They just locked them in one of the attic rooms in their large mansion, and forgot about them. Then after a few months, they sent someone in to clean up the mess.

TERRORISM AND CHILD ABUSE

Al-Qaida provided money to US mafia and IRA groups for the production of 'child batches' to be brought up 'outside of Christendom'. The objective was to produce a group of white child soldiers with a war-like background, without Western ethics. To achieve this, Al-Qaida sponsored groups of white outlaws and criminals recommended by the IRA, to breed or procure children to be brought up to fight for the cause from their earliest years. Al-Qaida money flowed to these gangs, who prospered unsupervised, in whatever way they chose. The people that I met running Al-Qaida batch kids, were child traffickers, paedophiles, and people who had been in prison and had no job, including some that had been classified as criminally insane.

They took the money, spent it on alcohol and drugs, denied the children adequate food and clothing, and abused the children and their female supervisors. The female supervisors were typically single parents and drug addicts, incapable of running their lives without assistance. They were forced into a life of slavery that involved limited use of electronic weapons, control and training of kids, drug trafficking and prostitution.

Sexual exploitation of children is not considered wrong by Al-Qaida. This approach is commonplace across the Arab world. Under the IRA-Al-Qaida contract for funding of the local terrorist unit, it was specified that young children should be supplied to the Daesh 'warriors' for sexual refreshment, to be accessible several times a day. A child brothel was set up for this purpose.

The Al-Qaida contract required that Daesh males must never be seen walking outside, and must not be visible from the air. This

meant that they had to get into vans inside garages, and be transported into other areas, shielded from view. In my area, there was a secret underground walkway which enabled Daesh to reach terrorist buildings within about five hundred yards of their dedicated safe house. The child brothel was located in the summer house, where there were two shower rooms and a changing area. The children were also transported in a van to different locations in the evening.

The Al-Qaida batch kids were kept outside formal education. Some could barely read and write, and their main skills included petty thieving, prostitution and illegal drug distribution. The boys had some weapons training, including martial arts, how to throw fire bombs, and how to use electronic and electromagnetic weapons. The girls learned to use electronic weapons, and to operate synthetic telepathy equipment. In 2015 Al-Qaida stopped funding child batches in the West, on the grounds that they didn't produce the desired results. Al-Qaida realised that the money provided for them was being siphoned off, and that the end product, the future generation of soldiers, was not fit for purpose.

It is common knowledge that the IRA have paedophiles in their midst, although I have met soldiers within the Republican movement that are totally opposed to such things. A house owned by an IRA family near where I lived was being run as a child brothel for children aged four to eight years old. Some of the children in it had been trafficked from France. I used to see a four-year-old child and her mother speaking French in the supermarket. They lived at the brothel house, but after eighteen months the mother disappeared, leaving the child. It turned out that the mother had been a Creole interpreter, working with the regular intake of Algerian Daesh illegal immigrants that arrived very week in our terrorist unit.

The brothel was supervised by Esme, the Anglo-Pakistani terrorist. She tortured the children with a microwave gun to make them take part in brothel activities, and carried out a painful process on their colons, which triggered voiding of the bowel, to make it more hygienic for the Algerian clients, and the elderly white paedophiles that patronised the establishment. The Algerian clients

women tried to run the child brothel, but their numbers reduced, as the deaths within the terrorist community increased.

The posts of child managers were advertised, and a married couple in their thirties, from a mafia unit in Canada, applied for the job. They were given a week's acclimatisation, to see if they liked the work. It involved a lot more than the official position suggested. They were constantly required to put up people for the night, and host events for visiting groups bringing young children. The applicants were doing alright, and seemed likely to accept the post, when they went down with acute food poisoning. This affected others staying with them, and the entire operation had to close, owing to the debilitating nature of the attack.

It later emerged that the poisoning had been deliberate. Esme, the Jihadist, had wanted the job. She and other local terrorists, who had not been offered a chance to apply for the post, felt aggrieved, and found a way to express their views. Unsurprisingly the newcomers decided not to stay after all.

It was a lovely sunny Autumn day. I went into the garden. I could hear a group of kids laughing and shouting and talking to adults about two hundred yards further down the hill. The absence of brothel managers was already beginning to take its toll on discipline within the IRA women's group. The child brothel, now without Al-Qaida funding, was trying to carve out a new role for itself, by training its young charges in synthetic telepathy technology and surveillance of images on the MRI viewer. The kids were bouncing up and down and laughing, as usual.

A belligerent grey-haired IRA man in his late fifties ran up to the kids, shouting at them aggressively.

'What are you up to? Stop doing that!'

He raised his arm threateningly, as if to strike a child.

He had a reputation for bullying children, and I immediately disposed of him. They put his body in the potting shed.

'Thank you, thank you!' shouted the kids waving at me. They bounced even more.

'How did he die? There's nobody there,' said a disbelieving woman terrorist. *'She* didn't do that'.

'Wave back!' the kids shouted to me.

I had never done this before. I sat on the garden bench, where I knew their remote camera could pick me up, and waved at them several times, smiling. The kids crowded round their remote camera viewing screen.

'There she is! She's waving!' they cried.

They were so close that I could hear them with my external ears, as well as on Syntel – in stereo! The adults joined the kids looking at the viewer. I heard an IRA woman muttering, 'Oh Christ! Oh God! I didn't believe it. She is over there.'

'That thing didn't take out the manager,' another woman sneered. 'Look at her. She couldn't have done it. Some men with weapons did it.'

While not needing to prove anything, I felt that this was a defining moment for that group. Sure, they heard things and saw things via their viewing screen, but they never communicated with me except via Syntel. I didn't really exist in their reality. I wanted to break through that barrier.

The sneering lady, a pretty brown-haired woman in her thirties, wearing a long, flowered frock, was walking towards the house up the path. I let my gaze slip under her feet. She fell backwards and ended sitting on the ground.

'What happened?' the others shouted, laughing.

'Nothing,' she said. 'I just slipped'.

'OK,' I thought.

She went into the kitchen to get a cup of tea.

'Where are you now?' I asked.

'Sitting at the table,' she said

'Stand back,' I said.

Then I blew around the kitchen and spiralled the movement up in the air. The china and cutlery clashed as they flew upwards and then downwards.

'Oh, my God,' she said again.

She called her husband, and together they cleared up the mess. He was understandably annoyed with me. I pointed out that his wife had tried to say that I didn't really exist, and he accepted my

argument. As I left, I could hear others in the group whispering together.

'I can't believe it!'

'You see, I told you so, but you wouldn't listen.'

The kids danced and pranced round them, shouting triumphantly, 'She did it! She did it!'

I had proved that I existed independently of my ultrasound voice. I had made contact.

US MAFIA CHILD TORTURE PROGRAMMING PROJECT

The movie *The Manchurian Candidate* is a well-known example of how a type of psychological warfare method, similar to brainwashing, worked in practice. The North American mafia used this approach to create fearless killers, 'super-soldiers' who would attack on command, and go on attacking until death. Those created in Britain had a metal plate inserted into their heads, through which electronic stimuli could be transmitted remotely, activating various behaviour patterns. The electronic stimuli could give the recipients the strength of ten in energy terms.

I discovered that the North American mafia were working with Al-Qaida to produce a generation of programmed child super-soldiers, not only in the Middle East and North Africa, but in North America and Europe as well. The Al-Qaida 'batch kids' were meant to go through all the stages of electronic torture, brainwashing and programming, and to emerge in their teenage years as combat-ready super-soldiers.

Only scientists and clinically trained technicians can carry out that type of torture programme. Mindless brutality does not achieve the same thing. The North American mafia sent a group of scientists to take forward the super-soldier programme in our area, and they looked for suitable children to receive this horrific treatment. Thankfully, they rejected our local child brothel kids entirely, as being too deprived to be usable. Their IQ scores were too low, and they could not read or write.

But there were exceptions, including a young lad called Kevin. I will never know who his real father was, but there were an official

father and mother with responsibility for his upbringing. He was in junior school up to the age of about nine years old. Every day, an Asian Daesh soldier escorted him and his sister back from school in the afternoon. But after the age of nine, Kevin's school were told that he had moved away from the area, which meant that he left the state education system. He became a child soldier, trained in martial arts, electronic and electromagnetic weapons.

What I did not realise was that, every morning before breakfast, he attended trauma-based programming sessions, during which he endured electric shock 'therapy' that would drive most sane people mad. There was no one he could call. He either lived with it or died with it. Most of the British-based terrorists were unaware of this project being conducted by the North American underground research centre in their midst. When they found out, they were as shocked as any normal person would be. This was something Al-Qaida had not specified in the 'Batch Kid' Initiative.

I heard some IRA staff discussing this in a garden nearby. They were expressing disbelief, and they asked Kevin why he hadn't told them about it before. He replied:

'We aren't allowed to talk about it... It's not something you could understand'.

He sounded like a tired adult now, no longer a twelve-year-old sporting with his friends.

Another young kid called Daisy was also subjected to this awful torture, day after day. She was sent to the secret underground research compound, in the company of North American mafia personnel. I saw her being told to go for her treatment, and she was shaking her head, saying she didn't want to. I felt helpless. You see, I had long ago reported my concerns about the child brothel to the British constabulary, and they had assured me they were looking into it; but that, with no hard evidence to go on, they could not promise much.

'Couldn't you watch the place, and see who goes in and out?' I asked.

'We don't have the resources for that,' they replied.

'What about drones?' I asked, 'Couldn't they monitor the place?' The policeman gave me a look as if I had suggested that Santa's sleigh might fly by.

'Drones?' he said. 'There's no such thing. You've been reading too many science fiction novels.'

Of course, that was some time ago. Our police have been reorganised, and specialist teams now work in many disciplines, but that was how it was then.

One day I saw a boy of about twelve walking in a field crying. His body was covered in black mud, and I could tell that he had received a torture punishment, most likely for failing to complete some task successfully. I picked him up and put him in a large aerial cage, suspended from wooden beams, like a kind of tree house. I lined the cage with carpets, easy chairs and tables, and enclosed the boy in a light beam, to remove any pain and suffering.

I first started to create these aerial cages when people asked me for asylum, to take them out of danger. Inside the cage, they could not be reached by the terrorists, whose technical equipment frequencies were not high enough. Once the threat of torture was removed, the refugees relaxed, became human beings, and settled happily into their new environment. Being at a higher than normal frequency, they did not need to eat, drink, sleep or take drugs, and they felt neither heat nor cold. They had no needs and were completely content. Eventually, they passed on to a higher stage, where I could no longer see them, but their passing was peaceful and happy.

I expected the young boy to undergo the same transformation, but he did not. Once the threat of torture was removed, and he was clean and free from pain, he retreated to the back of his new home, and told me to leave him alone. I was just going to do that, when he shouted after me, 'I suppose you're going to leave me to starve now, are you?'

He assumed an expression of self-satisfaction that belied his young age, as he contemplated his ability to control me through my sympathy - as he thought. He looked like a little old man. I was reminded of the Artful Dodger from Charles Dickens's *Oliver Twist*.

Something was clearly wrong. I examined him closely, and, in the rarified frequency of the tree house, I could just discern a metal plate inside his head. I wondered if the boy was being manipulated remotely from outside via the cranium implant, but that could not be the case, as he was now above the range of those who would harm him. I reached my hand towards his head, and into the area where the cranial implant was. It was secured with metal pins. Slowly I began to ease the pins out, one by one, and then I lifted the metal plate out of his head.

As the metal plate came off, things happened very quickly. The boy's face changed to that of a young child about three years old. Smiling and happy, he flashed past me, and went to wherever he was destined to go. The tree house was empty.

I was shocked to realise that what I had just seen was the young boy before the metal plate had been inserted in his head. It was as if he had been 'paused' at that moment and had not gone any further with his life. Whatever his artificial persona had been made to do after that, had nothing to do with him. He left this world free and innocent of all that took place while under the control of external forces.

I wondered how many of the terrorists I had dispatched had been forced into the same state by the child soldier programme. It looked likely that their future life, whatever it might be, was much more hopeful than I had guessed. But what a terrible thing to do to children. I remembered the words from Sunday School when I was a kid:

'But whoever causes one of these little ones who believe in me to sin, it would be better for him to have a large millstone tied round his neck and be drowned in the depth of the sea.'

Matthew 18:6, *English Standard Version*

After I found out that the North American mafia were doing experiments locally on young children to turn them into brainwashed cyborgs with cranial implants, I suspected that the underground research centre was where it was happening, but I had nothing to go on. Then one night I was attacked by some IRA technicians from a nearby building. I located the staff in a room full of electronic

equipment, screens and monitors that I had not seen before. I removed all the staff permanently, and rolled over to go to sleep.

Some piece of equipment in that room must have been on, as no sooner had I closed my eyes than I saw an entirely new scene, courtesy of the electromagnetic computer system. It was a large hall, constructed in pale green metal – the official colour of the research base. It looked like a modern prison. I was standing on an upper level gantry that looked into the darkened area below. There were six beds, with five children lying asleep.

A girl of about nine years of age was standing up in bed wearing a nightdress. She had shoulder length brown hair. Facing her was some kind of search light positioned on the gantry above. Some remotely operated mechanical equipment seemed to be moving towards her body. Instinctively I felt that the girl was about to be harmed. Using visualization, I imagined a cylinder around her with calming light inside, and a mirror on the outside, which I hoped would reflect back any laser activity.

The girl seemed entranced.

'How lovely!' she said.

She stood poised in the cylinder.

'I feel so safe now.'

My heart sank, as I realized that some bad things must be coming her way, and that there was nothing much I could do to stop it in the longer term. Killing the perpetrators didn't achieve much as they were immediately replaced by others.

The North American mafia's electric shock torture programme for kids includes intensive night-time trauma-based training events. I looked up at the spotlight. There was an electric cord connecting it to the machine. I 'blew' at the equipment, to see if I could melt or interfere with it. It worked. I heard a noise. A man dressed in what looked like a black wet suit was coming towards me. I stood back out of sight. He picked up the equipment and dragged it to a wider part of the veranda, opposite some large lifts. By the lifts was a trolley bed, like those used in hospitals, and lying tucked up in it was a boy of about six years of age. One of those horrible spotlight machines

was connected to his back. I had no idea what was going on, but I knew it was evil.

I flew at the man, aiming at his head again and again, to dislodge his communication equipment, and remove him from the planet. The lift suddenly opened, and another man came out, also dressed in a black wet suit. I did the same to him. Then a third man appeared out of the lift, and, as I disposed of him, I realised that I had left the little girl still standing in her safety cylinder.

'I can't leave her there forever,' I thought, so I quickly released her and found myself back in my bedroom.

I had never felt so low, leaving the poor little girl defenceless. If I had ever called on a higher force to intercede, now would be the time. I imagined myself talking to some disembodied spirit.

'Can't you send someone to fix things?' I pleaded. The answer I gave myself was not what I wanted to hear.

'Why do you think you are there? That's your job'.

'But I can't rescue the kids properly,' I continued. 'No matter how many operatives I remove, they just replace them'.

Then it occurred to me that I ought to notify the British military. I knew that their priority was preventing the planning and carrying out of acts of terrorism, and that child abuse wasn't in that category. But the kids were being trained up to carry out suicide bomb attacks or similar, at some future date, which should count for something. I needed to find out the exact location of these operations, so that the British Military could find it.

Next day I decided to investigate further. I guessed the underground base might be somewhere in the precincts of the research centre, and I began looking for a large green plastic barn with no windows that I had seen before. But from above, there was nothing to see but some rather nice residential houses in a large secure compound. The compound was reached through a private car park with a high fenced gate with a punch lock. I was looking around the back to see if any neighbouring properties might be involved, when I suddenly heard a man shouting

'It's an underground base, here I am.'

Via the electromagnetic computer system, I looked down inside the research centre and found myself back in the underground facility I had seen the night before. A man in a black wet suit was behaving strangely on the gantry level, hopping onto the safety rail, shouting and waving his hands. He was obviously able to hear my thoughts and seemed to want to help me. But the balance of his mind appeared to be disturbed. The man was now shouting at his supervisors, 'You can't stop me!'

The large lift doors flew open, and a fearsome piece of electronic hardware appeared. It could have come out of a James Bond movie. It was about four feet square and had two search lights like the front of a train. It made a roaring noise. Underneath were two rotating brushes. There was a place for a driver, and an operating panel with flashing lights, but no driver was there. It was being driven remotely along the width of the gantry, sweeping all before it. There was no escaping its onward path.

'You won't get me with that old hoover,' shouted the man, and he plunged off the safety rail into the hall below.

I never saw him again. Looking from above again, I tried to take stock of what had happened.

'How far down is that underground facility?' I wondered. 'Surely our British military would be able to spot it, if they sent a scanner over it?'

I reported my suspicions to the military, and in the days to come, there were so many aircraft and airborne scanners over the area that it became a routine event. It was not until later that I found out that the child torture area was part of a larger underground base, where a range of illegal activities, including experiments on human beings, were carried out.

One evening, I was camping in my father's garden, enjoying the night sky, when I was attacked with electronic weapons, coming from the North. As always, I was linked by wi-fi to the terrorists' electromagnetic *operating* system. The terrorists were similarly wired up, but they were set up on dedicated *application* systems. This critical difference gave me a distinct advantage, as I was soon to discover.

I was able to look through trees and buildings and see whatever else was wired up on the system. I looked into the next garden, a mafia property owned by a wealthy sweatshop manager. I saw a large man, heavily built, lying on his stomach. To his right were a crowd of children aged about six years old. One of them was crouching in front of the man, pointing a small electronic laser at me. I reached out mentally and pushed the child to one side. The man swore at the kid and hit him with a laser gun. The child fell to the ground, writhing in agony.

'Next!' he shouted, and a small cowering girl was pushed forward to attack my body.

When the man hit the child, I just flipped. Burning with anger. I went for him, punching his body and his face as hard as I could. I suddenly noticed that the crowd of tiny kids could see me, and were standing behind me, mimicking my movements, punching and kicking with determination. I loved their spirit. Despite their terrible tortures, they wanted to fight back.

To my surprise, the man I was attacking seemed weak in comparison to myself. I noticed he had a lot of electronic weapons strapped to his arms and legs, and under his armpits, in order that he could deliver more powerful electronic hits to 'motivate' the kids. When I punched him, all the weapons strapped to his body started firing off at once, with him as the target. He fell to the ground, twitching and writhing. Two white-coated scientists who had been lurking in the background ran forward to his aid.

The man was carted off on a stretcher. An ambulance came, and I learned later that he died in hospital from a heart attack. His weapons had been the death of him. I hoped that the child torture programme had been at least halted for a while.

One day soon afterwards, I heard the kid called Daisy near my house, calling.

'Mummy, there's a man here… I'm frightened.'

Mentally logging onto the terrorists' electromagnetic computer architecture, I looked in the direction of the child's voice. I saw Daisy, and a man I recognised, a drug addict used regularly by the IRA for prison guard duties. He had just had a fix and had given

himself a bit too much. This often happened to local operatives, and usually in about ten minutes, they were back to normal, but this guy was looking as if he had intentions on Daisy. Instinctively I leaped to her defence, and found myself next to the druggist. He could more or less make out my form, and so could Daisy. I hit the man and he fell over, and lay on the ground. I stayed with Daisy, and five minutes later her 'mother' arrived. Daisy was OK again.

The following week an elderly couple of Arab ethnicity arrived at the IRA reception desk. They had a cargo of six Syrian children, whom they trafficked as a child brothel. They were allocated a safe house in the valley below. Plenty of Daesh people visited the terrorist unit, because it was on their list of safe places to stay in the British Isles, and I assumed that these were just breaking their journey in transit to somewhere else.

But this group had received an invitation from the local Faeces Group. The reason was that their kids not only provided brothel services, and knew how to operate electronic weapons, but they also did school studies at night, thus enhancing their usefulness within the terrorist community. The IRA wanted the local Faeces Group to learn how to do this, and to start educating their own brothel kids. The Daesh group was welcomed, and expected to stay for some weeks.

That night I was lying in bed, when someone shot at me with an electronic weapon. I rolled over, reaching in my mind to find the direction of the attack. I picked up the electric current and aimed a hit at the offender. I hit him on the head, and breathed sufficiently into his brain to put him out of action. Two other weapons shot at me, and I disabled the perpetrators as well. Then I surveyed the scene I had entered.

It was a classroom. There were six desks, and six little boys had been sitting in the chairs. Only three of them were conscious. The fourth and fifth boys were slumped over their books with electronic weapons beside them. I caught sight of the sixth lying by the window pointing towards my bedroom, his electronic weapon still in his hand. Unfortunately, I had hit all three of them.

The brothel madam, an old woman wrapped in dirty drab robes and a headscarf was sobbing to herself. I realised that she was not weeping for the kids. She was bewailing her loss of income. Her elderly partner, a fearsome looking black-bearded man, watched impassively. No doubt more kids could be obtained, at a price. The woman carried the three unconscious boys into the sleeping area, and laid them on small beds.

'I think they will recover tomorrow,' she said.

But the kids passed on to a happier place, where their tormentors could no longer reach them.

Next day I removed the ghastly old slave-drivers. The Syrian traffickers were no more, but three of their brothel kids had survived. I was just cooking my food when one of the kids hit me lightly with a small laser weapon. I followed the direction of the attack, and saw a small child of about seven years old. As I reached to remove the weapon from his hand, a tall, strongly-built Islamic State Asian strode into the room, scooped up the child and began to walk off with him. The child looked up and saw me.

'Stop, let me go, I want to go with the woman, she can help me,' he shouted.

'No, you won't', replied the soldier, 'I need you. You're mine.'

'What's he talking about?' I wondered.

A nearby IRA operative picked up my thoughts on Syntel.

'The kid is used to provide sexual services,' he said. 'There are only three left, and they are being over-used. That kid has already said that he wants to follow his dead brothers to a better place, and, as you removed them, he thinks you can solve his problem.'

'Well, I'm not going to,' I said. 'I am not here to help people to a better place. I've got a life of my own, and I'm busy cooking my food.'

The kid wriggled and escaped. He rushed up two flights of stairs to the top floor. There was a study room, with desks and a table for a teacher. He sat on the table. Then suddenly he began rolling and writhing on the table in agony.

'What's going on now?' I wondered.

Then I saw laser lights coming through the wall. Two people in the next room were hitting the boy with electronic weapons.

A big Islamic State soldier came in and went to grab the boy. I focused on the soldier's head, breathing into his brain area again and again. In about half minute the soldier was down. Another soldier came in. I did the same thing to him. Then another, and another. Altogether there were six men on the ground. They wouldn't bother the child after that.

One of the orange-clad men from the secret research centre could be heard climbing up the stairs. He had been watching the proceedings from across the road, and his job was to remove the bodies. He and a colleague would then administer an anesthetic shot to send each 'wounded' soldier to sleep, after which a lethal injection would be administered.

The Syrian boy could see me. He looked hopefully at me.

'Now then, sonny, you come with me,' said the kindly orange-clad man. 'We've got a play area with other kids. You'll like it there'.

'No, I don't want to go there,' screamed the boy. 'They'll hurt me. I want her to finish me. I know all about it. It doesn't hurt, and I'll be fine.'

I looked at the man.

'It's not something I want to do,' I said.

The man looked at me.

'There's not much of a life ahead for any of them, really,' he said quietly.

I knew he was right. The last thing I wanted was to witness further harm to the child, and I didn't trust the male perpetrators inside the encampment, especially with the stream of visiting terrorists that flowed through.

'OK,' I said to the boy. 'Let's sit down.'

He smiled confidently and sat on the table. I did not delay, but began breathing into his head as quickly as possible.

'I'll be asleep soon,' he said.

Those were his last words. The orange-clad man picked up his body and carried it away. Then he and his colleague dragged the

bodies of the six Islamic State soldiers down the two flights of stairs, and loaded them into a van outside. It was becoming just another day of death in the terrorist unit.

Did I do wrong? Of course I did. But what if I had not helped the boy, would that have been better? No. Was there another way I could have handled this situation? Well yes, there must have been, because there always is another way. But I just couldn't think of it then. That is the trouble with decisions on the battlefield. The realities of war come up and confront us, and we can only do our best as we see it at the time.

The IRA perpetrator attacks continued as before. One day, I saw a young kid asking to operate a piece of equipment with the intention of voiding my bladder. My policy was to permanently remove all such perpetrators as quickly as possible, but it was Daisy, the little girl I had known since she was about four years old, now completely programmed to hurt people, seeking to prove herself in order to win the approval of adults in her group. It was very sad.

I had so many memories of Daisy. She was an incredibly caring child. One day an Algerian Daesh torturer had been left in charge of the women and children in the child brothel, and was carrying out malicious electronic attacks on them for his entertainment. Daisy's foster-mother wanted to call for help, but her mobile was in the house. I heard Daisy say to her foster-mother, 'It's all right Mummy, you don't have to be hurt going into the house. I'll go instead of you.'

On another occasion, when Daisy's mother was lying on the ground after a ghastly beating by one of the terrorists, Daisy came and lay down next to her. Taking her hand, she laid her cheek against it.

'Poor Mummy,' she said.

Now it looked as if Daisy's life as a child was over, she was becoming a soldier. I wondered if there was some way I could avoid the inevitable. If I just overlooked her, the terrorists would use her to attack me more and more, knowing she would not be hit. Then one day she would probably die as collateral damage, in the confusion that was my daily battle field.

I remembered the Al-Qaida North American mafia research facility in Algeria. It was staffed by French people on the admin side, and they were not involved in the unethical research work. In particular, I remembered Pierre, a man in his early thirties who was responsible for the running of the buildings there. Perhaps he could find a place for children like Daisy. The North Americans had their own children with them, so there might be a school they could go to.

I went to the back garden where the batch kids were playing; it was their free time in-between their child brothel and terrorist training duties. The kids knew me as a friend and were not afraid that I would hurt them.

'You have to go from here now', I said. 'It is no longer safe for you. Soon some of you will be used as soldiers and you will be killed. Does your family have a safe place for you?'.

The kids looked hopeful, and, at the same time, despondent. They were used to rough treatment, and if they displayed the slightest interest or pleasure in anything, one of the terrorists would snatch the object of their happiness from them out of spite.

'We have nowhere to go,' said the eldest girl.

'Where is Daisy?' I asked.

'She's out there in the kitchen,' said the girl. 'Daisy, come here!'

Daisy came skipping out to join the others.

'I can take you away to a safer place,' I said, 'if you agree.'

They all nodded. These kids understood a lot, and they had seen me transport people all over the place in the past.

'Can you get together in a close circle?' I said.

They did so. Then I created a magnetic field envelope around them, and carefully lifted them into the warm sunlit staff common room in the Al-Qaida Algerian research facility. The children ran around excitedly.

As I expected, Pierre, the young manager came out.

'Who are these kids?' he said.

'They are Al-Qaida batch kids from England,' I said. 'Al-Qaida have stopped supporting their batch kids' initiative, and these children have no one to provide for them. Your outfit is funded by

Al-Qaida, so I figured that you might be able to help them go to school and grow up normally.' Pierre nodded.

'OK, but only for these ones. I don't want hundreds of them.'

My mind went to another little girl called Tess, now a teenager, whom I had also watched grow up. She belonged to the same batch as Daisy and the rest of the kids. She lived nearby, and had been forced into work as a drugs mule against her will, as she was too old to earn a living in the child brothel. But she always protested against these activities. She was exceptionally bright, and the local Al-Qaida representative had pleaded that the IRA should pay for her to have full time schooling, and use her on the admin side, but to no avail. The traffickers won the day, and she continued her life as a slave.

'There is one more to come,' I said. 'I'll bring her.'

But where was she now? I had no idea. My guess was that girls who worked in the mother and baby trafficking section in the next village would be able to help. There was a safe house where they all went when there was no work for them elsewhere. I visualised the house, and picked up its frequency. I found myself in the garden of a pleasant country cottage, which had been extended to increase its size.

I went in through the back entrance. It was a hive of household activity. Women and young girls were cleaning floors, washing and ironing clothes. I stopped one of them.

'Have you seen Tess?' I asked. The girl did not look up to see who was speaking.

'She's upstairs, helping Mary,' she said over her shoulder as she passed by.

I went upstairs, and soon found Tess. She was wearing an apron, folding linen in one room, while Mary was making beds in the next room. I took a breath. It was going to be difficult to explain what I wanted Tess to understand, and she might not be interested.

'Tess,' I said, 'The rest of your kids group have been rescued and gone to Algeria. Do you want to come too?'

'Go away and don't bother me', muttered Tess. Then she gave a quick look round and dashed into a kind of closet area.

'Yes, but do it quickly,' she said, clearly afraid what would be done to her if she was caught by one of her women captors.

Immediately I picked her up and transported her to Algeria, carefully setting her down in the administration common room. It was a lot for Tess to take in. I could see the last of the kids going through the swing doors at the other end of a long corridor,

'The rest of them have just gone up there,' I said.

Tess saw the last kids leaving. She recognised her little family.

'Thanks,' she said.

Then she ran and ran, till she caught up with the rest of them. The kids cheered when they saw her.

'Tess is here, Tess is here!' they cried, 'Now we are all together.'

Pierre was leading them into a family room where a woman was preparing lunch. There was a large wooden table with chairs set informally around it, and the kids spilled in there and sat down.

'Is that it?' said Pierre, looking enquiringly at me.

'Yes, that's it,' I said, 'I am so very grateful'.

Pierre smiled, and that was the last that I saw of him or the kids.

I would like to say that they all lived happily ever after, but, inevitably, that was not going to be the case, given the traumatised state that the children were in, and the harmful activities for which they had been trained. I heard later, from IRA terrorists locally, that the French contingent in Algeria had severed connections with their IRA contacts in the UK in disgust, when they found out how the kids had been treated.

There was a good deal of re-education required to explain to the kids about the meaning of right and wrong. They had to learn that they could no longer gain 'parental' approval by hurting people. All credit goes to the French people in the Algerian research base who were willing to put in the effort to rescue those kids.

BRITISH MILITARY AND SECURITY INTERVENTIONS

Under the IRA-Al-Qaida contract, eight Afro-Asian Daesh illegal migrants from North Africa were imported to our terrorist unit every Wednesday and Saturday. They worked for free for a week, during their registration and acclimatisation period, before being delivered to designated units across the British Isles. This work counted as training, after which they received a certificate stating they were fit for purpose as terrorist operatives in the UK. Some of them were offered full time jobs in the terrorist unit as interpreters.

The Afro-Asian Daesh migrants spoke Creole to each other, which no one else in the unit could understand. This gave them a distinct advantage, if they wished to keep secrets from the unit. On 25 June 2015, I noticed a group of them on the top floor of the house next door, gathering in a conspiratorial fashion. They stopped talking if other operatives came in. They were very jumpy and nervous. Something was obviously up, and they didn't want the IRA unit to know about it.

My suspicions increased next day, June 26th, when we heard the news about the massacre of British holiday makers on a beach in Tunisia, and Islamic State claimed responsibility. The attack was timed shortly before the Prime Minister was due to attend a celebration of British Armed Forces Day. The North African Daesh migrants could be seen hurrying up to the top floor, and whispering together. I began to wonder whether they had known in advance that some kind of terrorist attack was going to happen.

I reported my suspicions to MI5, mentioning that the Daesh migrants used Creole for their private communications. Up to that

point, our special services maintained a discrete aerial watch over developments in our area. From then on, aerial monitoring became overt.

It was a clear, sunny day, with blue skies, and I was outside digging, when a beautiful Chinook appeared over the next-door garden. It stopped in mid-air, just opposite the roof of the house next door. There were trees around the house, but they did not seem to be affected by the double rotor action. The Chinook stayed motionless for a moment, before twisting to the left and right without moving forward, as if rehearsing left and right turns. Then, suddenly, it leapt into an extraordinary manoeuvre, circling the roof, and flying sideways over the part where the Daesh migrants had been meeting.

'Wow! Wow!' I cried, falling into the flowerbed in my excitement.

The helicopter moved away into the distance. Ten minutes later, I heard it coming back. But whereas ten minutes before there had been a clear blue sky, now visibility was zero. A thick white fog had fallen over the entire area. I could hear the Chinook over the next-door roof again, but I couldn't see it. After five minutes, the fog began to clear, and I saw the Chinook taking off from the roof in reverse. It leapt into the air, and went East through the trees, barely disturbing a leaf.

One evening next week, I was coming back from a musical event. As I walked up our drive, I heard the noise of helicopters flying very low. Two flew over our house and into the garden of the house where the Daesh group lived. A bright light shone down from one of the choppers, and I saw something rolling and tumbling to the ground inside the brilliant directed beam. My guess is that it was some kind of monitoring device.

In the days after that, if I was attacked by IRA oscillators, manipulating my gravitational field, a helicopter would whizz over the secret research centre and disconnect their wi-fi satellite communications. This meant that the terrorists could no longer use their electronic equipment on line to attack me. At first, they just reconnected themselves. They then went through a learning curve as the British Military disconnected them several times a day. After a

while, the underground research centre, which managed their equipment, began to charge the Faeces Group a £500 reconnection fee, whenever this happened, which concentrated minds somewhat. The Faeces Group soon ran out of cash, but word got back to their Al-Qaida representative in France, and money was found for them to continue.

The secret research centre began developing alternative locations for technical support, because of the British military's increasing interest in their operations. One night I was outside in the drive, when I heard the sound of helicopters again, and two appeared, moving toward one of the new technical support locations. Then I saw what looked like shiny white spaghetti coming from one of the choppers. I recognised it as a directed laser beam. It hit its target. After that, the IRA's new technical installations were closed.

The British military, security services and counter terrorism unit have their work cut out preventing terrorist attacks on the British mainland. I was greatly heartened that additionally, there were times when they saw bad things happening to children, and intervened. On one occasion, after lunch, I could hear the brothel kids in their garden screaming loudly. Nothing out of the ordinary, perhaps, but an aircraft of a type often used by the special services was patrolling our skies. Its motor suddenly changed tone, and it turned left over the garden. Then it dropped vertically, like a stone. Now I could hear adults screaming. Then the aircraft soared up vertically again. I gathered from the IRA's Syntel chat-room that Daesh prison guards were sexually abusing children and women in their garden, using electronic weapons, and that the aircraft had put a stop to it.

'But hang on,' I hear you say. 'That's not very likely. Few aircraft can drop and rise vertically like that.'

All I can say is what I saw. It might not be an accurate description of what took place, but, by now, I have seen so much going on in the sky in our area that it seems there is nothing that our military aircraft cannot do.

There was a follow-up to this, a few days later. The child brothel was operating inside the third floor of the house which the aircraft had visited. A Euro-copter appeared outside the third-floor window,

and stayed there for nearly five minutes, while what could be described as a full and frank exchange of views, in sign-language terms, took place between those inside the chopper, and those inside the house. Apparently, there were several North African clients in the brothel at the time, who dashed out of the room with their trousers down, when the chopper arrived, leaving the female brothel managers and their male guards to face our Military.

On one occasion, my father and I went on a coach tour to see a stately home and gardens in the next county. The IRA decided to make this an occasion for one of their training courses, with twelve students being led out to practice trailing the coach with different cars, tracking and sniping at me as their human 'quarry'. They must have planned these attacks rather loudly, because the British military were waiting for them when they arrived. My Dad and I had a lovely day out, and we enjoyed watching various manned and unmanned aircraft passing overhead at frequent intervals.

At one point, we were having an ice cream on a park bench when a Puma, painted in pale green and brown camouflage colours, flew twenty feet above us to target a terrorist suspect, hiding some twenty-five feet away in a thicket. When it was time to get back on the coach, my Dad, myself, and several other elderly folk, watched with amazement as a helicopter hovered ten feet above the car park for about five minutes, before moving off.

Was all this just for my benefit? Of course not. The IRA, and their affiliates, are active on the British mainland. MI5 stated as much in 2012. Our military have their own way of dealing with them, and, on this occasion, twelve IRA trainees plus their teachers had turned up to cause harm covertly to British citizens, and were prevented from doing so.

During 2016, the IRA started importing groups of ethnic Chinese people from the Philippines. An ethnic Chinese woman who spoke French told me that Al-Qaida had a secret base in the Philippines, and that her people had been taken from there to a location on the border of Brazil and Uruguay, where they had learned how to detonate bombs. They were informed that they would be sent to Europe to assist the work of Islamic State warriors. Their first port

of call was Paris, after which they went to different countries in Europe.

These ethnic Chinese were experts in IT and specialised in virtual reality effects. Sometimes, if a terrorist attacked me and I defended myself, 'dragging and dropping' him from five hundred feet above the ground, the technicians would superimpose an image of that person getting up and walking away, so that other terrorists viewing the event via their computer system would not realise that he had died.

After a while, the Chinese group began to bombard me with virtual reality attacks. When I lay down to sleep, coloured lights would flare up in front of my eyes, with a dizzying series of violent images. I began wearing industrial goggles at night to shield my eyes from the transmissions, but the transmissions shifted to target my eyes from the back of the head instead. The effect was similar to that of the brainwashing techniques demonstrated in the 1965 espionage film 'The Ipcress File'. It was affecting my sleep.

I sent an email to MI5 describing these attacks. About three nights later, when I went to bed, there was total silence, no synthetic telepathy, no electronic sniping and no virtual reality attacks. I slept peacefully. Next morning, I woke at six a.m., to the sound of birds singing outside my window, something I had not heard for a long time. Then, as I lay dozing with my eyes shut, I saw a green bank and a tarmac path leading to an underground building. A fit young man in his early thirties, with a military-style haircut, came out of the building. He was casually dressed in jeans and T-shirt, his jacket slung over one shoulder. He gave a cheery smile to his colleagues in the building, as if sharing a private joke.

Then the force field was lifted – for that is what it was. The British military had created a force field which grounded the terrorists' entire electromagnetic operations for the whole night, including the operations within the secret underground base. The terrorists lost a lot of money, owing to their inability to carry out planned activities, and they got the message. The virtual reality attacks never happened again.

Daesh terrorists made no secret of the fact that they were here to combat the ideology of Christendom. There was a naiveté about this. They had not been in the UK for more than a few weeks, but they seemed to think they could intervene in the lives of local people and 'correct' their 'mistaken' Christian beliefs.

One Algerian Daesh migrant slipped out of his safe house, evading his supervisors, and walked to a local housing estate. He knocked on a door at random. A woman came to the door, her dog barking loudly. The man began to tell her that Islam was superior to Christianity, and that she should change her belief system. Understandably, the woman shut and locked the door, and called the police.

Daesh migrants were urged on by the IRA to plot attacks against local church goers, in line with Al-Qaida objectives to mount 'attacks on Christendom'. They targeted members of church choirs, using infrared scanners to locate them through church walls and direct laser beams at their throats, trying to disrupt their singing, making them cough uncontrollably. Some female IRA members, who attended their local Catholic church, distanced themselves from these activities. The IRA got round this, by allocating genetically modified humanoids to take the lead in guiding Daesh migrants in attacks on Christians.

I wrote to MI5 about these activities. The IRA were aware of this, but they let Daesh migrants continue their attacks, taking care to keep their own staff out of harm's way. They positioned Daesh soldiers where they could see a local choir practicing for Sunday service. To get a better view, the soldiers climbed onto tree stumps. As they aimed their electronic devices at the choir, a British military helicopter zoomed in and zapped the Daesh migrants with a guided laser weapon, hitting their electronic devices, and knocking them off the tree stump. The skin on the soldiers' hands was burned, requiring plastic surgery. The IRA gave up that strategy.

From then on, you could see small unmarked aircraft hovering discreetly, whenever the choir used the church for practices and services.

One day, I was walking to the bus stop after my music lesson, when in my mind's eye, I inadvertently caught a glimpse of a British military installation, presumably, via their own electromagnetic system. I saw rows of men and women sitting along benches, wearing headphones, and using laptops. The rows faced each other, but were divided by a wooden screen. A young lady was just removing her headphones, at the end of her work session. I realised that I had seen something classified that I should not have done.

'Awfully sorry,' I muttered, mentally; 'I didn't mean to.'

I was overcome with confusion, but, of course, it was OK. It showed that our military were logged on to the terrorists' electromagnetic communication systems, and were carrying out monitoring exercises.

Sometimes I caught sight of men and women in military uniform working at night in one-story concrete buildings, in the countryside. They had laptops, headphones and seemed to be interacting with aircraft. I wondered if they were driving drones.

One morning, I heard two low-level IRA operatives conversing via the Syntel system, using their code language. In this language, 'upstairs' meant the IRA officers' residence at the top of the hill, and 'downstairs' meant the building at the bottom of the hill used by low-level operatives. They were talking about the British military.

'The British military can't see me, now I'm upstairs,' boasted an IRA operative to his less fortunate friend, who was 'downstairs'.

At that moment, a man's voice came over the intercom.

'We can see you whether you're upstairs or downstairs!' he observed dryly.

Everyone gasped. It was the voice of one of our military, exasperated at the drivel he had to listen to from these terrorists.

The unsung heroes of this story are those dedicated members of the Counter-Terrorism Unit who were there for me, and for other British citizens, so many times, when we least expected it. They were the first law-enforcement people to make contact with me in 2012. It started when I cancelled my BT Broadband subscription, because the router was constantly being hacked by terrorists. I had to pay a severance fee to BT, and I was cheesed off about it. BT asked me

why I no longer required their services. I explained the situation, but doubted whether anything would come of it.

I was on my way to the hairdresser, when two men stopped their car on the other side of the road and one of them crossed over. He asked me if I could tell him where the nearest B&Q store was. We didn't have one in our village, and it would have been a twenty mile drive to the nearest outlet. The man was in his late fifties. He was casually dressed in a brown leather jacket and jeans, but I knew instinctively that he worked in law enforcement.

Once in the hairdresser, I was having my hair washed, when the other man in the car came into the salon. He looked even more like an ex-policeman, again in his late fifties, with dark grey hair, and grey clothes. He sat down on a sofa directly opposite me. Then he got out a camera, and there was a flash. A stylist immediately came up to him, and asked what he was doing.

'I was looking at my holiday photos when the flash went off', he said.

The stylist gave his hair a proper cut, while interrogating him in detail, asking about his recent holiday.

'Well,' I thought. 'If he had waited till I'd had my hair done, it would have been a much better picture.'

The two men evidently agreed with me, as, when I came out of the hairdresser, they were still there on the other side of the road. If they wanted a photo, they now got it.

After that, I got used to seeing experienced ex-policemen in all kinds of situations. It was clear that they were able to listen in to Syntel. On one occasion in 2013, the IRA seemed intent on getting rid of me, directing a light beam at me, possibly a carbon-dioxide laser, which delivered trapped droplets of a chemical into my nose, making me fall asleep. I was in the house when it started, and realised that I had to get into the fresh air immediately. I got as far as the garden, before I 'went out'.

I was not in a normal sleep state, and part of me was awake, but another part of me was going into hibernation, cuddling up cozily for a long winter.

'Get up,' ordered my wakeful self.

'Not yet,' said my sleeping self. 'I'm comfy now.'

It was lucky I was outside. It was half an hour before my mind cleared sufficiently to make the effort to get up. I went upstairs to the kitchen, to get a drink of water, and, as I looked out of the window, I saw a couple of ex-policemen hurriedly placing red traffic cones around the entrance to our house. There was a lorry in the background.

'They're coming in to get me out,' I thought.

'It's OK now, thank you,' I thought-spoke on Syntel. 'I'm all right again.'

The message must have been transmitted to the men with the truck. They put the traffic cones back in the truck, smiling, and drove off. The IRA were watching from across the road. They did not repeat that type of attack again.

At that time, we had a dedicated section of the Counter Terrorism Unit in the town centre. You could tell where they were, because they had technical communications equipment on their roof, including a type of bird-scarer. The terrorists' ultrasound Syntel equipment also scared birds out of the area, whenever they were broadcasting. When the Counterterrorist Unit switched their bird-scarer device on, all the birds went to perch on roofs out of range. When that happened, the IRA would warn their staff to keep their voices down, as they had a healthy respect for the Counterterrorist Unit, and guessed that they were listening in, using an ultrasound device.

Every Monday I went to have music lessons in the next village, and afterwards I would get the bus to a local café, and have hot soup and warm crusty bread. The terrorists would wait for me at the café, and would try to direct their electromagnetic weapons at me from close range.

One day, I was in the café, when the IRA turned up with twelve male trainees in vehicles parked in the public carpark nearby, so that each of them could have the opportunity to target me in turn. Suddenly I caught sight of one of those experienced law enforcement men waving a large tanker into a parking space directly outside the

café. It completely blocked the electromagnetic attacks. I could hear the terrorist tutors swearing and muttering on Syntel.

After that, on Mondays, whenever I went to the café, there was a weary looking law enforcement man sitting there, just drinking coffee, and talking on his mobile. The terrorists gave up their Monday stalking courses. I really appreciated the care taken to protect us British citizens, by these hard-working heroes.

On Remembrance Sunday 2016, our town held its usual Memorial Service, with the laying of poppy wreaths in memory of those who died serving their country. I was watching from the pavement, accompanied by a friend who was also a targeted victim of the IRA. We turned to follow the procession of Air Force cadets. Suddenly I caught sight of those brave men from the counter-terrorist unit. They had commandeered a municipal recycling bin lorry, and parked it across the high street. They stood guard on either side, wearing orange flak jackets, alert to the risk of terrorist attacks, to make sure that no vehicles were driven into the crowds of pedestrians.

TERRORISM AND DRUG TRAFFICKING

IRA units had to be self-financing, except where funds were provided by Al-Qaida for fulfilment of their objectives. Drug trafficking was one of the IRA's main sources of 'earned' income, as opposed to donations from Al-Qaida and US Republican sympathisers. The drug traffickers that I knew to be working with the IRA were Pakistanis. They had a base in Covent Garden, and their Godfather lived in Eastbourne. Drugs entered the country by different routes, Turkey being the main one. They trafficked crack cocaine from Kabul in Afghanistan. It was ready for distribution on arrival in the UK. The drugs arrived by boat at minor sea ports, and were offloaded in black bags and into unmarked vans. Our local drug traffickers had a large warehouse where drugs were stored underground, prior to distribution. On the floor of the warehouse there were two large metal sheets, which folded back to reveal the underground store.

The IRA combined drug distribution with attendance at terrorist training courses. The distributors did not pay cash for drugs, instead they brought young people to spend a day on the training course before collecting drug consignments. The drug distributors paid the training fees for their youngsters. This bolstered attendance on courses, making it appear that the courses were well attended and self-financing. That meant the IRA could claim that they had complied with Al-Qaida contract objectives for training courses. They settled up any outstanding balances privately with the drug traffickers.

IRA training courses were generally run for students belonging to one unit at a time. They came from all over the South of England,

the Midlands and Sunderland, camping in tents in gardens owned by the terrorists. At the end of each training course, the visitors' group leader was given a black bag of crack cocaine to distribute to his own area.

The Organised Crime Squad arrested quite a number of key people involved in drug distribution locally. According to the press releases, it took a year for the police to prepare their case, but they did their job well, as two weeks after the arrests, most of the perpetrators were charged, and given long prison sentences.

One of the oldest Pakistani traffickers used to live next door. He was a pusher, and offered free drugs to lower level IRA operatives. They were soon hooked. They could see what he was doing, but feared to refuse the drugs, in case they were victimised. Having drug addicts as employees undermined the effectiveness of the IRA, but their senior managers did nothing about it. They did not appear concerned about efficiency or effectiveness.

An ambitious Eastern European prostitute, originally from Moldova, known to associates as Danuza, sought to rise through the terrorist ranks by cultivating the company of senior IRA men. The group she wanted to get in with had their own special club. Entry was by initiation. Danuza was asked to kill a baby with her bare hands. She was unable to do it. After that, she quickly fell from grace, and was assigned to work with the Pakistani pusher. He was seen offering her free drugs on several occasions. We heard that she was going to move into his building. Then, one day, she ran away, back home to her own criminal family, who now lived in the Czech Republic.

She had more sense than most of her peers. She planned her escape around a visit I made to the Botanical Gardens at Kew, which is near Heathrow Airport. She was with a group of terrorists who tailed our gardening club's coach all the way to London. She was due to join the IRA's Metropolitan Group to target me with oscillators and other electromagnetic weapons when I was in Kew Gardens. Instead, she slipped away to Heathrow.

Two months later, she returned to the UK, and dropped in on our local unit to say 'Hi'. But she did not work there again. A

consignment of crack cocaine for her personal consumption had been left outside her door for two months. Nobody touched it till her return. Eventually she collected the crack, but I heard that, unlike many other young terrorists, she did not become a regular drug user.

The IRA avoided direct involvement in high-risk terrorist activities on the British mainland. Instead, they commissioned subcontractors to organise attacks on British citizens, in order to comply with the Al-Qaida objective of hounding and killing the white population covertly. In our area, the subcontractors referred to themselves as 'Our Group', but they did not belong to any unit or group. They were a mixture of Faeces Group operatives, prostitutes, child traffickers, paedophiles, former convicts, people with criminally insane tendencies, people in debt, and drug addicts. A lot of the staff used drugs, and some of the females worked for a drugs distribution network, run by Asians in London, but organised by Al-Qaida from Kabul in Afghanistan.

'Our Group' was managed secretly by middle management IRA women. They received a fixed salary from Al-Qaida to organise the receipt, distribution and cash management of drug trafficking. The women were control freaks when it came to the drugs business, so terrified were they of what might happen to them if they did not deliver expected results. The cash from drug trafficking went to fund the IRA.

'Our Group' organised bizarre job creation schemes for unemployed terrorists. The women held the Al-Qaida cash, and commissioned the services of male terrorists on piecework. The work the men had to do - targeting local people, nursing homes and the elderly with electronic weapons - was in line with Al-Qaida objectives. Work schedules were drawn up by the IRA in administrative offices referred to as 'police stations'.

Staff in the so-called 'police stations' had a menu of terrorist activities that the male operatives could buy tickets to complete. The tickets were paid for in advance by the women. If the work was carried out successfully, the men received further cash from the police stations. If they failed to do so, they were not paid, and lost the money that the women had given them to buy a ticket. The

genetically-modified robotic humanoids were made available to assist the operatives. Electronic attacks had to be launched from locations above the target. The humanoids positioned electronic pointers in trees and high buildings, to facilitate targeting of victims in their homes.

The police stations monitored the performance of operatives through a complex arrangement of microdot cameras, located on interior and exterior walls of buildings occupied by employees and targeted individuals. Plasma screens lined the walls of the police stations, and staff spent their time scrutinising them, checking what operatives were doing. There were print-outs of activities for each registered electronic weapon, which were reconciled to the schedule of assignments by supervisors.

There were weaknesses in this system, mainly due to poor independent review. Corrupt practices were widespread and went undetected. But management was never the strong point of the local IRA, who had a tendency to shoot the messenger, so problems were not reported up the line.

The exception to this was a breakaway group of activists who once had connections with an American cult. They appeared to be on good terms with Al-Qaida, particularly in North America, and when they spotted misuse or misappropriation of Al-Qaida's money they reported it. These activists were specialists in psychological warfare, which included using synthetic telepathy to harass targeted individuals and application of psychotic drugs. Both methods were intended to damage the perceived mental health of their victims. These specialists acted as advisors to the IRA in the covert disposal of 'enemies', but kept themselves at a distance in other respects.

The activists were supposed to collaborate with 'Our Group'. Initially, they provided instruction on how sick and elderly people could be 'helped on their way'. But they withdrew cooperation after a short time. In their view, 'Our Group' were an illiterate disorganised rabble, wholly lacking in principles or ethics of any kind – which was fair comment.

Non-IRA members of 'Our Group' did not receive a salary from Al-Qaida. They relied on income from drug trafficking, but

entitlement to that income was tied to arranging attacks on me. I decided to sever the connection between drugs and terrorism.

A female drugs baroness from London came to mind. I had met her once, locally. She was a nasty piece of work; focused solely on the accumulation of money. I tuned into her frequency, and aligned my electromagnetic 'Global Positioning Satellite' coordinates towards her. She was in her Covent Garden pad with her husband. They were in their kitchen, racing through their financial records, as they had a busy schedule of management meetings to attend, where reporting of profits would be important.

I prompted a thought in her husband's mind to visualize the location of these meetings, and saw a large brass-coloured ornate Victorian building, with steps leading up to a pillared entrance, which looked as if it might be in a street off the Strand.

I entered the building and was struck by the impressive foyer. There was a grand double staircase with a red carpet. The large vestibule led to two heavy dark wooden doors. Inside was a spacious meeting room with an enormous oval table. About twenty Asian men were sitting round it, all carrying bulky black dustbin bags, which I took to be full of drugs for distribution.

I briefly introduced myself to the chairman of the meeting, explaining that the people they were funding on Al-Qaida's behalf were attacking me, and that I should be grateful if they would order them to stop doing so, since this activity was in no way relevant to their mainstream business.

They looked like frightened rabbits in a car's headlights.

'Who are these people?' asked the chairman.

'Oh, I know them,' said one of the dealers, 'They live down South,' and he named a couple of those involved.

'Can you see to it that they stop attacking her?' asked the chairman.

'Uh, OK,' said the other man, looking a little uncertain as to how he would do it.

'I'll believe that when I see it,' I thought, but I thanked the chairman and left.

The attacks continued, so, in the days that followed, I began to remove groups of drug traffickers, room by room, throughout their London building, depositing them dead in the back garden of Al-Qaida's French safe house from a height of four hundred feet. Al-Qaida had to lay groundsheets over the bodies, and arrange for their collection by night in lorries.

The attacks on me continued, and no matter how many men I removed, the troops were replaced by others. It took a long time to achieve an impact, but, eventually, a decision was taken not to supply Our Group with drugs or use them as a distribution point anymore. At last, I was getting somewhere. (See Chapter Twenty-One on The Death Camp for details on this.)

I noticed that wherever IRA, US mafia and Islamic State soldiers were operating, there was always drug trafficking operating in parallel, supported by Al-Qaida. For a long time, I did not fully understand the significance of the connection. I knew a house in our area, operated by Asians, where the head man visited Kabul every month to arrange delivery of crack cocaine. He allowed Daesh people to stay in his house and to use it as a base from which to target British citizens with electronic, chemical and biological weapons, obtained from the nearby North American mafia underground research base. He also allowed terrorist training courses to use his facilities.

North American mafia operatives frequently visited the site, and they invariably turned out to be crack addicts, with poor work records, who were seeking a safe place to escape to from the hectic pace of North American gangland, particularly now that, as they reported, the American Military were going after them in a systematic way.

One day the IRA were facilitating a training course in electronic weapons for Islamic State Sergeant ranks. I noticed that the ISIS troops were all doing cocaine.

'I'm sure that the Islamic State officers' cadre would disapprove of that,' I thought.

I went to the safe house where the Islamic State officers lived inside the perimeter of the North American underground research

base. They recognized me, and knew that I would defend myself if attacked, but they were careful not to attack me, so a neutral dialogue was possible.

I knocked on the front door, and an Islamic State officer opened it. He looked at me in an enquiring way.

'Hi,' I said. 'I just called to let you know that some of your Sergeants group are doing drugs, cocaine, in fact.'

'Oh,' he said, smiling, 'You mean this stuff?'

Reaching behind him he took out a rucksack filled to the brim with white powder. Then he shook some of the powder out of the rucksack and made a line with it.

'You see, we use the powder like this,' he said, demonstrating.

I was rather shocked by that, and my expression must have showed it, as he smiled at my discomfort.

'We need it to help with our everyday work,' he explained.

'Thanks,' I said. 'I will not take up any more of your time,' I said, and left.

I wondered how typical these guys were of Islamic State in general. Were they all cocaine users, and was access to drugs a significant factor in their military campaigns in Syria and Iraq? It was now apparent why the Afghan drug traffickers had a pre-eminent place in Al-Qaida's arrangements. They were supplying basic provisions to the troops. *

*For a full analysis of the relationship between drugs and terrorism see *Shooting Up: A History of Drugs in Warfare*, by Lukasz Kamienski, published in 2016 by C Hurst and Co (Publishers) Ltd.

THE TIDE TURNS

Several times in this book, I report how I killed terrorists when they attacked me or other innocent people. In fact, it took several years for me to learn that I was technically capable of doing it via the electromagnetic computer system. This is how I first found out.

One sunny day I was preparing a liquid feed for my plants, when I heard a lot of noise, talking, and festivities in a nearby garden belonging to the terrorists. A tent had been erected, and a garden party was in full swing. It was a terrorist 'Funders Day'. Terrorist funders and their representatives had assembled at the IRA's grand house, for food and drinks, and discussions on how things were going. The following day they would proceed to the secret research centre for reports on return on investment, trends, and future expectations. The garden party nearby was a modest event for lower and middle level terrorists. Despite the festivities, work must go on, while there were hostages and victims to be attacked, and IRA operatives still had to be put through their paces.

I could see Stuart, the local manager, a small, bad-tempered bully of a man in his late thirties. He belonged to an IRA family, hence his position. He had been a works manager, preparing rented accommodation for the unit's increasing stream of visitors, but now he commanded the weapons divisions as well. He had two cars, both displaying his name on their number plates.

A group of low-level criminals and IRA cronies were gathered around the drinks table, to watch an elderly man being urged to attack me with an electronic weapon. Like Bill, the poor man had been a whistle-blower to his senior management, reporting internal corruption, but senior management decided to punish him for this

foolhardy act. From then on, the guy was always fair game for other terrorists.

'Please don't make me,' he begged, as he was hustled forward.

The manager shot him in the rear with a laser weapon, to motivate him further, and the others roared with laughter. A wave of anger rose up inside me, that I had never felt before. I reached out to the evil manager and started punching and hitting him. I wanted him dead. Using the power of the electromagnetic system that I was linked up to, I tore his jaw apart with my bare hands. I started tearing his head apart in strips, in an effort to prevent him torturing the poor man. I found that blowing at his body made it shrink back, as if burned, and I did so repeatedly.

After a while I stopped. What was left of his body fell to the floor. I turned around and saw the rest of the evil crew in full flight. It was my first killing. They had to send in some men to pick up what was left of the manager. Apparently, I had burned parts of his body to ashes, and there was a white scorch mark on the stones where he had been standing.

I spent some time thinking over what had taken place. Was the man really dead? If so, was there a possibility that I could repeat what I had done sufficiently to remove some of the prime movers behind the terrorist unit? It seemed unlikely, and I didn't relish the idea. It was tiring bashing people about from the electromagnetic dimension, which was at a remove from our reality. But there were serial killers living not far from me, and they were still trying to kill people.

The British military now had the IRA's technical activities locked down, but the terrorists could still wield some limited power, authorise killings, and profit from the money that Al-Qaida so generously provided. I remembered the deaths of neighbours, people in the town that I knew, and the death of my aunt. I wanted to kill their murderers.

There were three people in particular that I singled out. The first was an elderly woman called Rosemary. She was the grandmother of the Faeces Group, who had worked in Al-Qaida's death camps in Algeria and North America, and belonged to an elite North American

mafia family. The second was the well-known female torturer and IRA terrorist called Esme, who acted as Rosemary's personal assistant. The third was a man called James, who worked in the secret research centre. His job was to supervise the termination of nonconsensual human research subjects, when no more money could be gained from carrying out experiments on them. He called upon the services of specialist technical staff to assist him in this work.

I had never tried to gain access to the premises of these people, but I knew where they lived. Using my mind to navigate the electromagnetic architecture, I entered the house where Rosemary and Esme lived. I could see everything clearly. I found them both on the second floor. They could not see me. Esme left the room just then. I struck Rosemary as hard as I could, and began to demolish her body. She fell to the ground, motionless, and I hoped that she was dead. Then Esme returned, and I did the same to her.

Still uncertain whether I had achieved what I set out to do, I went next door, to find James. He was busying himself with papers out the back, a secretary was hurrying in and out with even more papers and refreshments. I waited till he was alone and began to attack him. He realised what was happening, and fell to his knees in prayer.

'What a pity you didn't pray earlier on, before ordering the deaths of all your innocent victims!' I shouted.

He could hear me, and turned his eyes heavenwards with a shrug of his shoulders, as if to say, 'I guess this is it.'

That is how it ends for terrorists. Those who live by the sword know what to expect.

After that I went to bed, still unsure whether I had managed to make an impact in our 'real' world, as opposed to the sometimes-illusory dimension of electromagnetics. When I awoke next morning, there was silence. Nobody attacked me. Later, I heard the Syntel team whispering to each other. It was a peaceful day. I was never able to confirm for sure what had happened, but James's car disappeared for three weeks. We learned that he was on holiday. Later, I saw his car being driven by a man I recognised as his

understudy or lookalike. James was never seen again, and nor were Rosemary or Esme.

One afternoon, when it was still quiet, there were military helicopters over the secret research laboratory. That was usually a sign that Daesh soldiers were being entertained in there. I mentally logged on to the electromagnetic system to see what was happening. Sure enough, I found a room full of Afro-Asians, receiving refreshments. But my interest was caught by what was happening in a gracious adjoining room. Who would have thought that the research centre had anywhere so grand to entertain its guests?

There was a circular table, with all kinds of refreshments, and sitting round it were the big, the bad and the ugly, plus their partners. They were in the middle of a discussion about return on investment, and it seemed that business wasn't doing so well. They were talking about the trauma-based 'Child Super-Soldier' side of the business, which the North American mafia were taking forward. They were working with teenagers, as well as young kids, and had to pick up a number of cases initiated and left unfinished by the American man who died of a self-inflicted heart attack earlier.

These children had been personally 'developed' by the dead American, and would not respond to programming from other scientists. The question was what to do about it. I looked at these elderly moneyed people, none of whom were British. They did not care about the human misery their investments created. But profits were not going up, and that was serious.

Leaping onto the table, I wished I had a long staff with a wooden knot on the end. I tried to imagine myself holding it. I had it. I whirred it around, knocking all the participants on the head. Some of them noticed something.

'Did you feel a breeze just then?' an elderly American remarked to his companion.

'Yeah, I did as well,' replied a man sitting across from him.

'Good!' I thought. 'Let's try something else'.

I imagined a large meat cleaver. Standing in the middle of the table I hit every alternate person on the head, disclosing a section of

their brains. There were about thirty people there, so I must have hit about fifteen of them.

'Ow! I've been hit!' a woman jumped up from the table.

'Honey, I don't feel so good,' cried another guest.

'Look, there's someone on the table!' shouted a third.

The guests all stood up and stepped back. Their hosts suggested that they should go to their rooms and rest before dinner. The suggestion received general support. After that, I saw medics discreetly passing between the guest rooms, with transparent gauze to wrap round the heads of the wounded. Some of them reported feeling liquid oozing from their heads, even though nothing could be seen.

I sat down and thought over what I had learned. It seemed that I could do a fair bit to the terrorists, just by wanting to, provided that I was in an electromagnetic environment wired for ultrasound. The best results came when I blew or breathed at people or objects. I was not sure why that was, but - OK, great! I would try that again, next time someone attacked me.

Pretty soon the opportunity came. A weapons operative was ordered in to try and give me an involuntary bowel movement. This was a fairly routine attack, for which I was always prepared. But with my new-found powers I turned on him, slicing his head open with an imaginary meat cleaver, and breathed into his brain with force several times. To my surprise, he fell to the floor, and was pronounced brain dead. It only took two minutes to do this, and didn't tire me out. A technician arrived with a couple of syringes, one to anesthetise him, the other to deliver a lethal injection.

I looked around the room where this scene was taking place. It was a typical office, set in a private house that had been turned into business premises. I blew at the furniture, pulling it up to the top of the house via the central stairwell. There were papers flying in all directions, and then a moment later, chairs came crashing down, hitting the terrorists, and damaging fixtures and fittings.

I moved my attention to the house next door, where the child brothel kids were having their meal. The room was rather refined, with cabinets full of cut glass and porcelain. I smashed the display

cabinets. Then I went into the kitchen which had lots of mugs and plates displayed on a Victorian style dresser. With one whoosh, all the china and cutlery went flying in the air, landing with a crash. The kids came running in, exclaiming delightedly at the unexpected entertainment. The well-heeled IRA female who owned the property also came running in.

'Oh, my cut glass! My cabinets!' she cried.

'Right!' I thought. 'It looks as if I can hit the bastards where it hurts, in their pockets. They didn't much care about loss of life, but hit their property and they suddenly begin crawling out of the woodwork.'

THE DEATH CAMP

When the terrorists realised that I could fight back, and win, the IRA, ever alert for a money-spinning opportunity, began to call up other units, offering them a new service.

'Bring your unwanted staff, and we'll downsize your business, for a fee,' was the message they were peddling.

This was timely, as since Al-Qaida's withdrawal from the British Isles, it was becoming clear that the Revolution wasn't going to happen, and that the covert part of the war had been lost. There weren't going to be large numbers of civilians in prison camps. All those ground troops, carefully amassed over time, were now an expensive embarrassment.

Every day, a new group of criminals arrived to be led out before me, and 'motivated' to attack me. They included the oldest, the grossest and the least employable of the criminal community, plus the most bolshie unwilling young trouble makers, all objecting to their lot and demanding special treatment. I could see why the terrorist units wanted rid of them. But if that's what they wanted, why hadn't they the guts to do it themselves?

Some of the units just wanted their staff bashed about a bit, to toughen them up, so that they could write that they were 'combat ready' on their CVs. They sent in their young braves, who had been in training for the event, eager to achieve advancement.

I decided that where possible, I would remove the bosses and managers, and not touch the slaves and youngsters, unless really necessary. That would put a stop to the money-making element in our terrorist unit's strategy, because other units would think twice about participating if they lost their managers but not their staff.

At first, this worked well. A mixed group of male and female terrorists arrived in the valley, and took up their positions excitedly. The females were seated around tables in synthetic telepathy rooms, while the males were lined up to attack me with electronic weapons. As the first one hit me, I cast my inner eye into the area. I saw a tall supervisory figure wearing black reinforced shielding gear. He looked a bit like a biker. I hit him, and breathed into his head. After half a minute, he fell to the ground unconscious, with no hope of recovery. The men from the research centre would soon be on their way to dispatch him humanely.

As their leader fell, the visitors let out a wail that echoed around the hills. The second in command bade a stiff goodbye to his hosts, and the entire team left, taking their money and their teenagers with them.

The local terrorist unit made a loss that day. But in the days that passed, they got wise to my tactics. The deal was now, 'Bring out your legacy managers and we will free up your workforce's promotion prospects.'

The junior terrorists were getting over-confident.

'It's all right, we can rip her apart. I've heard she only goes for the bosses,' they chortled.

They often arrived tanked-up, which wasn't so clever really, but considering the lives they led, and their future prospects, maybe it was understandable. In the end, I got fed up with the whole lot, and began laying about me, irrespective. If they attacked me, they got it. If they ordered attacks on me, they got it. If they mistreated each other, or preyed on victims, they got it.

My score went up from six to eight per day, then to fifteen to twenty, and, on one occasion, to over thirty in one day. I exceeded the two hundred mark. The men from the research centre who had to tidy up the bodies, found their business booming. At first, they buried bodies underneath the underground walkway, over thirty feet below ground. Soon this was no longer possible. The bodies were piling up, and had to be sprayed with preservative to stop them decomposing, while a long-term solution was developed. The research centre developed a laser cremation process that left no

traces, and caused no inconvenience to local people. They charged other units a fee for these services, and made a profit.

But something was wrong. No matter how many terrorists I hit, there were more than ever the next day. The IRA's local crack cocaine trafficking business was located in a valley just below me. Every day, small-time distributors would arrive to collect their little parcels, but they were being forced to spend a day in service to the IRA as payment for the drugs. The IRA was using these people as cannon fodder. If they died, then the IRA could keep the drugs.

The IRA had a contractual arrangement with Al-Qaida which stated that, if any of their troops were killed in action, they could claim 'restitution'. This meant that they could get financial compensation in order to replace the lost personnel. In practice, unit heads regarded this as an opportunity to cash in their chips, and use the money for other things. All the units were heavily over-resourced, and they had to give their staff free board and lodging. Getting them killed was a great opportunity, and the prospect of restitution as well made the death camp business very attractive. It also gave IRA henchmen chances to earn bonuses on all sides. They were being slipped sweeteners to get particular staff killed first. Unpopular managers, unruly teenagers, and ageing retirees - they were all on the list, and 'never would be missed'.

I decided to permanently remove the bodies of those I killed, so that restitution did not happen. At the same time, I had developed better methods of killing lots of them at once, quickly. I would draw a large net around a group of twenty perpetrators, and sealing the top of the net, would transport it to the African desert, where, from a height of about five hundred feet, I would open the net, and drop the people out of it. They all landed dead, saving me the trouble of dispatching them. I started doing this in a big way, and my tally quickly rose to three thousand.

Also, as described in the chapter on drug trafficking, I came to an understanding with those behind that side of the business. After I attacked their London HQ, they had moved to an underground warehouse by the Thames, with several floors below the river level. But their staff were still being used to attack me before collecting

drugs for distribution. I hunted them out by their frequency, and appeared in the office of the big chief. He shrank back in shock, knowing that the hooded figure in the long black robe, holding a stick like a shepherd's crook, could remove him and his staff.

'I am not here to kill you,' I said.

He relaxed.

'What is it, then?' he said.

'The IRA are exploiting your staff as unpaid attackers, most of whom will not live long enough to collect their drug packages, and the IRA are then pocketing them instead,' I said. 'Is there some way you could do things differently?'

The big chief thought for a moment. Then his face brightened.

'Leave it with me,' he said.

A couple of days later, the entire system had changed. The drug distributors no longer had to put in a day's work for the IRA in order to earn their crack packages. The drugs were paid for in advance at high level, and all the distributors had to do was to go to the valley depot and collect them. I was impressed at the efficiency with which this arrangement was executed. It shot the IRA's fox, and I never had any more trouble with that particular population of drug-trafficking villains.

The IRA had to look elsewhere for cannon fodder to come and attack me, so that they could make a profit on the dead bodies. They had their funders to consider. They continued to offer downsizing opportunities to other units, with the lure of larger financial inducements, should their staff prove successful in vanquishing me. I adopted a new tactic.

Using a device that looked like sugar tongs, I removed an arm and leg from each attacker and disposed of the limbs in the North Atlantic Sea. This method did not cause pain, but it prevented the IRA from claiming restitution, because operatives missing an arm and leg were not dead. But they could not continue in employment, nor could they be released alive into the outside world, where they might speak of what they knew. They had to be humanely put down by lethal injection, by IRA paramedics.

About this time, the technical staff employed by the nearby North American mafia underground research base all lost their jobs. The British military discouraged their bosses so much that they closed down, and withdrew from the British Isles. At first, they maintained a token presence, renting out their facilities to the IRA and Islamic State, but that attracted even more interest from the British Military, and, in the end, the buildings were left empty.

The unemployed technicians - IT and radio electronics specialists - went into business on their own, offering services from a building rented from the IRA. By now I had learned how to select entire buildings and drop their contents into the sea. This did not remove the bricks and mortar, but it wiped out the electronic architecture that supported the electromagnetic systems. You could tell when a building had been wiped, because, to those of us on the system, it looked like interference on a television screen, and an electronic wind current was blowing through, dislodging office papers that lay scattered on the floor.

It took the technical people forty-eight hours to rebuild the electronic architecture, but rebuild it they did, with enthusiasm, because they got overtime. True, it was harder to replace the staff, because technical specialists who understood the electromagnetic system were not easy to find, but the IRA offered even better pay, and technicians came from units all over the UK and Ireland.

The IRA's staff had, by now, downsized significantly. As their budget from Al-Qaida remained the same, they were able to offer significant inducements. However, individual families within the IRA went bankrupt, because they had mismanaged their funds previously. They borrowed money on the strength of collateral which they did not own, and got found out. This set off inter-tribal warfare between various IRA groups. But they all continued to attack me. I decided to try a different approach. Instead of killing the perpetrators, I hung them upside down by one foot from beams close to the ceiling of their police stations and work areas.

This sounds cruel, but the way it worked, the suspended ones were transported to a higher frequency than they were used to. They no longer felt pain, fear, hot or cold, hunger or thirst, and they were

out of the reach of their employers. They no longer had to work. Their slave life was over. What was intended as a warning to others, became a desirable outcome. You could hear all the suspended men chatting and laughing together, obviously enjoying themselves. Their in-work colleagues looked up at them enviously, hoping that they might share the same fate. Those on the ground might now be living in hell, urged on with cattle prods by their managers, but up above their heads they had before them the prospect of Purgatory, with a good social life.

In the meantime, the IRA were issuing invitations to groups that specialised in technical attacks to come and try their hand at removing me, with huge financial incentives. These guys were bussed in, and there would be as many as twenty coaches in their car park, each coach capable of carrying forty people.

I just did not want to spend that much time removing them. After all, I was living a happy life, which took up most of my day, taking music lessons, singing in choirs, gardening, going for walks and visiting friends. For an old pensioner, that was quite enough!

Then one day a group of technicians attacked me with very heavy electromagnetic oscillators, using six to eight oscillators at a time. I was angry about it. I created a huge cooking pot, and, after killing the villains, I popped some of them into it, and microwaved them. They came out cooked, smelling appalling – really appalling. Then I suspended their bodies in all the IRA work places, in the rooms of chief executives, in staff eating areas, in technicians' work areas, and in the private houses of the super-rich profiteers, whose businesses flourished on human misery.

At last, it worked. When the terrorists smelled the dead bodies, they vomited and left the buildings in droves. The bodies could not be removed by anyone except myself. Henchmen and technicians began applying for passes to work elsewhere. Buildings were closing everywhere. The death camp episode was over.

THE IRA TERRORIST CELL IN FRANCE

I decided to revisit Al-Qaida's hideout in France. I tuned into the memory of my last visit, described in Chapter Eight. Immediately, I could see the fine panorama of green fields, surrounded by rolling hills, and the high promontory, on which the beautiful nineteenth-century country house and garden had been built. The Al-Qaida boss appeared. He was still wearing the chunky crew-neck jumper, and old jeans. Beside him stood a man wearing black robes and a black hood. His face could not be seen. The robed figure walked down through the walled garden to a wrought-iron gate. He went through and down a set of steps to another door leading to an underground facility. I followed him.

Inside the room, three men were sitting round a table listening to their leader.

'Now your group will take this route,' I heard him say. 'I will take the others, using the other road'.

The man had an arrogant manner, and a Southern English accent. It turned out that they were IRA activists, plotting terrorist attacks on the British mainland. They had been prepared over a long period as sleepers, to blend in with the communities on which they intend to prey.

The robed Al-Qaida operative wished to interrupt the talk, and began speaking, but he was brusquely put down by the English guy in a less than respectful manner. In response, the Al-Qaida operative pulled a hand gun from within his robe, and shot him straight between the eyes. He died instantly. I would have expected a lot of blood, but there was just a red mark where the bullet went in. The dead man's colleagues played it really cool, as if such executions

were an everyday event. They turned their full attention to the robed figure and began interacting with him, in a courteous fashion. Then their boss emerged from an adjoining room, and ushered him in for a private interview.

At this point, I began to think that I ought to report what I had seen to the British Authorities. I went on the MI5 website, where you can email information, and described what I had seen. I did not have a location, and it could have been anywhere in France, but I tried to describe the countryside as best I could.

A few days later, I was being attacked by a group of Al-Qaida funded trainees sponsored by 'Our Group', attempting to void my bladder, upset my balance, and make me fall over. In the past, when this happened, I had 'dragged and dropped' the trainees into Al-Qaida's French garden, from three hundred feet. The tactic was intended to make Al-Qaida stop funding training courses, using me as a training aid. But it had little impact on Al-Qaida's funding arrangements.

This time, knowing Al-Qaida's discomfort at having to interact with females, I decided to pick up two female training course participants, and to deposit them alive in the French garden.

As I transported the young women into the garden, I could hear a loud mechanical noise and a lot of invective going on, in a language that wasn't English or French. An unmarked French plane, of a type similar to those sometimes used by the British military where I live, was swinging up and away into the sky. The Al-Qaida guy was clearly annoyed about this, as he was throwing stones at his robed accomplice and shouting at anyone who would listen. The robed accomplice was ducking the stones in a tolerant way.

When the two female terrorist trainees arrived, in their neat knee-length skirts and tops, the Al-Qaida guy took a look, and raised his eyes to heaven. Without further preliminaries, he hurried both of them into the underground facility at the bottom of the garden, where the IRA were working.

One of the women immediately asked to use the toilet, causing extreme embarrassment to all the men, as their toilet had no door. But the girl wasn't bothered anyway. In a bizarre moment of

modesty, I decided mentally to create a curtain for everyone's convenience.

At that moment, we heard a military aircraft flying low outside. The IRA men suddenly started leaving the main room at speed in all directions. I guessed it must have been a targeted sonic device that caused the men to rush out like that. They were as desperate as flies buzzing against a window.

One man pushed through the curtain into the toilet, climbed over the girl's knees as she sat there, and dived out of a window. As he emerged in daylight, the French plane shot him with some form of electronic laser beam, and he lay dead on the ground

Then we heard a banging and cracking sound, as the Al-Qaida guy and several of his team, opened the windows of the underground facility from the outside. The head guy helped the English group leave through a back window, while his team formed a human chain, passing what looked like sports bags full of equipment from hand to hand and out to a white van parked in the lane at the back.

'Hurry now, you go first and get in the van!' directed the boss to the first female.

She ran for it. Then we heard the plane coming back. Everyone outside pressed up against the back of the building. The plane strafed the wall with some kind of beam effect. There was a hissing sound as it just missed us.

'Quick, up the garden and through the house. The van will pick you up there!' the head guy ordered.

Everyone ran. Then the plane came back, really low, and hit the leader of the English terrorists. He fell dead. Everyone else dropped to the ground except the Al-Qaida team.

'Run! Run now!' ordered the Al-Qaida guy.

The remaining English IRA terrorist and the other female trainee got up and ran. They made it. The van had whizzed round to the front of the building at high speed, and they piled into the back, closing the doors as it took off down the road.

What struck me about the incident was that the Al-Qaida boss and his team did not appear overly troubled by all this, like seasoned soldiers of many a battle campaign. I was also surprised that the plane did not attack any of the Al-Qaida team. It was as if the pilots

were deliberately targeting the English IRA activists, and knew which they were.

I wondered about the note I had sent to MI5. Could they have identified the Al-Qaida location from the poor-quality description I had given, and communicated with their French counterparts? I will never know, but what is certain is that the South of England IRA terrorist cell was busted, and did not reform there again.

Where did the female terrorists go? I had heard the men talking about putting them on a train in Brussels, but they would need travel documents for that. Maybe that was something that could be organized for them. So perhaps the girls made it back to the UK after all.

THE SIEGE OF EXEBOROUGH

I often wondered where the numerous terrorist training groups came from, but apart from their accents, which enabled me to identify Northerners, Southerners, Londoners and Midlanders, I did not have much to go on. One day, I picked out a young man, and asked him straight out where he came from.

'I am not allowed to tell you that,' he replied conscientiously.

I tuned into his brain imaging, and saw a picture of the place that he was not allowed to name.

'Oh, I see, it's a building with a black façade and no windows,' I volunteered.

The young man gave a gasp, and withdrew from me.

'You mustn't tell on me…don't say you spoke to me,' he begged in obvious confusion, realizing what I had done.

But it was too late, because I had the frequency of the building, and that was all I needed. I moved my mind through the walls of the building, much in the same way as an infra-red scan would do.

Inside, I noticed that the building had windows with one-way glass that looked black on the outside, and the room I was looking into was crammed with terrorist operatives engaged in remote electronic attacks on victims in their area, using Global Positioning Satellite and wi-fi, together with CDs of biodata previously compiled by the technical research team, to enable them to identify their targets.

There were four darkened rooms bristling with male operatives, all engaged in such work. It was night, but I could see that the building was on a main road, somewhat back from the pavement, with stairs leading up to the entrance. I felt enormous frustration that

the terrorists should continue on like this without being apprehended, especially as I was fairly sure that their activities must be known to the Authorities.

'Perhaps it's because of lack of evidence of wrongdoing,' I reasoned. 'What if I could provide such evidence?'

'I know!' I thought. 'If some Islamic State or Daesh soldiers in possession of their weapons were found on, or outside, the premises, that would give the police a reason to search the building, and then the terrorists would be found out.'

On an impulse, I located a safe house where Algerian Daesh illegal immigrants were being harboured prior to placement in terrorist strongholds across the British Isles. I isolated one of the Daesh soldiers and 'dropped' him in the road outside the building. Then I raided another safe house where Islamic State soldiers were hiding, and dropped them outside the front door of the building, on the pavement. The men I dropped were not badly hurt, and were able to answer questions.

As soon as I did that, some cars screeched to a halt, and helpful people got out of their cars to render assistance to the casualties. Ambulances and police cars arrived. The police had obviously seen these type of Daesh and Islamic Sate terrorists before, and they held back the ambulances till they had searched the men for weapons. The men were carrying hand guns, and they were asked to give them to the police, after which the emergency services went in. Having established that they were dealing with armed men, the police called the Counterterrorism Unit.

The police themselves were armed, indicating that they had intelligence about the nature of activities in the suspect building. What happened next, however, was a surprise. One of the police, covered by his colleagues, approached the front door of the building, and as he went in, he was hit with a barrage of bullets. The policeman fell to the ground, wounded, but not seriously injured. Another policeman rushed to his aid, and the IRA fired on him as well. Then a third policeman was hit. Things were not looking good.

At that moment, we heard a helicopter making a loud noise over the roof of the building. Three tall men in battle fatigues, armed with

semi-automatic weapons, abseiled down on ropes. Two stood on the roof, while the third went down to the ground and covered the front hall entrance.

The two men on the roof lifted the skylight and entered the building. Shortly afterwards, a procession of men, meekly holding their weapons out in front of them, emerged from the building, under close surveillance from the third soldier. They deposited the weapons in a large polythene container held by another policeman, and were directed to line up against the wall and remove their shoes. The police then put shackles on their ankles, and slow-marched them to waiting dark blue-vans organised by the Counterterrorism Unit.

The Counterterrorism Unit blocked the road on both sides with vans and traffic cones, and started directing traffic away from the area. One of the Special Services men said, 'There's a room full of Algerians up there, and they haven't come out yet.'

The Daesh Algerians finally emerged. They were all excessively overweight, and had trouble getting down the stairs, but they marched proudly out of the building into the waiting blue vans, and were taken away.

I was shocked that policemen had been injured. One of the men was in a lot of pain.

I prompted a thought towards one of the ambulance men. 'Why don't you give him an anaesthetic?'

The ambulance man then took out a syringe and administered a painkilling drug. Maybe he was going to do that anyway.

After the siege was over, the police and counter-terrorism team went into the building and brought out crates of electronic weapons, and semi-automatic rifles. Since then, the building has been closed, and I guess it will not be used by terrorists again.

DESERT ADVENTURES

After the siege of Exeborough, the local terrorists redoubled their attacks on me, importing groups of men from as many as five different units a day, lured in by the promise of large financial rewards, and special bonuses, should they manage to terminate my existence. One night, faced with a barrage of full-on electromagnetic oscillators, laser hits, masers (microwave laser beams) and internal organ attacks, I had to do something, as there were too many of them to cope with individually. I decided to use 'drag and drop' to deposit them *en masse* in the African desert. I was not exactly sure where, but I scanned for a place that looked far away from human habitation, and found one where the desert had rocky outcrops and was fringed with green. I then dropped the perpetrators from a height of about four hundred feet, to ensure that they were dead by the time they landed.

This worked well, but it did not deter the terrorists from attacking me. They seemed unaware of what was to come. Their supervisors did not pass the information on to their colleagues waiting in the wings, with the result that a large number of dead people were soon lying in the desert.

The next morning, I noticed a dark black area where I had dropped the bodies. It was a horde of vultures, doing their bit to recycle waste in a positive way. I noticed one large white bird that looked like a stork. It tried to get into the melee, but the vultures would not give way. Then, somewhere in the background, I saw some animals.

The first animal I saw was beige, like the desert sand. I wondered what it could be, as it had long back legs but its face was

so matted with sand that it was unrecognizable. It had a hang-dog look, and was terribly thin. I saw a beige-coloured fox following it, also terribly thin. Then a strange animal with a dark head, a bit like a donkey, or so I thought, appeared. It held its face to the ground, constantly sniffing the dry sand. It was covered in dirt.

As the sun rose higher in the sky, I realized that the first beige animal was a lioness, in the last stages of hunger. There were bodies all around, and she could tell that, but her eyesight seemed to be poor, and she was feeling her way cautiously. Then a third large animal showed up with the lioness. I guessed that it was a lion, as it had vestiges of a dark mane, but it was painfully thin.

Next day I checked in on the animals to see if they were still there. They were, but what a change. The lion's mane was now clear of sand and showed that the lion was a full-grown male. He was lying stretched out on the ground, chewing on a thigh bone. Gruesome maybe, but for him, it looked as if he had just had his first meal in weeks.

The lioness was lying on her side, and, at first, I thought that she had died of hunger, till her ear twitched. She was sunning herself, and digesting the protein meal that might have saved her life. She was still very weak, but, if lions could smile, it looked as though there was one happy cat stretched out in the sun.

I continued to direct the bodies of vicious attackers into the desert, and over the next few days, the lions continued to improve. The male lion had time to attend to his grooming, and his coat now looked healthy. He had put on some weight, and had much more energy. When he saw bodies falling from the sky he would leap onto some nearby rocks, in order to reach them more quickly. I knew that he was going to pull through.

I was less sure about the lioness, whose poor eyesight was a serious drawback. But even she had put on some weight, and I saw her washing her paws and face. When bodies fell from the sky she would look upwards, even though they were nowhere near her. I think she had lost some of her teeth, and she was timid of approaching a body in case it turned out to be alive. All the animals had a well-developed fear of humans, dead or alive, and they would

watch a body for a long time before approaching it, in case it attacked them.

The lioness would turn over the bodies and pat them with her paws, to make sure they were really lifeless, before picking up the smaller ones in her mouth and carrying them off to a sheltered place, where she felt safe to eat. The white stork danced attendance on her, and was rewarded with whatever was left.

I looked up the lions up on the internet, and found that they were described as East African lions, which despite their name, can be found in a belt below the Sahara, horizontally across Africa.

Then I saw the third animal again. It was definitely a strange kind of lion, and now that it was in better health it was clearly a male with a short dark mane that extended not much below the top of its neck. From what I could see on the internet, it was a West African lion. It was in the right place, but these animals are rather rare, so I could not be sure.

I always warned the terrorists when they attacked me that they would go to help hungry animals in Africa, but though they had by now heard about this, they took little notice. Still, at least they were of service to the planet when dead, if not alive.

One day, everything changed. I was dropping a group of terrorists into the area, when the local IRA tried to prevent me with a strong anti-gravity device. The device did not stop me, but it slowed me down, and I only achieved an altitude of about ten feet above the desert floor. The men spilled out onto the desert, still alive, largely unharmed, but hundreds of miles from civilisation. Later that day I checked in on them, and saw some of them sunbathing on top of a rocky hill. It was the first day off they'd had in years.

That night, I saw that they had lit a fire at the bottom of the rocky area, in a cave that had been used by the male lion to sleep in. Now he had been chased away, and they were cooking and eating. There was nothing obvious for them to eat, but I had seen them picking meat off bones. There were a lot of dead bodies lying around on the sand, so it is possible that they survived on the bodies of their dead comrades. I guessed that there was a water source at the bottom of the rocks, because the birds and animals never seemed to suffer

from thirst, and there were tropical trees and shrubs growing there. The men had now congregated in that area.

A month later I looked in on the men to see if they had survived. They were doing well. A pale-skinned man in his seventies appeared to be their leader. His face was red with sunburn and he wore a handkerchief draped over his head. He wore no trousers, just underpants with a shirt over them. Beside him was a small white boy of about seven who brought him whatever he asked, scrounging among the dead bodies for clothes and the contents of pockets. The boy seemed cheerful and content, although it became clear that he was being used by the old man for sex.

Down in the oasis area, I saw several neatly constructed round wooden huts on stilts with roofs made out of leaves.

'The terrorists could not have built them without help from local people,' I thought. 'They must have made contact with civilisation'.

A few minutes later, I saw a black African, of Sub-Saharan appearance, busily employed in loading provisions into a storage area. I wondered how the young boy had arrived. Our local IRA informed me that when I had started to place people alive in the desert, they had studied the landmarks and terrain, and had concluded that the location was somewhere on the border between Algeria and Mali. They had then contacted the Al-Qaida research base in Algeria, and had asked them to send out a search party. There were enough men in the desert to justify starting a small enterprise, and they proposed to begin with drug trafficking, sourced from Algeria.

A member of one of the ruling French-Canadian IRA families in our area was sent out to manage the new enterprise. The next day I visited the growing village community, and saw the Frenchman sitting at a wooden table in the sun. He was in his early forties, dressed in a khaki polo shirt and shorts. I recognised him as Jules, a local IRA manager. He was much more relaxed than in the past, now that he was away from his supervisors, and was clearly enjoying the warm weather.

The village looked neat and tidy. An officious white woman, who had accompanied Jules, was organising some white children. I

194

suspected that child trafficking was going on, but if so, the regime was not as brutal as the one in our area. The children were allowed to participate in the work of the village, and there were no punishment weapons in evidence. It looked as if the children were having some schooling, and were being trained to be useful in their community.

I was visible to the villagers, and an African man came up to me.

'Excuse me, Miss,' he said, 'Next time you come, can you please bring some bigger women's clothes? My wives can't wear the ones on the dead females that you dropped off.'

I searched my mind for oversize female terrorists whose wardrobes I might raid. There just weren't any.

'I'm terribly sorry,' I said, 'But I do not know anybody who has clothes the right size.'

I did not like to disappoint him, but there was nothing I could do. Anyway, I did not intend to revisit the village, now that it had turned into the usual terrorist organised-crime outfit.

However, I was back two days later. The reason was that I had to rescue a small girl from some ghastly brutal child brothel runners who had moved into our area after the Al-Qaida batch kids left for Algeria. I tried not to get involved, but there was a lot of noise and screaming going on, a few houses down the valley, where the child traffickers lived. I looked in on what was happening. I saw a man and a woman both hitting a girl of about six, who was unwilling to participate in child brothel activities.

The child looked up, saw me and held her arms out towards me. What could I do? I got rid of the evil pair and picked up the child. But where could I put her? She was not an Al-Qaida batch kid, so I could not ask Al-Qaida to take her in. The only place I could think of was the African village. I was fairly sure that child trafficking was going on, which is always terrible, but the regime was not cruel, like our local child brothel had been. With a heavy heart, I deposited the child on the rock that looked over the African village below, and watched to see whether there was a possibility that she might find some shelter there.

At that moment, the little boy I had first seen, came climbing up the rock, as if he had heard something worth investigating. When he saw the little girl, he gave a happy cry.

'Natalie! It's my friend Natalie!' The little girl brightened up, and laughed with surprise. The little boy took her hand, and led her down to the village. Jules, the French IRA man, gave me an enquiring look.

'I really am sorry about this,' I said. 'But I had to rescue her from a bad situation at home.'

'Oh, it's OK,' he smiled. 'We've got loads of kids here. She'll get along fine with them'.

I had reservations about the whole thing, but Natalie was looking so much happier that I felt it could have been worse.

I was still looking for alternative places to dump the hordes of terrorists that were being bussed into our area, with the objective of attacking me. Sometimes I had to relocate over one hundred bodies a day. I looked on the internet at a picture of place in the Syrian desert where some murderous Arab terrorists had filmed videos showing people about to be decapitated. I tuned into the frequency of that area. My thinking was that if there were murderers living there who spent their time executing people, a few more bodies wouldn't bother them.

The first time I visited the area to drop bodies, I found myself in an empty desert at sunset. There was no sign of life at all. But when I returned with more bodies, I saw three Middle Eastern men dressed in Bedouin clothes and carrying rifles. One was on horseback. They were going through the clothes of the dead men, and pocketing anything of value. In the distance was a battered old truck, and a young man in Western clothes was sitting in there.

The next time I visited the area, there were several Bedouins waiting. The men had put all the bodies in the truck, and were looking at the sky in an expectant way.

'They must be very poor,' I thought, 'if they are prepared to spend most of the day hanging around in case anything should turn up.'

There was no evidence to suggest that they were terrorists. They seemed to have formed a friendly alliance amongst themselves, and were quite happy just sitting out in the warm evening air chatting.

It occurred to me that I could recycle some of the IRA and Our Group terrorists' vehicles, and give them to these desert people. I turned my attention to the car park of one of the local terrorist installations, and tried placing an electromagnetic field around a small car. Then I lifted it into the desert environment, and when I was sure that I was fully 'there', surrounded entirely by desert sand and a starry night sky, I carefully placed the car on the ground.

The Bedouins became extremely excited, and ran towards the car. At first, they could not open it, so they pushed it down the hill and out of view, shouting loudly.

'Hmm,', I thought. 'It would be better if I could get the car keys as well, next time.'

I watched the terrorists' car park, until a man drove in and got out of his smart BMW. He held the keys in his hand, and, as he walked away, turned to lock the car. Using anti-gravity, I snatched the keys from his hand, and placed them on the top of the car. Then I quickly airlifted the car into the Syrian desert and dropped the keys right next to the car door with a clunk.

The Bedouins gave a great shout, and the young man in Western dress sank to his knees, pulled out a rosary that hung round his neck, and thanked Mother Mary for her gracious gift. Then he raced to the car, picked up the keys, and jumped inside. Two of the men piled inside with him, and the rest climbed on the roof, waving their rifles. The car slowly started to move round and round in circles in the desert, while the Bedouins fired their weapons into the sky in celebration.

After that, if our local terrorists tried to harass me, I would head straight for their vehicles, and airlift them to the desert, sometimes in groups of ten or twelve. The Bedouins started a second-hand car business, and the price was right for scores of local people who timidly approached to inspect the cars, and bargain over the bonnet, before being given a set of keys from a large stock which the Bedouins had now acquired. It was heart-warming to see local

families packed into the cars, driving away with bemused dream-like expressions on their faces.

HM PRISON SERVICE

It seemed that no matter how many terrorists I disposed of, the IRA, backed by Al-Qaida, were determined to replace them with others from other terrorist units within the British Isles or overseas. I decided to adopt a different approach. Why not drag and drop them into UK prisons? I had no idea what would happen if I did, but it was worth trying. I had visual memories of one or two prisons, which I had seen on television, and I started by dropping terrorists, one at a time, into these locations.

The first place I picked was a high security jail for violent male prisoners. I dropped an IRA officer in his forties into the hospital wing. A doctor and a prison officer were in the room, discussing a patient. They looked up and saw him.

'What are you doing here? How did you get in?' shouted the prison officer.

The terrorist turned white with shock, and stuttered a few words. The prison officer grabbed him by the shoulders and marched him off to a lift.

I dropped an IRA weapons technician into the corridor. He quickly dashed through the swing doors and up a staircase. He was seen on CCTV, and two prison officers began climbing the stairs, looking for him. He froze, but when they came too close he made a run for it down the other staircase, where he was met by another prison officer. He was frogmarched away.

I could hear some prison officers in a nearby room, discussing how the terrorists could have got in, breaching prison security. Meanwhile, an IRA weapons operative foolishly attacked me with a laser gun. I dropped him outside the building. He ran round the back,

pressing himself up against the wall. A prison officer walked past without seeing him. The terrorist followed him into the building. There was a shout from two prison officers behind him.

'Oh, I see, he came in from out there.'

The three terrorists were put in handcuffs and marched to a waiting van. They went to a detention centre.

A young woman terrorist wearing a red frock, which designated supervisor status, started screeching obscenities in my ear. My mind went to a woman's prison that had been closed for some time, but was still used as a temporary holding bay. I placed her in the corridor. You could see the CCTV cameras placed along the top of the wall. A minute later, a sturdy woman police officer wearing a bullet-proof vest, with a lot of keys in her belt, pushed through the swing doors and nabbed her. The female terrorist struggled and swore as she was taken away.

I could see a row of toilets at the end of the corridor. I dumped another white-frocked woman terrorist into one of the cubicles. Her outfit showed she was an IRA trainee. Two women police offices extracted her, and sent her off to join the red-frocked terrorist in a van. They were taken away to a women's detention centre. Then the women prison officers went round securing all the windows.

I went back to the prison later, and saw women police officers patrolling the areas where the terrorists had been seen. They were trying to figure out how the terrorists had got in. Then they walked over to a reception room, where several other women prison officers were looking at a prison announcement on their laptop.

'Look, there's been a break-in in a men's prison in Yorkshire, just like us,' said one of them. 'See, there are photographs of three men.'

A senior woman prison officer came into the room.

'I've been in contact with our central security people,' she said. They want us to post our experience on the HMP intranet, so that other prisons can be alerted in case there are any more cases.'

I was impressed by the proactive approach of the HM Prisons security people. I looked up a list of UK prisons on Wikipedia, and found photographs which I could use to tune into the locations of

each prison. Then, the next time some IRA women from 'Our Group' used Al-Qaida money to commission electromagnetic attacks on me, I dumped them in a high security women's prison. The prison had caged-in areas with bars, and locks on the doors. It looked very intimidating.

The IRA women I selected were child brothel managers and drug distributors, trained in the use of synthetic telepathy for psychological warfare. They commanded groups of trainee teenage girls, who they put in to bat against me. These girls had to read my mind, repeating my every thought in an irritating manner, and making hostile comments about me. They were being prompted by a senior woman IRA manager, linked in by webcam from a gracious mansion, safely outside the battlefield area.

My policy was to place younger girls in a young offender's institution for women. When I dumped them in there, they were immediately detected via the CCTV screens, and motherly women prison officers came out and picked them up. The women prison officers displayed a lot of compassion.

'Come with me, Dearie', said one of them to a young Asian girl, aged about eleven. 'You go in there and have a wash, and take off that outfit you're wearing. Then we'll get you something to eat'.

The young girl had to ask the woman guard to help her, as the plastic pinafore she was strapped into was tricky to lift over her head. These uniforms had unique barcodes and tracking devices in them, so that the IRA could see where all their employees were and identify them. When the girl took off her battle dress, the IRA could no longer locate her, or identify who she was.

After getting the girls cleaned up and fed, the woman prison officers took them to a reception room, where they were asked to give their name, address, and any previous time they had been in prison. The girls were then taken away in a minibus to a detention centre.

I was surprised to find that in high security prisons, the prison guards could see me. It was something to do with the electronic security in the prison. They asked who I was, and why I had brought the women in. I explained the situation, and what crimes each one of

them had committed. Once in the prison environment, the women terrorists were visibly cowed, and admitted carrying out attacks on me and other British citizens. They enjoyed the unusual attention being paid them by the Authorities.

The IRA women were not taken to detention centres. They could be seen, promenading in a line round the prison garden every morning. I dropped a child brothel manager into the caged part of the prison. The woman prison officer expressed her disgust at her crime, saying, 'Come along, you horror, let's get you inside.'

On one occasion, I dropped an Eastern European woman terrorist from Romania into a barred woman's prison. When the woman prison officer went to get her, she drew a knife on her. That was a mistake. The woman prison officer was armed, and tasered her. I watched as two men carried her body out on a stretcher.

The IRA were constantly urging teenage boys from the Al-Qaida child soldier batches to attack me, in the hope that I would remove them permanently from the planet, saving the IRA further food and lodging expenses. I started putting the lads in a young offenders' institution. I was surprised at how many of them had been in prison before. This reflected the IRA policy of incriminating their troops at an early age.

I scooped up twelve lads from the garden of an IRA safehouse, where they were being ordered to participate in attacks on my bladder. I deposited them on the floor of a large room inside a young offenders' prison. The boys spilled out over the floor, looking around them in a bemused way. A kindly prison officer came in and did a double take when he saw them.

'Hey, you're back! Good to see you!' he said, smiling.

One young lad burst into tears and rushed towards him with open arms. The prison officer gave him a hug.

'I know, lad, I know,' he said in a consoling voice.

The other boys were smiling at each other, as they recognised their old home. It turned out that they had only recently left this institution. They were picked up by members of the IRA and transported to our area, where they were due to continue their apprenticeship as terrorist trainees.

By now, there were several friendly prison officers pushing a trolley and ordering the boys to sit on the floor. Bread rolls and cups of water were handed out to everyone. The prison offices righty guessed that these lads had not eaten for some time. A few of them needed a fix as well. They were separated out from the rest, and the prison doctor was heard asking what they were on, and offering them suitable alternatives which would ease their problem temporarily.

I was surprised to see what a soft regime was being meted out to these young offenders. But it turned out that this was no ordinary institution. It was a place that deprived youngsters with sad family backgrounds were sent to. Often, these kids had never had a real home, and the prison officers tried to make up for that.

In the following days, I could hear boys asking when the next airlift to the young offenders' institution would be happening. They did not want to miss it. Older kids, who could no longer be categorised as young offenders looked wistfully at the lucky youngsters. One of them begged me to put him back inside a man's prison, as a second best. I did so. As he arrived, he was challenged by a prison officer.

'What are you in for?'

'He hasn't done anything', I said, 'He's a volunteer.'

'I just wanted to get back into XXXXX prison,' said the lad.

The prison officer laughed, and ruffled the boy's hair. Then he patted him on the back.

'Be off with you,' he said, nodding in the direction of the canteen.

As the Prison Service got used to these unscheduled arrivals, I had opportunities to chat to the prison officers. They knew a lot about the lifestyle of the kids, but what they had not realised was that the IRA was systematically using prison as a kind of school for crime, and were outside waiting to take them away as soon as they had served their term.

The men's prisons were generally firm but fair regimes. The prison officers were used to handling unruly inmates and did not tolerate misbehaviour. When I delivered hardened terrorists into their care, they rounded them up immediately, recognising them as their

lawful prey. But nobody wanted to take the genetically- modified mutants. The prison officers groaned when they saw them arriving.

'Oh no, not another one of those things,' said one officer, as he herded the diminutive figure towards the registration area.

'Well where do you want me to put him, then?' I replied.

'OK, OK,' the officer replied, 'I guess we'll have to take him.'

But the prison officers were generally supportive. They understood what I was doing, and seemed to agree with it. They realised that these terrorists were part of a covert war on British citizens, and they had orders from their Authorities on how to handle them. No one asked me to stop bringing the terrorists in.

The officers who worked in specialist security prisons were the most clued-up people I had ever met, with regards to electronic and electromagnetic weapons. Organised criminals now use covert technologies routinely for their communications, and, in high security prisons, there are advanced systems that stop gangsters outside from communicating with those inside. I met prison managers who were aware that prisoners might have cameras in their eyes with wi-fi send/receive transmitters. What prison managers did not appear to realise, was the extent to which organised crime was interpenetrated by the IRA and other terrorist groups.

One Prison Governor at a large modern prison expressed interest in meeting some of the IRA managers, and in receiving examples of their electronic and electromagnetic weapons. I delivered both to his prison. He asked someone from MI5 to come and talk to him about this. Then I was asked to take examples of the microwave laser guns, known as 'fasers', to a location operated by Special Services. These fasers were a new type, greatly enhanced in comparison with earlier versions. They had several power settings, and could deliver a radiation beam to the brain which mimicked the symptoms of dementia at lower levels, and which could simulate an ischaemic attack or a stroke at higher levels.

The Prison Governor chatted to me about my background and experiences with the terrorists. When he realised that the microchip at the back of my head was what enabled the terrorists to track me, and sell access to me for target practice, he wondered whether

something could be done to block the signal from the chip permanently. This did not happen, but I appreciated his enquiry.

One night, I was being attacked by a group of weapons operatives in a large IRA building, and I selected the electromagnetic architecture for entire building and dropped it into a large modern men's Category A prison. As I did so, all the lights in the prison went out, and I could hear officers checking the fuse boxes. After a few minutes, they had everything working again, but they could hear strange noises, like people talking, on their prison public address system. It was IRA radio engineers talking about their work, and they could be heard in any of the prisons that had special security features.

Dropping the IRA building's electronic architecture into the environment of a high security prison, connected the IRA's electronics to the prison wiring. A group of technical specialist prison officers began to take an interest in this. I dropped several more IRA buildings into the Prison Service. They asked me how I had done it. Then the technical specialist prison officers put on head sets and sat at their laptops.

'I wonder…' said one of them.

'Let me try something…' said another.

They had found out how to get into the IRA's electromagnetic environment. Then they began creating tools like sugar tongs, to pick up terrorists that they could see attacking people, and drop them in their prisons. Soon all the top security prisons were in on this. Then one night the IRA decided to fight back. A very stupid IRA manager, in charge of the electronic weapons division, shot a woman prison officer in the backside with a laser gun. It was a cowardly thing to do. She was not too hurt, but she was very angry.

Several prison officers from men's top security prisons immediately retaliated. Leaning in from several locations they hunted for the man who had done it. Two of them found him at the same time, and both of them tasered him. Electricity flashed from his head to his feet in a loop. I was sure he must be dead after that. One of the offices recovered his body, and announced that he was still breathing. He was taken away to the prison sick bay.

After that, I didn't have to bother so much about dealing with terrorists. I was lying in bed one night when an IRA marksman, using telemetry, hit me with a laser gun. Before I had time to roll over and look into the matter, a prison officer had picked up the culprit with the sugar tongs, and that was the last I saw of him. I got a bit more comfy under my duvet and went back to sleep.

'This is the life,' I thought.

It was such a relief to meet people from our Authorities who understood all the terrorist technologies; who knew what was going on; and who cared about what was happening to victims of covert terrorist attacks. I began to feel that things were looking up.

But how come HM Prison Service were so advanced in technology that they could start picking off terrorists in the electromagnetic environment? It turned out that they had recently got a technology upgrade, in response to the growing numbers of mobile phones and SIM cards being seized in prisons, and the associated security risks. These risks had been identified as long ago as 2009.

One night, while I was going to sleep, some IRA weapons operatives and their supervisor attacked me with laser guns. I looked over to where they were, and saw two gentlemen from HM Prison Service and one lady prison officer looking down into the terrorists' electromagnetic environment from above. They towered like giants over everything, picking the terrorists off and dropping them into large brown reinforced paper bags the size of dustbin liners. Then I saw rows and rows of them positioned across the country, around what appeared the Pennines, and all the way up to Northumberland, busily picking off thousands of terrorists and bagging them up.

When the bags were full, the prison officers took them back to their prisons, where other staff took each terrorist out separately, and carefully placed them on the ground. As the terrorists touched the ground, the magnetic field which had kept them in their covert environment dissipated, and they expanded to their normal size.

The terrorists were then frisked for weapons and having handed in their guns, were escorted to a registration area, where their personal details were recorded. Then they were sorted into groups, and transported to detention centres in different parts of the country.

I have heard senior IRA staff speculate that, five years ago, they numbered over a hundred thousand in total, although many left voluntarily for other shores, when the British Military started to clear them out. That night, the dedicated staff of the Prison Service made a significant contribution to cleaning up the pollution of evil that has been afflicting this country, bringing in least ten thousand terrorists.

I GO TO NORTH KOREA

As the weeks went by, the IRA imported more and more Daesh troops from North Africa, providing them with false identity papers, including EU passports. It seemed a waste of tax payers' money to drop them into HM Prison Service, so I began to look for prisons overseas. Iran was an obvious choice, as they were no friends of Al-Qaida. I looked up Iranian prisons on the internet, and found three that seemed suitable.

All three prisons had high walls with barbed wire on the top. The first one I chose was near Tehran. I selected eight genetically modified Daesh dwarves from Algeria and six full-height men from Tunisia, and dumped them over the wall in the prison grounds. There was a lot of shouting, and prison guards came running out, their rifles pointed at the interlopers. The Daesh men all put up their hands, and were instructed to get in line, facing the back of the colleague in front of them. Then they were told to put their hand on the shoulder of the man in front, and to march inside.

Inside, the prison duty manager was sitting at a desk. He asked for the leader of the North Africans to sit down in the chair opposite him.

'Why are you here?', he asked.

'We were forced here by a woman,' said the leader of the Tunisians.

'Why has she forced you here?' asked the prison manager.

'We were sent to attack her, as part of our UK training,' replied an Algerian.

At this point, I decided to make an appearance in my long black puffa-coat and hood.

'They are all Al-Qaida,' I said.

The prison manager smiled.

'You know Al-Qaida are our enemies,' he said.

The North Africans nodded. They did not know where they were, but they could tell that they were not among friends.

The prison manager looked at me.

'We will take them,' he said. 'We need plenty of gardeners here.'

'Thank you,' I said, and I left.

Later that day, I looked in to see how things were going. All the Algerian dwarves were in the prison kitchen garden, digging away with little spades. The Tunisians were levelling the stony ground further up the hill. The place looked like a waste land. Clearly there was lots of work for all of them for the foreseeable future.

Next day I dropped in another consignment of Algerian dwarves. This time, the prison guards were not alarmed.

'Look,' cried one. 'The young gardeners have arrived!' The prison guards smiled and waved to them.

The men marched into the prison manager's area, and were seated around his desk.

'We haven't eaten our evening meal yet, and we want to meet our friends,' said their leader.

'You've missed the last meal for today,' said the prison manager. 'And your friends are fast asleep in their bunks, but you can join them tomorrow.'

The Algerians were duly marched off to their room.

Word soon spread to other Iranian prisons. When I dropped off twelve Tunisians and six Algerians at a high-profile prison outside Tehran, the prison guards came running to watch, clearing a space where everyone could view the teleportation event to best advantage. When the Tunisians appeared, everyone clapped enthusiastically, and when the Algerians appeared, there were cheers.

'It's the young gardeners!' they shouted.

They continued clapping and cheering as the men lined up, each one touching the shoulder of the one in front of him, and marching off in an orderly fashion.

'Hmm,' I thought. 'That is all very well, but the celebrity status wouldn't last long if I dumped all the 'prisoners' I've got in there. The Iranians would not welcome thousands of them. I'll have to find a more sustainable solution.'

It so happened that my internet searches for prisons in countries not favoured by Al-Qaida had turned up a rather gruesome Daily Mail report about the conditions inside prison camps in North Korea. In fact, the Daily Mail had run several reports on what a North Korean whistle-blower now living in the States had divulged about these prison camps. What I read turned my blood cold. We have not forgotten the prison camps of Nazi Germany, and I never thought to read of such things yet again.

My first reaction was shock. Then I wondered what, if anything, could be done to help the poor people being tortured and starved to death, often just because a member of their family had fallen out of favour with someone in authority. It seemed that there was nothing anyone could do.

I looked up North Korea in Wikipedia, and discovered that despite its poverty, it was endowed with excellent mineral resources, and spectacular mountain scenery. In other situations, there would have been a thriving tourist trade, including ski resorts, if it had not been for the horrific regime, which terrorised and repressed its own people to an appalling degree.

Then a mad thought occurred to me. Even Al-Qaida and Islamic State are not quite in the same class as North Korea, ghastly as they are. Al-Qaida has a secret underground base in Algeria. What if they could be interested in secretly developing something similar in North Korea, while putting up a front as a private commercial organisation that specialised in running prisons to international standards in different countries? North Korea was desperate for cash, and might even let them in, and Al-Qaida's friends might be willing to come in on things, if rights to exploit minerals were somewhere mentioned in the deal.

How would this help? It would mean that prisoners would get food, and be kept in more humane conditions, and perhaps North Korea would like to have some modern prisons that would enable it

to demonstrate to the world that it was cleaning up its act. And I would have a place to dump the IRA sub-contractors known as 'Our Group'. It is true that these terrorists had been in league with Al-Qaida, but in recent times, Our Group had been caught stealing money from them, and seemed to be working against them, though it was not clear who for. There was no love lost between those parties.

Looking back, I wonder why I thought this was a good idea, but I think I was emotionally affected by the reports I had read about North Korea, which coloured my judgment. I decided to visit one of the prison camps in a remote mountainous area, which I had seen pictured in a Daily Mail article. The acreage of this camp was enormous in comparison with the number of prisoners kept there. The prison huts which contained the prisoners were little more than chicken coops, which made me shudder. It seemed suitable for development.

After that, whenever Our Group or the IRA attacked me, I 'hoovered up' about a hundred at a time, and dumped them in the grounds of the North Korean prison camp. I provided the prisoners with the basics - food, water, tents and blankets – which, by now, I produced by visualising what was required. Soon the visitors outnumbered the North Koreans, who retreated to the other end of the prison camp. One day, I was walking through the prison camp woods, making sure that all my prisoners had enough to eat, when I met some North Korea prison guards, spying on me.

One of the men, their leader, came up to me.

'What are you doing here?' he said, grabbing me roughly by the shoulder.

I knocked him down, and then regretted it, remembering that this was not a good start to the relationship with North Korea's prison service, if my plan was to come to fruition.

'I'm interested in buying this property,' I said.

The man picked himself up and walked over to his men. They went into a huddle, talking excitedly. Then the man came back to me.

'You want to assist us here?' he asked in disbelief.

'Yes,' I said.

'It could be possible,' said the man. 'We will consider and come back to you.'

'Good,' I said, and I left.

That weekend, the local IRA was hosting a training event for Islamic State troops imported from North Africa. Normally on these occasions, I raided all the delegates, and put them in prisons overseas, but this time, I went in search of the organisers. The event was being run by some senior ranking Islamic State officers, whose regular job was putting new recruits through their paces in a Western country. They tried to look like the British Army, with smartly pressed khaki uniforms and maroon berets. These guys had seen active service in the past, but they were now in their fifties, and did not get involved with fighting any more.

I requested an audience with the head of the training event, who held the rank of Commander. He was of Arab ethnicity, from North Africa, a thin, quiet man, called Nasim. He agreed to meet me, a little cautiously.

'You know that I am teleporting Our Group terrorists to North Korea?' I asked.

'Yes,' said Nasim.

'I told the North Korean prison manager that I was interested in buying the prison camp site, and running it as a commercial concern,' I said. 'Of course, I could not do that by myself, but the project might be attractive to people within Al-Qaida, and if the North Koreans agreed to the proposal, I wondered if your people might consider providing security for the camp, as armed guards.'

'How so?' asked Nasim.

'It's a massive site,' I said. 'Hundreds of square miles, big enough to hold another Al-Qaida base like the one in Algeria, and it would need at least two thousand visible guards on the surface, to protect the perimeter. Underground, to protect Al-Qaida's business interests, you would need another two thousand initially. You see, mineral extraction could be part of the deal.'

Nasim began to look interested.

'But the proposal would have to be at country level,' I continued. 'A country which has friendly relations with North Korea would have to make the proposal, through their diplomats.'

'I think I know of a suitable country,' said Nasim. 'But leave it with me, I must consult several parties. It would not be easy, but North Korea offers many opportunities. If such a project went ahead, could I count on your continued support for the first year?'

'Certainly,' I said.

I did not tell Nasim about my plan to rescue the North Korean prisoners, and give them food and medical attention, so that they could live safe and well in their prison compound.

Nasim came back to me the next day.

'We have provisional backing from the parties concerned,' he said, 'but we need evidence of North Korea's interest first.'

'I will look into it,' I said.

I went back to the North Korean prison camp, and found the leader of the prison guards.

'Representatives of country X would be ready to meet with you to underwrite the project, if you would like to name a place and a contact,' I said.

The prison camp leader got on the phone and spent some time in discussion with his senior officer. Then he made another phone call. Finally, he turned to me smiling.

'We prefer to hold the meeting in Hong Kong. If country X would like to make contact with our embassy there, a date and time can be agreed.'

I passed the message to Nasim, and later that day, he returned.

'It can be done,' he said, 'but I need your help. I have to be the other side of the world within an hour. You can do that, I think.'

'Do you have a photo of the man you want to meet?' I asked.

Nasim produced his smartphone, and called up the picture of a man in Arab robes.

'OK, let's go,' I said.

I encased Nasim in a transparent tube and pulsed the tube with golden light, to help counter the effects of jet lag which accompany long distance teleportation. Then I teleported Nasim into the

presence of the man in the photograph, and set him down carefully, supporting him discreetly, to make sure that he did not fall over on arrival.

The two men greeted each other warmly, and the Arab potentate, who I will call Suleiman, led Nasim into a meeting room where a number of men were waiting to meet him. I waited outside. Well, actually I was doing some washing and cooking, but I kept an eye out for what was going on. An hour and several phone calls later, the men emerged.

Suleiman came towards me.

'We need to be in our Hong Kong office today,' he said. 'Can you transport us all? I have a photograph.'

'Of course,' I said, looking at the photograph.

It was a picture of a senior Arab diplomat sitting at his office desk. I gathered the group into a circle and teleported them into the presence of this man. He had several staff with him, waiting to greet the party. Then I said goodbye to Nasim.

'Do you need to be taken back to the UK?' I asked.

'No,' said Nasim. 'I can go by plane.'

'Good luck,' I said, and I left.

Two hours later, I got a message from the South of England Islamic State group that the purchase had gone through, and that a depot had been allocated for all supplies, including weapons and food. I made contact with Nasim's Aide de Camp, and started teleporting Islamic State volunteer troops to the North Korea prison site. These guys had volunteered to become anonymous security guards for the moment, as neither Al-Qaida nor Islamic State could be mentioned in North Korea.

There were many things to organise – tents and mattresses, rice bags, large containers of biscuits, so that there was something for people to eat if no other food could be provided, laundry basics and soap and mirrors so that the troops could shave. I transported them all to the prison camp site, and waited for the new prison camp manager and Nasim, who were staying in a hotel in the village, to arrive and take possession of the site.

The site manager, an urbane man in his fifties called Haroun, of part French, part Algerian extraction, arrived in a black limousine, accompanied by Nasim. They had a military escort, a truck load of North Korean soldiers followed behind the car. When Nasim arrived, the Islamic State soldiers all stood to attention. Nasim saluted them, and told them to gather round. Then, standing on a large wooden pallet, he introduced Haroun, and gave the troops a pep-talk about their new duties. He divided the men into three groups, day shift, night shift, and general day support.

The handover had been accomplished. The North Koreans retreated to an adjoining prison camp site, and left Haroun in charge. At last my moment had come. I raced to the prison huts to rescue the prisoners.

The huts were too low to stand up in, and so dark that you could hardly see what was going on in there, which was just as well, as I was not ready for the horror of what was inside. There were skeletal bodies tied in sitting positions by ropes, like battery chickens. I was not sure if they were alive or dead. Quickly, I went from hut to hut, untying everyone. Then I created small plastic water bottles, with 'designer water' that I had pepped up to provide all the basic nutrients for life, took the tops off the bottles and handed them in to each hut. Leaving the hut doors open, so that light and air could come in, I stood back to see what would happen.

'How could they move at all, after being tied up like that for such a long time?' I wondered.

I visualised golden light over each hut, as this seemed to help restore bodies that had been damaged in an electromagnetic environment. It was all I could think to do. After about five minutes, a skeletal arm reached out of one of the huts, and placed some empty bottles on the grass. Then a tiny little old woman crawled out, dragging herself along by her arm. She had no hair, but there was a light in her eyes, and a look of hope on her face. She found a place on the grass and lay there.

Gradually, more men and women crawled out of the huts. Not all of them did. Some of them were dead. I decided to give the survivors a thin gruel made from rice, with rice grains in it, as it

seemed unlikely they could take much more than that. The new kitchen staff began cooking bowls of rice for all the troops, and for the 'Our Group' prisoners I had dumped there before. They all lined up and got their rice. Then I created hundreds more of the special water bottles, and piled them up for people to help themselves. I placed large baskets of biscuits around the prison camp site, and refilled them when they emptied.

The Our Group prisoners were invited to volunteer to work around the camp. Teams of women took over the cooking and laundry work. There was a clear stream flowing from a lake above the camp, and people were using it for drinking and washing. This was not ideal, but at least it was a start. Next day, some bulldozers arrived and a team of builders from Russia started to create a sewage system, with pipes leading all the way down the hill.

Nasim caught my eye, and beckoned me over to what had become the military part of the camp.

'We need to build underground now,' he said. 'Can you do that?'

I had never tried to do this, but it seemed logical that if I could create things by visualising them, I could construct underground areas for living in.

'OK,' I said. 'But I need you to tell me exactly what you want things to look like, as my idea might not be the same as yours'.

'I'm not too worried about that,' said Nasim. 'Just create an underground space where the troops can sleep securely, with entrances that can be guarded.'

I stepped back and set about hollowing out an underground living area, using a high intensity laser. The underground site looked a bit like a huge crypt, with arched ceilings and pillars to support the roof. Then I levelled the floor, and provided a sand and aggregate underlay, pouring concrete on top. I put down two hundred mattresses on rubber bases, modelling it on what I had seen in British Army surplus shops. Finally, I piled up hundreds of dark grey blankets, as the site was already becoming cool at night.

I created a series of large tents for the Our Group men and boys, and a separate tent area for women workers, all with bedding and

blankets. Pretty soon we had a proper camp site going, with two hot meals a day cooked in the kitchen by the women, and lunch portions delivered under contract from a local firm. I added more and more Our Group and IRA prisoners, whenever they attacked me. Everything seemed to be going reasonably well.

But things weren't all that they seemed to be. One night, I caught two North Korea prison guards diving into a prison hut and punching and kicking an old man, who died shortly afterwards.

'Why did you do that?' I asked.

'It is my job to do that,' said one of them. 'You've taken away my prisoners, and I can't do my job without them.'

I was so disgusted that I executed them both, and hung their bodies in the air so that everyone could see them. This was not diplomatic, but I didn't feel diplomatic about it. Soon a delegation of North Koreans arrived at the gate, and asked for an explanation of what had happened. Fortunately, I had ready a United Nations report on atrocities in North Korea prison camps, which quoted their leader as saying that prisoners were kept in humane, comfortable, conditions. I pointed out that the two prison camp guards had clearly broken their own country's laws and acted contrary to the wishes of their leader.

There was a silence, and the North Koreans withdrew. An hour later, a young Russian man on a bicycle asked for admittance to the camp site. He took out a poster with large black letters on it in North Korean, and nailed it to a tree.

'What does it say', I asked the man.

'It says that the men who died were punished for breaking Government laws', said the Russian. 'I have instructions to post these notices in every prison camp in this area.'

'Good,' I thought.

But Haroun, the site manager, did not agree.

'Please try not to kill them,' he said. 'You're making my job more difficult.'

I got the message, but it was impossible for me not to notice that the North Korean prison guards were climbing into the camp at night and stealing sacks of rice. I did not arrest them, but I reported their

activities, and Nasim redoubled the troops on night duty. Then I caught a man dressed as an Islamic Imam, wearing a long black robe and black hat, entering through one of the many underground tunnels already dug by the North Koreans, and going round the camp, begging for money from the troops.

Then, one day, Nasim asked to speak to me. He kept his voice low.

'We are expecting trouble tonight. I need a hundred more troops urgently. Can you help?'

'OK,' I said.

Given that all the troops had to be volunteers, this was not an easy task to achieve at short notice. Quite often, the cadets, fresh from their training, wanted to prove themselves in battle, and looked down on security guard duties. I went up above the earth's atmosphere, and surveyed Europe and Africa, trying to sense the frequency of suitable troops. I found them in underground hideouts in Algeria, Ireland, France, Austria and Morocco.

All the men agreed to be imported into the camp, where they were equipped for work on the night shift. Nasim addressed the new recruits, explaining the likely threats, and procedures for dealing with them.

'If you get into a confrontation,' said Nasim, 'fire over their heads; but be careful not to hit them.'

Just before the night shift started, one of the men asked,

'If we've got to be discreet about our positions, how do we draw attention to any problems? We can't shout out to each other.'

'You will have to use lights,' said Nasim.

We hadn't got any lights of course, so I created a huge basket full of high-powered LED torches, and the troops took one each. Then they set out around the perimeter of the camp, along the boundary that faced towards the village. At around midnight, some young men could be seen making their way up the road towards the camp border gate. They had a North Korean prison guard with them. When he got to the gate, he showed his pass and asked to be let in. The guards on the gate had only arrived that day, and were a little worried about what to do. They waved their lights towards their

colleagues further up the hill, but they did not see them. At that moment, a silver sports car arrived, and a man with shoulder length black hair, wearing a fur and leather coat, got out. He looked like a Russian.

'What is the meaning of this?' he demanded, 'Why can't we go in?'

He gave a nod to some of the young men, and they began to scale the barbed wire fence, putting cloth down, to cover the spikes. At the same time, the North Korean prison guard tried to push past the troops. One of the troops fired two shots into the air. A moment later, five experienced troops came running down the hill from the other side of the camp gate, and took control. They pointed their guns, and ordered them all out.

The intruders withdrew. As they left, the man in the fur could be heard saying, 'I suppose we'll have to try a different prison camp next time.'

I guessed that he was from the Russian Mafia, who played a part in the North Korean underworld.

As the men turned the corner of the road, one of the young men rushed up to the camp border, and scaled the first fence. There was a second fence with barbed wire on top, and, as he tried to climb it, one of the troops further up the hill shot him in the arm. The young man managed to climb back over the fence, before lying on the ground, clutching his arm. A car sped up and took him away.

I went to find Nasim. He already knew what had happened.

'They won't go to the Authorities,' he said. 'North Korea has strict punishments for law-breakers.'

'I will go and see if I can help,' I said.

Calling up the young man's picture in my mind, I looked to see where he was. The young man was lying in bed. His mother was by his side, crying. An older man was trying to get the bullet out of the young man's arm with a knife, but it wouldn't come. The young man was screaming. I quickly anaesthetized the wound with an electromagnetic field, and, using suction, eased the bullet out of the wound. The older man bound the arm with a bandage, and he and the boy's mother discussed what to do.

'He will need stiches,' said the man.

'I know someone. Let me call him,' said the mother.

She looked on her mobile and found a number. After a short conversation, she looked up, relieved.

'He will come within an hour,' she said. She clearly felt more secure about calling a doctor, now that the bullet had been removed.

I directed a golden light towards the young man again, and he breathed a long sigh. Then he went to sleep.

After that things went more smoothly in the camp for a while. There was no more trouble from the Mafia, and the North Koran prison guards kept their distance. I was pleased to see that the elderly prisoners that had survived were beginning to put on weight. They could now eat two modest meals a day, and spent their time resting against the wall of the old kitchen building. They hardly talked, but they looked content. I had converted the punishment huts into proper rooms with bunk beds, and checked on the prisoners several times a day.

Then, one day, I noticed that one of the old women prisoners was missing. I asked where she was, but none of the prisoners said anything. I tuned into her picture in my mind and found her in the next prison camp down from ours, which was still run by the North Korea prison guards. The Russian man from the village who provided us with our mid-day meal was there, serving the same meal to the prison guards. Three children aged about seven years old were running around laughing and playing.

The old woman was lying on her back, completely passive. Suddenly the Russian man said a word to his kids, and they ran over to the woman and started pinching her hard all over. The North Korean prison guards pointed at them, laughing. The old woman just lay there, unresisting. She was long past being able to do anything about it.

I snatched her up and took her back to our camp, using all the electromagnetic aids I could muster. She recovered, and in a couple of days, was back with the others, leaning against the kitchen wall. I spoke to the kitchen staff, and explained that the well-being of the old prisoners was key to the future of the camp, and was our

justification for being there. They took it to heart, and were very good at looking out for the prisoners.

I made the women kitchen staff some special cream pashminas in appreciation of their work. The kitchen staff loved them and wore them immediately, but when the Russian catering service arrived for the mid-day meal, the man took a look at them, and said something to one of them women. She immediately took off her stole and gave it to him, and he gave her some coins. I noticed that he had produced far more food than our camp would need. I followed him down to the next camp, and sure enough, he was selling the food to the North Korean prison guards. I guess we had to expect this sort of thing, in such a poor country, where even basic food was scarce.

Next morning, Nasim waved me over to speak to him.

'We have to get on with the underground developments,' he said. 'We should build a mining area, below ground, where exploration for mineral extraction could begin. We have some mining engineers arriving next week.'

'I will carry out a preliminary review of the area,' I said. 'Where would you like me to start?'

'Right at the back of the camp, at the very top,' said Nasim.

I withdrew my view to the beautiful mountain area above the camp. The lake shone in the sun. Our camp was covered by a canopy of trees, so nothing was visible from above. I went through the forest, and selected a place suitable for a clearing. We needed an entrance to the underground facilities, and there would have to be an electromagnetic shield over it to ensure that it still looked like a canopy of trees from above. As I removed the trees and levelled the ground, I noticed a strange looking rock, cut at ninety degrees into the hillside.

'That has to be man-made,' I thought.

I ran my hands over the rock, and found what seemed to be a huge door, which opened outwards. I opened the door and looked down into a deep pit below. There was what looked like an enormous piece of metal, shining with a bright white light, red embers were glowing all over it. I could see North Korean workers pushing wheelbarrows to and fro all over the site.

'What is going on here?' I asked myself. 'It looks as if the North Koreans have already got a mine down here, and maybe they are smelting iron ore.'

I went down into the mine, which curved round under the mountain. The iron-smelting plant, if that is what it was, came to a halt, outside two huge metal doors. I went through, and found a completely different industrial plant in operation. It looked as if chunks of rock were being ground into a white powder. There was a chemical process, where the powder was treated in some way, and then another set of huge doors with windows in. I looked through the doors, and gasped. I recognised the machinery in this part. It was a vast centrifuge plant, used to enrich uranium. Workers wore protective clothing, and masks. There was no doubt about it. Our camp was located over a uranium enrichment plant, and there was no way that our plans for mineral extraction could run in parallel with that. So that was why the prison camp was so secretive and remote. It was a cover for North Korea's nuclear activities. It didn't make much difference whether the nuclear fuel was being produced for civil or military purposes. We just couldn't carry out our own mineral extraction processes so close to all that.

I returned to the camp with a heavy heart. Nasim saw my face. He offered me a chair next to him.

'What have you found?' he asked.

As I described what I had seen, Nasim's face also fell. He put his hand over his eyes for a minute. Then he looked up at me.

'We have to vacate the camp,' he said. 'We must pull the troops out of here. I cannot discuss it on the phone. Can you go to our friend Suleiman, in country X, who negotiated the contract with North Korea, and let him know what has happened? If he thinks we should quit, can you ask him if he is willing to take the troops?'

'I'll be back,' I said.

It was easy to locate Suleiman, he was sitting at his desk in his office. I materialised in my black robe and hood. He looked up and smiled, offering me a seat.

'Has Nasim sent you?' he asked.

'Yes,' I replied. 'There is a matter that could not be discussed on the phone.'

The potentate laughed.

'But of course, that is to be expected. After all, we are talking about North Korea.'

I told him what had happened, and he did not seem particularly phased.

'You can bring the troops here to me,' he said.

'Please, can you show me exactly where?' I asked. 'There are rather a lot of them, and I wouldn't want to make a mistake.'

'Come with me,' said Suleiman.

We went in his incredible maroon sports car. As he drove through his estate, servants saluted and bowed when he passed. He waved and smiled to them all, as if hailing old friends. We drove through a pleasantly landscaped wood, eventually emerging by what could have been a huge football pitch.

'This is the place,' he said.

I thanked him, and left immediately. When I got back to the camp, Nasim had already organised the troops. They were packed and ready to go. Nasim had spoken to Our Group, and offered to transport them as well. Some accepted, but many of them opted to stay in North Korea. It emerged that they had been carrying out their own secret diplomacy from their headquarters in the Seychelles. They had planned to subvert all the plans for the camp, and were working with the North Korea prison guards, against the project. They were also in league with the local mafia, and had been involved in the attempted break-in the previous night.

The leaving party assembled together, in the centre of the camp, and, when Nasim gave the signal, I lifted them all on to Suleiman's football pitch. There were smiles of relief all round when they arrived, and Suleiman arranged for everyone to be taken care of and transported to whichever country they wished. I shook hands with Nasim, and said goodbye.

Then I raced back to the camp, and picked up all the North Korean prisoners. I went straight to South Korea, and asked if the prisoners could be received as asylum seekers, as they had been

imprisoned and tortured by the North Koreans. The South Koreans agreed, and opened a reception centre for the prisoners. I looked in two or three times in the following week, and was pleased to see that all of them were being properly cared for, including the very elderly people that I had got to know during this crazy interlude. At least one good thing had come out of it. The prisoners had been rescued.

Shortly afterwards, we heard that Al-Qaida had stopped funding Our Group, and had put a price on the head of each Our Group employee, because they had tried to subvert the North Korea project.

Some months later, the media was full of stories about how North Korea had staged its sixth nuclear test blast at its Punggye-ri base. US monitors measured a powerful 6.3 magnitude earthquake near the testing site, estimated to be up to ten times more powerful than the device dropped on Hiroshima with an aftershock possibly caused by a rock cave-in. Chinese experts feared that another blast could 'blow the roof' off the mountain at its base. The mountain, believed to be above the underground chambers where North Korea staged the tests, was the same one that I had seen above our prison camp site.

THE SINISTER CITY

After the North Korea debacle, I was thinking over what could have made Our Group go over to the North Korean side, when everything would have been in their favour if they had stuck with Al-Qaida. I was also puzzled about the fact that one group of Arab terrorists, who wore white robes with black headbands and black coats were affiliated to the Al-Qaida group, while a different group of Arabs found mainly in Malaysia, wore pink and blue pastels headbands and coats, and were enemies of Al-Qaida.

I found that the pastel Arab group were behind an American firm which offered wi-fi security technology for cranial implants used by the US mafia and the IRA. Secretly, the American firm was hacking into all the cranial implants, and the pastel-clad Arabs were dictating counter-instructions to their enemies through their implants. I had caught some of the pastel Arabs doing this, and presented them to the US mafia. The pastel Arabs had confessed, and the US mafia had started using shielding devices on their heads. But I suspected that Our Group had also been subverted. Apart from child super-soldiers, only senior ranks used cranial implant prostheses to keep in touch with their high-up VIPS.

Recently, I had tracked the high-up VIPS to their headquarters in the Seychelles.

The Seychelles hide-out was a desert island dream. Warm sunny weather, glorious private beaches, large yachts for drug traffickers, and mansions with roof terraces that were laid out like gardens, with views across the bays. Black and Asian servants served meals to the top brass of Our Group on the roof terraces. But the quality of these top brass was anything but top-notch. They were just the usual

bandits, traffickers, and mercenaries. So how did they get to those high positions, and who was behind them, I wondered.

I drew my mind away from the earth and looked down on our beautiful blue planet, trying to discover a low-frequency source. There was a strange brown frequency somewhere in the southern Indian Ocean, near a small French territory called Amsterdam Island. Far below the ocean floor there was a man-made construction, in the architectural style of twentieth-century brutalism – square concrete, with square windows looking out on to artificial yellow lights in the rock. Inside were a series of large open-plan offices on several floors, with old-fashioned computers on the desks. The walls were painted a dull orange colour. Each desk had a transparent glass viewing facility, and men were sitting at the desks in white shirts, with brown ties and brown trousers from the 1950s, staring into their viewers.

On the floor below were some meeting rooms. There were twenty men in dark brown fifties suits sitting in one of the rooms. Their leader announced that it was lunch time, and they got up to leave. I stopped three of them, appearing before them in my dark coat and hood.

'What is this place?' I asked.

'We work here,' replied one of them.

He seemed to accept that I had the right to be there. The men had the demeanour of people who take orders from others.

'What is your job?', I asked.

'We view what goes on up above, and report matters of interest to our superiors,' said another.

'Where are your superiors?' I asked.

The man pointed to huge transparent corridor, outside the building, which looked as if it was encased in glass.

'They are in our main offices. You can reach them by monorail.'

'Thanks,' I said.

I went and stood on the platform. I heard a noise like the wind blowing through a rocky glen, and a gleaming blue metro-style train appeared. It was suspended from a rail above it, apparently by some magnetic force. The glass doors opened, and I got in. As we took off,

it felt as if we were moving at hypersonic speeds, and yet, inside the train, it was peaceful and quiet. In less than a minute the train arrived in a station. It was lit partly by artificial light and partly by natural light from the exit points, where stairs led to the outside world. On the other side of the station were two metallic lifts. The door of one of them opened, and a man in a brown suit got out. I went in, and studied the floor buttons. It looked as if the top brass lived in the penthouse suite, so I pressed the top button.

Half-way up, the lift stopped, and a man dressed as waiter got in, pushing a large trolley covered with delicious looking sea-food and fish dishes. We both got out at the penthouse level. As I looked to my left I could see a large dining room, with many tables, lavishly laid for a banquet, and next to it, a spacious roof terrace. Opposite the lift, there were two tall glass doors, leading to a very large meeting room, with a huge oval table. There was a high-up meeting in progress. Thirty fit-looking senior men with grey hair were sitting at the table. They wore suits of an unusual silver cloth, their lapels embroidered with a platinum coloured edge. There was something menacing about them, as if they would be dangerous to approach.

I went out on to the roof terrace, and looked out. There was a high grey metal arch, reaching across the road and up the hill. On the opposite side of the road was some kind of futuristic multi-storey car-park. A dark shiny limousine with smoked windows drove slowly past. Then I heard a loud noise. An aircraft was passing low, obviously near an airport. With my mind, I entered the aircraft. I was expecting an ultra-modern interior, but it was surprisingly low-tec. The walls were lined with the sort of beige plastic that went out in the fifties'. Two air hostesses, dressed in uniforms like ice-cream sales girls from fifties' cinemas, were serving boiled sweets to the few passengers sitting in the plane.

The aircraft landed, and the passengers walked down the aircraft steps and onto the tarmac. There was a large metal shed like a bus shelter, with a man collecting tickets at the gate. The people passed through the gate, and some walked down the road. A few women were sitting on seats around the bus shelter. A bus arrived, and the women got on. I decided to follow one of them. She pressed the bell

half a mile further down the road, got out of the bus, and walked round the corner into a residential cul-de-sac. There was a row of bungalows, with red tiled roofs. They should have looked homely and welcoming, but there was a sense of desolation about them, as if no-one lived there.

The woman went in through the door of one of them. Inside was a staircase leading down to a lighted corridor, with rows of doors. The woman walked along the corridor, until she came to her door. She unlocked it, and I saw another set of descending stairs, leading into her one-room home. The bungalows at ground level were just for show. The people lived two floors down, underground.

Opposite the bungalows was a large park, with a wood of enormously tall chestnut trees, with huge conker cases lying on the ground. I planted myself at the top of one of the trees, and looked out over the forested area. The sky was grey, and it felt cold. I could see the city, with its silver metallic architecture. There was a strikingly tall spire coming out of the highest building, and on the top of it, what looked like a circular metal tube with two spokes crossing in the middle. I hardly had time to take in the view, as at that moment I was nearly hit by a stone.

'There she is,' cried a voice. 'I nearly got her!'

'Try again,' said another.

I quickly descended to ground level. A group of casually dressed men in their early twenties were walking away from me. An older man, in dull grey clothes, challenged me.

'Why are you here?' he said, 'It is not permitted to walk above ground.'

'I am a visitor,' I said. 'If it is not permitted to walk above ground, how come you are allowed to?'

The man smiled, taking in the situation.

'You must be from the other Earth outside,' he said. 'Here, poor quality people with no educational ability can only live in the lower residential levels. But those who prove themselves worthy are permitted to live above ground.'

The man looked complacently at himself and his departing friends.

'Thank you,' I said. 'I will leave you to your world.'

I reviewed what I had found: an undersea base where people were spying on our world, connected by a hypersonic link to somewhere that looked very much like our earth. There appeared to be a repressive regime that condemned its people to an underground existence, while some fat cats were living it up in the penthouse. Their preference for fifties clothes and décor was puzzling, especially as the limousine I had seen looked contemporary. And why were there 'pretend' houses, with people living below them?

There was something strange about all the people I had met. It was hard to define, but they were not like Earth people. They looked the same, but there was a lack of questioning about them. They came over as bland and brutal at the same time. What was missing? There was a lack of individuality and personal expression. It occurred to me that, perhaps, these people were not able to create new things for themselves. That could explain why they had a spy base looking at what we were doing. Maybe they just wanted to copy us, and maybe the last time they checked up on our buildings and clothing was in the 1950s.

But how did these people fit in with our world? Were they in some parallel reality? I was unsure, but what I had discovered so far made me think that these people might represent some kind of threat to us, especially as, despite their preference for fifties retro stuff, they clearly had advanced technologies.

I decided to report my suspicions to the Authorities. But who should I approach? After some thought I decided to approach MI5, but I only knew one man from that organisation, who had attended a meeting with the governor of a large British prison in the Midlands. On that occasion, the prison office governor had asked me to bring in some 'faser' weapons used by the IRA and Our Group, and I had delivered them to several people, including the British Military, and a lady in Special Services.

I had reservation about the MI5 official, as he did not seem to be up to speed on the threat from electromagnetic terrorism, although his organisation certainly was. He worked in Whitehall, and, in my view, was more of a 'pen-pusher' than an operations type. Perhaps

Special Services would be better. I tuned in on the Special Service lady, and appeared in front of her desk. She was a little surprised, as she was eating her sandwiches at the time.

'Oh, hello!' I said. 'Do you remember me? I sent you some fasers once.'

'Oh!' said the lady, whose name was Madelaine.

She raised her voice.

'Bertram,' she shouted, 'I think this one's for you'.

A man's head appeared round the door of the adjoining meeting room. Now it was my turn to be surprised. It was the Whitehall pen-pusher whom I had just maligned in my thoughts.

'Oh yes, come in please,' he said, not looking very pleased.

I went into the meeting room and sat opposite him. There was an adjoining room at the other end, and the door was ajar. Looking through, I could see some men and women in military uniform operating technical equipment. One of them was operating a glass viewer similar to those used by Our Group. I saw myself in the viewer. I guessed she was checking me out.

Bertram beckoned to a plain clothes Special Services lady and she came and sat next to me, staring rather closely at my forehead. I smiled and waved back.

'Well, what have you got?' Bertram addressed the woman in military uniform who had been scanning me.

'She's clear,' said the woman.

Bertram looked at me disdainfully. He leaned back in his chair.

'Honestly!' I thought to myself. 'Talk about a pansy resting on its laurels'.

I had inadvertently made a pejorative reference to the cap badge worn by the Territorial Army's respected Intelligence Corps. At that moment, the military woman in the room next door gave a giggle and covered her mouth. Then, in a loud whisper, she said to her male colleague, 'She thinks he's a Reservist.'

Obviously, she had picked up my thoughts via synthetic telepathy.

Bertram gave me a look.

'All right, what's this about?' he said.

'I've found some very strange people who are spying on all of us, from an underground base under the Indian Ocean. Would you like to meet a couple of them?'

Bertram was not as phased as you might expect.

'Oh, all right. Bring them in, then,' he said.

'Where shall I put them?' I asked.

Bertram nodded to a door on the other side of the corridor.

'Can you put them in there, please?'

'Will do,' I said.

I went back to the undersea base, and found the group of brown-suited men, who had just come back from lunch. Selecting two who looked like suitable spokespersons, I explained that we wanted to ask them some questions. Then I transported them into the interview room. The room was modestly furnished, with two arm chairs, a bookcase and a side table. The men were somewhat bemused, but sat down in the armchairs. I left them to it.

Half an hour later, I got a call from Madelaine.

'Excuse me, can you please take your two gentlemen away? We need people more senior than that.'

'OK,' I said.

I returned the men to their under-sea office, and went in search of the silver-suited VIPs.

'They all look pretty important,' I thought.

I selected all thirty of them, just as they were going in to their banqueting room, and put them in an aerial cage suspended above the garden area used by Our Group. Then I singled out their leader, and brought him into the room next to Madelaine's, where she and Bertram were now sitting.

'Perhaps you could stay for this, if you wouldn't mind,' said Bertram.

I nodded and sat down at the table with the other three.

'Thank you for joining us,' Bertram addressed the VIP politely. 'We haven't met your people before. Would you mind if we asked you some questions?'

The VIP did not reply.

Bertram beckoned to two women, hovering in the other room. They looked to be Special Service personnel. The women came in and sat next to the VIP. They stared intensely at him, as if scanning him at close range, which is what they were doing, using nanotechnology equipment concealed somewhere around their eyelids.

Then suddenly, the VIP ejected a prosthesis from above his own eyelid, as if in a tit-for-tat exchange. One of the women screamed and put her hand over her eye. She had been shot.

'Right,' said Bertram. He called out to two heavily armed guards in the corridor, who immediately appeared.

'Kindly escort our visitor to the research laboratory,' he said.

As the guards took the silver-suited attacker away, two medics were attending to the Special Services woman. I doubted whether they could save the sight of her eye, but hoped for the best.

'Come with me, please,' said Bertram.

We went down some stairs, passed a security check, and reached the entrance to the research laboratory.

'Maybe it's better if you don't come in,' said Bertram. 'Can you just wait out here?'

I nodded, and sat down on the stairs. An hour passed, then the door opened, and a hospital trolley was wheeled out. I saw the VIP lying face upwards. His eye prostheses were still open. It was not clear whether he was alive.

Bertram came out.

'Pity,' he said, 'We still had some questions to ask him.'

We went upstairs to the meeting room. Madelaine was waiting for us.

'I don't suppose you've got any more like that?' said Bertram.

He looked at me knowingly.

'Just one would be enough.'

'Actually, I've got twenty-nine like that in an aerial cage,' I said. 'Where do you want them?'

'We'll have to use that room in the basement', said Madelaine.

She led me down some stairs, and showed me where to drop them off. It had been used for social events at some time, and had several three-piece suites in it.

I went back and got the rest of the silver-suited VIPs from the aerial cage. Then I carefully deposited them in the large basement room. I checked to make sure that they had landed safely, but I couldn't see them at all.

'Maybe I didn't achieve the manoeuvre properly,' I thought. I did it again. Still no result.

Then I looked round the room. The twenty-nine VIPS were there all right. They were all pressed up against the walls, and their silver suits had faded into the background, achieving near-invisibility.

Some armed military personnel arrived, and I left them to it. All this was way above my head.

Just then, some low-level operatives from Our Group attacked me outside our house, with laser guns. They had been excluded from accessing me until now, because I was technically out of their area. The moment my mind returned to normal, they seized their opportunity.

'All right,' I thought. 'You can go and meet the people who seem to be giving you orders'.

I picked them up, and dropped them in the parallel reality Earth, in a large room below the VIP's conference room. The room could be described as a 'brown study', in that there were dark wooden panels all over it. The room had an enormous meeting table. There was a massive brown desk at one side, and the arched ceiling was so high that it felt like a cathedral.

A large heavily built man in his fifties with dark hair, was lying back in the Chairman's seat, with his feet on the table. He was smoking a cigar. When I dropped the Our Group rabble into his office, he called some guards, who marched them smartly off. I repeated this procedure several times. Then I went to see what had happened to them.

They were in a prison area, tied to iron rings embedded in the walls. There were two metal bars over the area of their faces. In front of them, guards were wielding various weapons. There was a lot of

noise, and the guards seemed to be hitting the Our Group lot in the face. I saw a woman Our Group member and went over to her.

'Are you in pain?' I asked.

'No,' said the woman, 'They are just hitting the bars.'

'How strange,' I thought.

A dark-clad manager came over to me.

'It doesn't work with people from your world,' he said. 'Now, if it was our lower people, they would be totally intimidated, and return to their work stations in a submissive state.'

The manager had a fairly repellent frequency. It reminded me of people I had met in North Korea. At that moment, I heard a senior Our Group woman outside our house giving orders for some weapons group men to attack me with electromagnetic weapons. Immediately, I lifted her up and dumped her in the prison. When she arrived, I could see from her uniform that she was a member of the US cult that advised the IRA. I was expecting to see her tied up, like the rest of the rabble, but instead, the large man with the cigar came over to her.

'How nice to see you,' he said. 'Please come upstairs.'

I watched as she was escorted to a VIP reception point.

'OK! OK!... interesting,' I thought.

Then I went over to North Korea, to one of the notorious prison camps, and picked up a head prison guard. I deposited him in the cigar-smoker's study. Again, there was the same response. The North Korean was welcomed as an honoured guest.

I had seen enough. It was obvious. These guys were in league with the best of the worst on our planet.

'So this is where the people driving all those cranial implants hang out,' I thought.

I decided to pick up the cranial implant trail of a senior Our Group manager, and see if I could track it back to the sinister parallel reality Earth.

I watched a senior Our Group man, receiving instruction via his cranial implant. He was sitting alone at his desk, on the top floor of his mansion.

'Let's see where his wi-fi trail goes,' I thought.

I followed the light trail up into the ether, expecting it to emerge in the office of one of these brown-suited freaks. I was determined not to lose it, wherever it went. My focus held on to the light trail as it sped into outer space at hypersonic speed. After a while, I saw a spherical dark brown object. It was hard to make out, as, unlike stars, planets and gas clouds, it did not shine at all. If anything, it absorbed light into its mat surface. I reckoned it was about half the size of our moon, and it was clearly man-made.

The asteroid, if you could call it that, was constructed like a submarine, with interior decks of different levels. It had a lot of antenna on the top, with a large mast, on which was a round transmitter, held in place by metallic cross-bars, just like the one I had seen in the sinister city. The light trail finished up in a large office. But it was hard to make out who was sitting at the desk. Everything was dark brown, and if there was light, it was dark brown as well. In spite of that, I could tell by frequency sensing, that the furniture was of a human type, and that there was someone sitting at the desk.

This set-up did not look like the centre of an organisation. It felt like a subsidiary body. I examined the metal wheel on top of the ship, and picked up a transmission coming from outside, leading far away into the galaxy. I decided not to track its path, as it could be light years away. Instead, I tuned into the frequency of the transmission, and found myself in a different world. It was a brown earth-like planet, with forests, and canopies of green trees. There were no buildings that I could see, except for one massive brown metal spire, of the same style as on the ship, and a round wheel with cross bars, stuck on the top.

The spire descended into the earth, and as I followed it down, I could see huge architectural spaces, clearly man-made, like enormous underground cities. But there were no people walking about. At the top of the city structures, there were rooms which appeared to be for very senior people, and then a complex honeycomb of structures leading far down into the earth. I learned later that ordinary people in this culture never went near the surface, and were not permitted above ground. I tried to make out what the

senior people looked like, but all I could see was a dark brown out-of-focus area, possibly caused by shielding devices.

Could this civilisation be the source of the maleficent instructions being cascaded to terrorists in our world? The whole place had a bad feel about it. What was needed was some higher frequencies to lift the energy. I remembered a 'cloud-buster' device I had seen on the internet, produced by a firm in Wales, which was said to help the energy of our planet. I mentally copied and pasted one onto my visual screen. I radiated it with pulses of golden light, and magnified it to a colossal size. I placed this device as close to the centre of the alien world as I could, deep inside its rocky centre. Then I multiplied the number of devices, doubling the number each time, until the devices filled the entire contents of that world and were beginning to show above the surface. I visualised the brown world as a ball inside a basketball net and filled the net with intense golden light. Then I stepped back.

The brown sphere began to glow from inside. Then lights started shooting out all over the surface. The surface was expanding, and, as it struggled to contain the frequency reaction inside, cracks started appearing. There was an enormous explosion of light, and the brown fragments of that world were sent hurtling into space at tremendous speed. At the same time, I could see trails of light leading off through space. I followed them, and found some twenty brown spaceships parked in a remote circle around our planet, each with their spire and wheel transmitter. They were hundreds of thousands of miles away from the earth, and absorbed light, instead of reflecting it. They were hard to detect.

As the trails of light reached the dark ships, they began to glow, and expand. Then they also began to crack, exploding in a shower of galactic fireworks. But now there were thousands of trails of light snaking their way towards the earth.

'They're going to hit all the cranial implants!' I thought. 'I wonder what will happen when they do?'

I returned to the Syrian desert and my Bedouin friends, knowing that they lived across the road from a group of Arabs that were enemies of Al-Qaida, and likely to have implants. As I arrived, I

heard a tremendous wailing going on. One of the Arab houses had its windows pushed wide open.

'My master has had a heart attack,' cried a senior Arab manager.

I switched my gaze to a Malaysian underground base, where the pastel Arabs supervised a group of technicians involved in remote electromagnetic attacks on their enemies. There were no Arabs visible. The technicians were not working. They were looking round and talking to each other in hushed tones. Above ground, in the car park, I saw an Arab with a pastel coat lying on the ground.

Then I went back to the UK and checked on the numerous senior Our Group officers, who seemed to do nothing but sit at their desks day and night, issuing orders for their servants to carry out. Not one of them was at his desk. Everywhere I looked it was the same. In New York, the US mafia's headquarters had posted a list of the deceased. People were standing silently looking up at the board above their heads.

Although rather shattering, this was quite logical to me. After all, we already knew that people whose cranial implants had been subverted were responsible for all kinds of terrorist attacks across the world. But I was not expecting so many people to be affected. Even senior people in Al-Qaida had been hit. I never guessed how many of them had had the implants.

That night, there was silence in terrorist headquarters across the world. All the secret communications lines had been burnt out, and terrorist decision-makers across the planet were lying dead, awaiting burial.

THE SIEGE OF EXFORD

After the demise of the sinister city, it began to feel as if the terrorists' electromagnetic world was beginning to go extinct. And thanks to our British military, the counter-terrorism teams and the Royal Air Force, the activities of the Al-Qaida/IRA terrorists had diminished to such an extent that several IRA regiments had been obliged to merge, most notably those known as the Exford Regiment and the Metropolitan Regiment, which included London and the surrounding areas.

Following the merger, the Metropolitan Regiment put pressure on the Exford element to resolve its problems in our area by seeking to take back control from the British Military. As a result, groups of male and female terrorists from several units were drafted in from both central and outlying areas, and ordered to cooperate with the Islamic State and Daesh terrorist cells. They began a series of concerted attacks on me and other targeted individuals over a ten-day period, in an effort to re-establish sovereignty of the area.

Whenever they tried to attack, the British military sent helicopters and aircraft to disconnect their wi-fi routers and melt their electronic installations. The military took out the IRA satellite links to their shared systems across the British Isles, and hit the weapons of perpetrators with guided lasers. While all this was going on, I began thinking what I could do to highlight some of the more covert electromagnetic activities of the terrorists, going on behind the scenes. Exford was the nearest large terrorist centre, with a specialist science research centre, where unethical scientists, sponsored by the North American mafia, conducted industrial espionage, and

attempted to spy on defence and space research in neighbouring British government facilities.

I decided to repeat the method which I had used in Exborough. I went into Islamic State and Daesh safe houses in our area, dragging and dropping their soldiers onto the road and car park outside the secret mafia science research facility, where they lay with minor injuries. I also placed a Daesh soldier on the roof of the building. The county police and ambulance service services were soon on the scene, and started measuring the distance from the roof to where the Islamic State soldiers had fallen, to try and establish what had happened. They worked out how the terrorists might have got onto the roof, but they were puzzled about the placement of bodies on the ground in relation to the roof.

Our local terrorists were trying to stop me dragging and dropping their men, using a hand-held anti-gravity device. I seized the device from them and placed it in the car park outside the science research facility. Almost immediately, a member of the counter-terrorism team found it, and took it away, warning the police to be on their guard, and not to approach the building.

The area was cordoned off, partly because the Islamic State and Daesh soldiers were found to be carrying hand guns, and there was as risk that others could be nearby. I arranged for another Algerian Daesh soldier to fall a few feet, slightly hurting his head. He was immediately seized by the police, and disarmed. He began shouting that he had been pushed off the roof by a man in a black-robe and hood. Although he had entered Britain illegally, the terrorist could be heard demanding his rights as the ambulance men took him off to the County Hospital with a police escort.

There were US mafia scientists in the secret research building. I looked into one of the rooms, where a man with grey hair was having a meeting with two visitors. They had a sheaf of papers which they handed to him before they left. I gathered that the papers contained information about a confidential industrial development. Just then, the police could be heard, obtaining access to the building. The scientist was in the middle of putting the papers in a filing cabinet, when he went out to see what was going on.

On an impulse, using electromagnetics and anti-gravity, I selected the entire filing cabinet and lifted it out of the building. But where to put it? My mind raced through possibilities.

'I know,' I thought. 'I'll take it to MI5. But what is the best way to do that?'

I remembered the well-known buildings that could be seen near Vauxhall railway station, with the green glass and decorative roof technology shining in the sun. In a second, I had dragged and dropped the filing cabinet on to the top of the roof of one of those buildings.

'What will happen next?' I wondered. 'Will anybody notice?'

A moment later, I saw a man on the roof. He had emerged from a stairwell. At the bottom of the stairwell was another man. I watched as two men checked the filing cabinet with electronic devices. Then they manoeuvred the filing cabinet down the stairs onto a two-wheeled trolley, and disappeared with it.

I returned to the Exford area, and went to see what was going on at the County Hospital. I found the Algerian Daesh man in a private bedroom of his own. A policeman was sitting by his bed, taking notes, and a nurse was standing on the other side of the bed, bathing a gash on his head. The Algerian was demanding food and drinks, which were brought, and he lay back in bed, talking loudly about the important role which he had played in Al-Qaida's operations in the European theatre of war. Two other policemen were standing guard outside the door, chuckling to themselves.

Eventually, the nursing staff decided that it was time for their patient to take a rest, and a calming medicament was administered, after which the Algerian lapsed into a deep slumber. Owing to the pressure for beds, the hospital wanted to use the private room for a more seriously ill patient, and they asked the police whether they could move the sleeping Algerian to a small ward containing three elderly men. The police agreed, and positioned themselves discreetly on chairs at a short distance from the ward.

At that moment, I saw four other Daesh Algerians from our area peep round the door. How had they got there? Somehow, they had

sussed out where their injured compatriot was, slipped past the police, and had come to visit him.

They surrounded the sleeping Algerian's bed, and their leader tried to wake him, but he did not respond.

'We must rescue him,' said one of them.

They began lifting the man out of bed, in an attempt to remove him from the hospital. A nurse, who had been tending to another patient in the ward, spotted them and came running over.

'What do you think you are doing? Stop that!' she cried.

The Algerians were taken by surprise, and, feeling threatened, one of them pulled a gun on the nurse.

'Don't try to stop us,' he said.

The nurse gave a loud scream, and dropped the treatment tray she was carrying. The police outside came in, and seeing what was happening, ordered the Algerians to get away from the patients and go towards the end of the ward. One of the policemen was armed, and he drew his gun, but all four Algerians had guns as well.

Luckily, as it turned out, one of the County Hospital managers had seen the Algerians moving towards the ward earlier on, and, noticing their unmistakeable resemblance to the Daesh patient, had alerted the police station about ten minutes earlier. The manager was hovering outside in the foyer, worrying about what might happen to people in the hospital. To his relief, a large dark blue van drove up and parked outside the entrance to the hospital. Three strong men dressed in military uniform emerged, armed with semi-automatic weapons. The manager raced with them to the ward, and they burst in, in time to defuse what was becoming a rather difficult situation.

On seeing the soldiers, the Algerians dropped their weapons, and the soldiers put cuffs on their hands. Then the hospital manager brought in four wheel-chairs, and the soldiers put the Algerians into the wheel chairs, and wheeled them out of the ward, across the foyer, and up a ramp that had been brought out from inside the blue van. The van doors closed, and the soldiers and their Algerian captives disappeared.

Back in the ward, the Algerian patient continued in his slumber, as did the other three ward occupants, who had missed the whole

thing. It was as if nothing had happened. In an adjoining room at the back, the nurse was being comforted by another nurse, while a policewoman took her statement.

An hour later I tuned into my memory-picture of the four Algerians standing round their colleague's bed. I knew it would lead me to them wherever they were.

I found myself in an official looking hall, where there was a kind of caged area, containing three of the Algerians. There was a large corridor running through the centre of the hall. In an adjoining room, with the door ajar, there was a table with a telephone. Two well-dressed men were sitting on one side of it. On the other side, sat the fourth Algerian. He was saying nothing. An interpreter was sitting a little behind him, translating what was being said to him, into some kind of French, possibly Creole.

The Algerian continued to say nothing.

'You'd better put him in Room Three,' said one of the men.

I watched as the Algerian was escorted a few yards down the corridor into a suite containing an outer room with a table and three chairs, and a small but adequate inner room, with a bed, wash-basin and toilet. The lights were controlled from outside, and remained on. The Algerian was locked in. He went into the bedroom. There was a small window with iron bars on it. Standing on the bed, he looked out into the corridor. He pushed a piece of paper through the bars, and a man walking along the corridor stopped and picked it up. He smiled and said hello, before handing it back and walking on.

The Algerian reached for something in his underwear. It was a small cell phone. Lying on the bed, he began trying to dial up. At that moment, a woman soldier marched into his room and confiscated the phone. She left, locking the door again. Obviously, the room was under constant CCTV surveillance. The Algerian lay on the bed and turned his face to the wall.

I gathered that the three other Algerians were located in similar rooms a few yards away from the first. During the next day or so, I checked in on them. There seemed to be no change in their circumstances, except that food and drink was brought at various times. Then, on the fourth day, I saw the first Algerian sitting at the

table. The two well-dressed men came in and sat down. One of them took out a notebook to record what was said.

'I understand that you are willing to talk to us,' said the first.

'Yes,' said the Algerian, speaking in English.

Then, in a matter-of-fact way, he continued.

'There is only one thing I wish to say. I am here to kill white people for Al-Qaida.'

'I see', said the well-dressed man, not giving anything away by his deadpan tone of voice.

The Algerian lapsed back into silence.

'Is that all you wish to say?' asked the man.

The Algerian did not reply.

The two men smiled at each other, got up and left. In the circumstances, there was no need for any further interrogation.

The Algerians were held in their rooms for a further two days, and then they were no longer there. I found out later that they had been sent to a military detention centre, where their cases would be considered in due course.

It was recently reported on the radio that the British government was working with the Government of Jamaica to build a prison there, into which Jamaicans convicted of offences in Britain, could be placed, under a bilateral agreement. I wondered if a similar arrangement might in time be agreed with the Algerian government.

WINDING UP

After this I arranged similar siege events at selected terrorist installations up and down the country. Using the same formula as I had done at Exborough and Exford, I attracted the attention of the Authorities to the presence of armed terrorists bearing illegal weapons, and openly admitting to membership of proscribed terrorist organizations including the IRA, Daesh, Al-Qaida and Islamic State. In the following weeks, the Authorities took several hundred men into military custody. Terrorist locations disclosed included a centre in the North East between Durham and Sunderland, Milton Keynes, several along the South coast of England, and four positioned around Greater London, near the Ring Road.

Meanwhile the attacks on me continued, and I removed more and more terrorists from the planet. By now I had killed over eight thousand – according to IRA records. Whenever I removed perpetrators, I deposited their bodies outside the British Isles. This meant that their bosses were unable to claim 'restitution' money. IRA units were not averse to downsizing, but after quite a long war of attrition, they were not only short of men, but also short of cash.

One day, after over two hundred men had been lost, I heard someone shout, 'OK, that is it!'

Then the two ringleaders behind the attacks removed the shielding on their faces, which they used to conceal their identity while on the electromagnetic system, and stepped out into the open. They had decided to surrender. Their junior managers also unmasked, put down their weapons and stepped out into the open, as if they had been playing a cricket match. They seemed to think that

stumps would now be drawn, that everyone would shake hands and that we would all go in for tea.

I was incensed that they thought they could dictate the end to this war, which I had not sought, and in which they had been the aggressors.

'It's not over until they're all dead, as far as I'm concerned,' I thought.

I began removing all of them as usual. However, as I was going through their buildings, picking off survivors, I could tell that some of the men were only there under duress. I discovered a group of men in their fifties who had long ago given up pretending to participate in their unit's work. They sat at their desks reading the newspaper. When they saw me coming they prepared themselves for death. But that did not feel right to me.

'You can't stay here,' I said, 'Where would you like to go?'

Some of them had friends in a Canadian unit. The original terrorist group locally had been IRA sympathisers who had come from Canada, and there had been many Anglo-Canadian terrorist exchanges over the years since then.

There was a Canadian mafia safe house in Ottawa at the top of Lake Hudson, near a place called Cape Victoria, where some of these guys had retired from active service, and lived in a large mansion in the country. The men said they would feel comfortable going there.

I knew the location, so I asked them to group themselves together in the centre of the room. Then I lifted them out of their environment and into the Canadian heathland outside the mansion house. The men were initially out of breath and a bit jet-lagged by this sudden transfer, and sat on the ground, taking in their surroundings. The weather was cool, and the air was fresh and bracing. There were pine woods in the background, and a spacious green hillside sloping down from the house.

They hadn't been there two minutes when they were spotted by the inmates, who immediately recognised them as their English friends. The Canadians came running out to greet the new arrivals, and escorted them into the house, where a warm welcome awaited them. One of the men from Britain got left behind, and I brought him

to the front door separately. The door was flung open, and there were cries of:

'There he is! Come in, come in!'

I looked in through the door and saw a high-domed hall with a log fire blazing. The new arrivals were sitting in a semi-circle in large comfy carved wooden chairs, with blankets around them and hot toddies in their hands. The stress of their former job, with its seven-day a week regime had gone from their faces. I don't know what happened to them after that, but it can't have been worse than what they had before.

So, finally, there were no local terrorists left in our area, although the threat to national security from overt Islamic State attacks still remained. I'm sure there were plenty more covert electronic terrorist units dotted about the British Isles, and I am equally sure that our British Military and the National Counter Terrorism Security Office and HM Prison Service are continuing to deal with them as discretely and efficiently as before, without causing alarm to the public.

As for me, I have not relapsed into a state of false security. I am acutely aware that the threat to our families, our towns and our way of life still exists, and I am alert, in case the terrorists ever return. If they do, I will be waiting for them.

NOTES

This book is about how Al-Qaida and their allies planned a covert war to take over the Western World by stealth relying largely on electromagnetic weapons. The battle lines were drawn around ordinary people's homes and towns. Some of the terrorists looked like us, sounded like us, and lived in the same street. British people were targeted using classified technologies stolen from Western countries' military, NATO and agencies responsible for international space stations. Attempts were made to infiltrate local authorities and law and order, and influence people in the public eye.

The terrorists lost the war, but this book is a warning, to remind us how different things might have been were it not for our security services and the British military. We became complacent and assumed that we would always have peace in our own land. Some people begrudged spending public money on defence, law and order, and our enemies saw their opportunity. They came in disguise, and we were not all sufficiently alert to what was going on around us.

The oil riches of Saudi Arabia and other oil-producing countries, mainly in the Middle East, brought new-found economic power to a group of people previously living much as they had done since the Middle Ages. Some within their ranks were frustrated by the mismanagement of their aging rulers, and what they saw as Western exploitation. Al-Qaida was born out of this environment, with the dream of revisiting the holy wars that brought about the expansion of the Ottoman Empire. This time they would win, and transform the Western World into Islamic Caliphates.

Al-Qaida's strategy was to infiltrate North America, working with the US mafia. The events of 9/11 were a product of this

partnership. They then planned to launch an all-out attack on Europe, starting in September 2011 – another 9/11. With the IRA and similar groups as additional collaborators, their original plan was to bring about a military coup in Britain, to be unveiled in time for the 2012 Olympics, in the spotlight of the whole world.

Thousands of terrorist foot-soldiers from North America, Ireland, Pakistan and North Africa were being amassed in Britain, ready to subdue the local populace, using 'undetectable' electromagnetic weapons. Not all were well-trained, and some were just economic migrants, but they all swore allegiance to the Islamic cause.

Several thousand sleepers within the British populace, mainly subcontractors for the IRA and Al-Qaida, were activated, with the intention of becoming a paramilitary police state, designed to keep British citizens in virtual prison camps, after the planned invasion from the Middle East, Asia and North Africa took effect in 2012.

Both the IRA and Al-Qaida had been actively involved in various parts of Africa for some time, particularly South Africa, Libya and Algeria. Illegal immigrants from North Africa had been promised large British houses and possessions, as a reward for their part in the uprising. Sources within the IRA told me that they had planned terrorist attacks on the London Stock Exchange and Tower Bridge, as part of a pre-emptive strike, to mark the beginning of the overt 'European theatre of war'.

We may smile at the naiveté of such ambitious objectives. They would never have succeeded. The IRA would agree with that. I learned from the IRA that when Al-Qaida asked them to come in on the 'holy war', they called on their most experienced Brigadier to advise them how to respond. He could see that the war was doomed to failure, but the IRA had consumed so much Al-Qaida funding in the past, with little to show for it except the creation of wealthy robber-barons, that he felt they had no alternative but to agree to Al-Qaida's request.

In the run-up to 2012, so-called 'sleepers', funded by various terrorist groups, including the North American mafia and the IRA, were called to awake. Some had been located in Britain for as long as

twenty-five years, quietly blending into the local communities. In Europe and North America, the terrorists sought to infiltrate the operations of local authorities, where there was less scrutiny from the centre of power.

In Britain, the sleepers, largely family members of IRA and IRA sympathisers, had been placed in posts in social services, privately-run health care units such as nursing homes, mental health institutions, the police and schools. Some of these people lived inoffensive lives, and were never called upon to act. Others were drug dealers, ex-convicts, people traffickers and child abusers. These were ordered to start the killing of British citizens covertly, beginning with the elderly, in nursing homes and hospices, or those living alone. They also targeted whistleblowers, if they reported terrorists to the Authorities.

Al-Qaida funded the smuggling of thousands of illegal immigrants into the UK, many of whom had received weapons training in North Africa. These people were absorbed into local communities, where their ethnicity went unremarked upon. Large groups were located in Birmingham, Bradford, Manchester and Greater London, particularly East London. Islamic activists were placed around smaller sea ports across the British Isles, where drugs and people trafficking operated. They mixed with UK-born people who left to fight with ISIS in Syria and Iraq, and returned, seeking to radicalise youth. Where I lived, Al-Qaida was bringing in sixteen Algerian, Moroccan and Kenyan Daesh illegal immigrants every week, together with twelve experienced Islamic State soldiers.

The terrorist attack on Westminster Bridge in 2017 was carried out by a man from the Asian community who had recently lived in East London, Forest Gate, for a year before moving to Birmingham. He had also worked in Saudi. His current wife lived in Stratford. The subsequent terrorist attack on civilians on London Bridge was carried out by three men from Barking.

To those like myself, who lived for many years in the Ilford area, this came as no surprise. We watched as the entire area became a hotbed for drugs and people trafficking. The connection between these activities and terrorism appears with regularity. I noticed a

strong familial connection between groups in East London and groups in Birmingham. The Daily Telegraph, dated 23 March 2017, reports that a recent study found that a tenth of all Britain's convicted Islamist terrorists, twenty-six in total, came from just five council wards in Birmingham.

In Europe, we have learnt the hard way that tolerance of suspected terrorists and containment rather than eradication of organised crime lead to a deterioration of society and our way of life. They also create a fertile breeding ground for future acts of terrorism. According to Express.co.uk, dated May 23 2017, figures revealed in a quarterly Home Office report showed that:

- The number of potential terrorists being watched in the UK at the time of the Manchester bombing had swelled to nearly three thousand five hundred.

- Latest figures show that the three thousand potential terrorists monitored since 2015 has grown after the return of UK-born people who left to fight with ISIS.

- About four hundred ISIS-trained fighters are believed to have returned from war zones in Syria and Iraq.

Our Authorities were always alert, and they operated discreetly, within the laws provided for that purpose, to deal with the threat, without avoid alarming the public unduly. On 16 September 2010, in a speech on the threat to national security, the Director General of MI5, Jonathan Evans, said:

'We have seen a persistent rise in terrorist activity and ambition in Northern Ireland over the last three years… we cannot exclude the possibility that they might seek to extend their attacks to Great Britain, as violent Republican groups have traditionally done…It is also clear that many of the dissident Republican activists operate at the same time as terrorists and organised criminals, with involvement in both smuggling and the illegal narcotics market, despite public denunciations of drug dealing'.

On the subject of Al-Qaida, Jonathan Evans said,

'The fact that there are real plots uncovered on a fairly regular basis demonstrates that there is a persistent intent on the part of Al-Qaida and its associates to attack the UK…Some of those we see

being encouraged or tasked by Al-Qaida associates to mount attacks here are not people with the skills or character to make credible terrorists. [I can vouch for that] Others are.'

The security services of the world worked together to ensure that the 2012 Olympics took place safely for participants and spectators. On 25 June 2012, Jonathan Evans said:

'At the forefront of our minds are the Olympic and Paralympic Games. The security preparations for the games have been long and thorough…We are working as part of a mature and well-developed counter-terrorist community in the UK and with the close support and co-operation of friendly Services overseas, who have been extremely generous in their assistance.'

The 2012 revolutionary coup planned by Al-Qaida did not happen, faced with the cooperation of military and security forces from numerous countries. The order went out from Al-Qaida to terrorist collaborators that the 'revolution' had been postponed until 2015. The reason given was that preparations were not ready in time for 2012. But in 2014, Al-Qaida instructed its employees to withdraw from the British Isles, owing to the proactive initiatives of the British military and security services. This was tantamount to admitting that they had lost the war in Britain, although they continued to fund terrorist groups active on the British mainland, including Islamic State.

Al-Qaida had bases in both Ireland and France, from where it supported the planning of attacks on Britain. After Al-Qaida's withdrawal, the North American mafia and IRA were left supporting private armies they had amassed to run prison camps, which would never now be needed. They were not out of pocket, but their *raison d'être* had shifted dramatically. Gradually their leaders began to leave the British Isles for destinations like the Seychelles, the Caribbean, Ireland and North Africa.

Those unable to leave the UK were left in limbo, as their glorious revolution faded into a fantasy world of extremism. The emphasis had by now shifted to the overt terrorism of Islamic State. Those terrorists still funded by Al-Qaida continued the covert war against British citizens, including myself, mainly because they could

not see any way out that would not be construed as failure. Activists not close to the centre of power were losing Al-Qaida funding, and reverting to banditry and organised crime, in order to earn a living

By 2015, Islamic State was a key player on the terrorist stage. It held territories in Iraq and Syria, and created armies in over a dozen countries. (Source: *Washington Times*, January 4, 2017.) As Al-Qaida began to withdraw its own staff from the UK, Islamic State were coming to the forefront increasingly in Europe. British Jihadists who went to fight in Syria, returned to the UK and continued to support Islamic State.

Al-Qaida's policy was that those planning terrorist attacks should do so outside the country they were targeting. Al-Qaida was funding the importation of Islamic State officers to the UK to plan attacks on the European mainland. Islamic State officers planning terrorist attacks on the British mainland were mainly based outside the UK, although they controlled terrorist cells within Britain.

As the ISIS campaigns in Syria and Iraq began to stall, a confidential US Government report by the National Counterterrorism Centre, circulated on 28 December 2016 to counterterrorism agencies across the country, stated that ISIS had abandoned trying to put together huge plots such as the September 11 attacks, and warned counterterrorism agencies of a 'new landscape' where lone killers could strike and massacre quickly. This report reflected terrorist attacks in Nice and Berlin in 2016, and anticipated the 2017 UK terrorist attacks on Westminster Bridge, Manchester and London Bridge.

According to the *Washington Times*, the report said,

'The steady rise in the number of lone actor operations is a trend which coincides with the deepening and broadening of the digital revolution as well as the encouragement of such operations by terrorist groups, because intensified [counterterrorism] operations have disrupted their ability to launch larger plots...

Lone actors now have greater capability to create and broadcast material than a decade ago, while violent extremists can contact and interact with potential recruits with greater ease'.

The report warned of the danger posed by small autonomous cells or individuals who do not report to a central command. It highlighted an ISIS terrorist training magazine, published online, which recommended the use of vehicles to mow down civilians in Nice or Berlin-style attacks.

(Sources: *Washington Times*, 4 January 2017, Daily Mail, 5 January 2017.)

While each of the subsequent terrorist attacks in Europe had its own idiosyncrasies, it is my contention that the covert electromagnetic infrastructure painstakingly constructed by Al-Qaida over many years in European countries, including the UK, as described in this book, provided a network of support which made it easier for terrorists to operate. There were safehouses within the electromagnetic environment in the UK and France, ready to receive and conceal ISIS officers plotting terrorist attacks.

On 10 July 2017, Baroness Manningham-Buller, former Head of MI5, said in the House of Lords:

'On the tempo, it is clear that the pace has accelerated markedly. During the five years I was privileged to lead MI5 -2002 to 2007 - we had fifteen significant plots, three of which were not detected in advance. These were: 7/7, evidently; 21/7 two weeks later, when the detonators failed to work; and Richard Reid, the shoe bomber, who was stopped by an alert air hostess.

'Now we know from the Home Secretary that after Westminster [the attack on Westminster Bridge on 22 March 2017] and before Manchester [the Manchester Arena attack on 22 May 2017] my former colleagues and the police detected and prevented from materialising five other plots in as many weeks. That shows there is a very high level of plots indeed...

The second factor is the scale of the problem – we have already heard the figures – which I think is genuinely unprecedented. I am not one to exaggerate, but when we are told that MI5 has five hundred active investigations, involving three thousand subjects of interest – as well as a vast pool of some twenty thousand other, on whom it cannot focus at the moment, but about whom there have been past concerns, and whom it would like to go back to look at, if

time and resources allowed – it is pretty serious. Even I find this scarcely imaginable.'

(Source: Hansard, 10 July 2017, pages 1091 – 1092.)

There are a lot of assertions in this book. What evidence is there to support them? I spoke to many terrorists, and learned who their masters were, what training they had received, how they occupied their time and what attacks they had carried out. Some of the evidence is based on personal experience, including observations of the activities of the British military and security services. But personal contacts and personal experience alone do not constitute evidence in a court of law. You need the evidence of at least two witnesses for that. Some of the points made in this book are supported by reports in the press, or official statements by the Authorities. Others are not. Where there is only my own report of what took place, it is obviously nothing more than that. But it is my expectation that future events will tend to confirm or support what I have described.

Other victims of terrorism have told their own stories. There are points of convergence, but on the use of secret technologies to construct the covert electromagnetic terrorist environment, published material is scarce. Some of the technical developments I describe are hard to accept. I realise that, and do not expect to convince a skeptical reader. But my hope is that more about the covert use of these technologies by criminals and terrorists will enter the public domain at a future date.

Some of the statements in this book may be incorrect. I have no special expertise in terrorism or sonic and electromagnetic technologies, being just an old pensioner, so it would be surprising if I had got everything right. But I have reported what·I heard, saw and experienced, to the best of my ability. My reason for doing so is that these developments need to be recorded and brought to people's attention, so that if they are faced with such a terrorist threat they will be able to recognise it. I always reported anything significant to the Authorities, and as the book demonstrates, the Authorities always took such reports seriously and responded appropriately.

Technologies behind secret terror attacks

Much of what happens in this book is consistent with mainstream science. Occasionally, I give references to internet articles and websites which provide scientific insights into what is going on. You don't need to check them out, but if you do, it will become apparent that modern science is already in the realms of what we describe as science fiction. I use Daily Mail Science articles a lot, because they reporting cutting edge scientific developments in a way that is understandable to non-scientists like myself.

The terrorists that attacked me operated in an environment that was underpinned by ultrasound and electromagnetic technologies. Ultrasound imaging can show you sights that the human eye cannot normally see.

A number of terrorist groups, including Al-Qaida, Islamic State, the US mafia and the IRA, have been working together using a multinational ultrasound and electromagnetic computer architecture, designed by the US mafia, which gives super-normal sight and sound, and which you can enter, like a secret world, once you put your wi-fi headphones on. In that environment, you can speak to each other without others hearing you, - in this case, via private commercial satellite. Add MRI scanning technologies, and you can see each other without others seeing you, and you can be linked, as if by Skype, across any distance. If you have the right receivers and transmitters, you can live in an entirely different world, which is invisible and inaudible to other people.

Using these technologies, terrorists constructed secret offices, secret communications systems, secret towns and a secret global network that interpenetrates our everyday world. This global

electromagnetic and ultrasonic architecture enabled them to carry out covert attacks with much less risk of discovery.

This book demonstrates how covert use has been made of ultrasound as a communications medium for terrorists and organised crime, working together. They can talk to each other silently, and all you can see is someone listening to their smartphone, using earphones or an earpiece. Most of the terrorists have micro-chip transmitters located within their heads, which enable them to locate each other, and send and receive silent communications.

These technologies are already available in the outside world. There are computer games on the market that can be controlled using the mind alone. You just need a wireless headset that links you up to the application software using ultrasound. This is described as the brain-computer interface. On 1 December 2012, Scientific American listed six electronic devices you can control with your thoughts.

See: www.scientificamerican.com/article/pogue-6-electronic-devices-you-can-control-with-your-thoughts.

Other futuristic devices include using thought to drive your car, controlling a prosthetic arm by thoughts and controlling a toy helicopter.

See: www.hongkiat.com/blog/brain-controlled-gadgets.

Using the electromagnetic architecture, US mafia technicians created a virtual reality environment, within which employees operate on a different level from the everyday world. This environment could be extended to your house, by hacking into your house wiring, if you have old-fashioned electrical arrangements. A favourite hacking entry point used by terrorists is the time clock that operates the thermostat in some gas boilers. It is easy to hack into them at close range, if you obtain the remote-control device provided with the gas boiler.

Many terrorist offices look like underground call centers. There are rooms full of people sitting at desks with laptops and headphones. But they are deep in another environment, communicating across the road or across the globe. In some cases, they are manipulating avatars, designed to conceal their identity while carrying out electronic and electromagnetic attacks on innocent

people remotely, using locators for their victims that work like Global Positioning Satellite coordinates, linked by wi-fi to a private commercial satellite.

Al-Qaida planned to use these covert technologies to take control of people inside their homes, and to create invisible prison camps in which people could be restrained, managed and killed, without anybody realising it. This was planned as part of Al-Qaida's war on Christendom. The process was insidious, proceeding a little bit at a time. The objective was stark - to kill white people and replace them with non-whites.

The targeting of old people's homes went ahead in advance of other types of attacks, because old people didn't move around much. They sat in the same chair, and spent a lot of time in bed, making them easy targets to find. If they reported attacks, they were unlikely to be believed, and if they died, no one would be very surprised, because of their age.

That does not mean that old people did not notice if they were being attacked. From what I heard, they often watched calmly and fearlessly, fully aware that no one would ever believe them if they reported what was happening to them. I was told that one old lady gave her youthful attacker an old-fashioned look.

The Al-Qaida initiative to wipe out Christendom began in September 2011. In 2013, a British government document, made public by the Health Service Journal, revealed that statisticians had noted an unexplained increase of about twenty-five thousand in deaths of elderly people, mainly women, between the summers of 2012, and 2013.

(See: www.telegraph.co.uk/news/health/12158930/Biggest-annual-rise-in-deaths-for-almost-fifty-years-prompts-warnings-of-crisis-in-elderly-care.

And:www.independent.co.uk/news/uk/home-news/thousands-of-unexplained-and-unexpected-deaths-among-elderly-revealed-in-leaked-government-analysis-8731985.)

There is no causal link between these statistics and covert terrorist attacks on the elderly; but if there was a link, a rise in deaths of elderly people would be the first thing to look for.

See: www.bbc.co.uk/news/health-40608256

It must be stressed that there is nothing to link these figures with covert terrorist attacks on the elderly, but given that the IRA have been funded by Al-Qaida to target elderly white people in 'Christendom', it is interesting that the increase in life expectancy trends reverses around 2011-2012, which is when the Al-Qaida objective kicked in.

An IRA terrorist called Karen T, told me that she had started her terrorist training with attacks on old people's homes in Devon, and had known the perpetrators involved in the scandals that resulted in the closure of the notorious Veilstone care home there.

Electromagnetic Weapons

In this book, there are a lot of references to the use of electromagnetic weapons, both by terrorists, and in some cases, by the military of NATO allied countries. What are we talking about? I read on Wikipedia that when used against humans, electromagnetic radiation weapons can have dramatic effects. Such as an intense burning sensation caused by Raytheon's 'Active Denial System'. Also, more subtle effects such as the creation – at a distance – of a sense of anxiety or dread, intense drowsiness, or confusion in an individual or a group of people. Three military advantages of such weapons are:

1. That the individual or group of people would not necessarily realize that they were being targeted by such a device.

2. That microwave radiation, like some other radio frequency radiation, can easily penetrate most common building materials.

3. That with specialized antennas, the radiation and its effects can be focused on either an individual or a large area such as a city or a country.

Potential military/law enforcement uses for such weapons include:

1 Capability to influence an enemy force to flee rather than stand and fight, by imposing on them a sense of great anxiety or impending disaster.

2   Ability to convince captured enemy combatants that the greater sense of physical well-being which seemed to accompany their being even slightly cooperative was much more desirable than the overwhelming sense of uneasiness and dread associated with their being uncooperative or hostile.

3   Ability to impose a feeling of overwhelming drowsiness on an already weary enemy force.

4   Ability to deprive an enemy force of sound, uninterrupted sleep for a prolonged period.

5   Capability to persuade, indirectly the close comrades of an enemy soldier that the soldier – perhaps an infantry soldier who admittedly hears voices or strange noises that no one else is hearing – is mentally unsound and is not to be taken seriously. Such feelings, voices, or strange noises and dreams can be imposed on the enemy with some precision by specialized, microwave-type radiation antennas.

See: www.en.wikipedia.org/wiki/Directed-energy-weapon

This book describes how terrorists used similar devices to target British civilians covertly, in the knowledge that their activities would go undetected.

The terrorists could locate me by means of the microchip transmitter they had inserted in the back of my head. Having located me, they could direct their electromagnetic attacks at me. They could make use of clinical devices normally used to save people's lives, to cause actual bodily harm to their victims. For example, a clinical device designed to keep your heart beating, could also be used to stop the heart, and could be operated by remote control, using wi-fi.

Some remote attacks rely on 'telemetry' to find different parts of the body and to obtain feedback on whether they hit the target or caused harm. I also read on Wikipedia that Telemetry is an automated communications process by which measurements and other data are collected at remote or, inaccessible points and transmitted to receiving equipment for monitoring. Even though the term commonly refers to wireless data transfer mechanisms, e.g. using radio, ultrasonic or infrared systems, it also encompasses data transferred over other media such as telephone or computer network,

optical link or other wired communications like power line carriers. There are many modern telemetry systems that take advantage of the low cost and ubiquity of GSM (Global System for Mobile communications) networks, by using SMS (Short Messaging Service) to receive and transmit telemetry data.

See: www.en.m.wikipedia.org/wiki/Telemetry

Terrorists also use infrared sensors to define the outlines of bodies inside houses.

Once the British military came on the scene, they blocked any radio wave attacks that they detected. This meant that the terrorists were restricted to low-level microwave radiation and electromagnetic technologies. If they strayed above the limit, the British military sent an airborne craft that disconnected their electrical equipment from the commercial satellite and burned out their wi-fi routers, using automatic targeting.

Fantasy and science-fiction reflect reality

Writers and film producers have made use of so-called magical events, where people can do superhuman things, both good and bad. In most of those books, ordinary people carry on living their lives in the background, unaware of what may be happening around them. The Harry Potter movies, the Twilight movies, and science fiction movies like the Matrix series and Avatar are examples. I suspect that there are people who have experienced ultrasound and electromagnetic environments for themselves, and have used that experience to inspire their work.

Recently I went to see the movies *Ghostbusters II* and 'Fantastic Beasts and How to Find Them'. When the special effects came on, I felt a surge of recognition, because I'd been there, and had done things like that. I also felt sure that some of the people behind the special effects must have been there too.

You can regard the advanced science events described in this book as fiction. But that does not mean that the events described didn't happen. It could mean that they happened outside normal human perceptions, using technology enhancements. Remember the last Harry Potter book, when Harry temporarily dies? The

environment goes faded and beige, as if a thin transparent curtain was drawn across it. That is how an electromagnetic environment might look if you only have part of the technology to perceive it.

Synthetic telepathy may be used as a form of psychological warfare in which an external technology picks up and matches your private brain waves using what is known as 'brain entrainment'. The technology can then broadcast voices to your wavelength. It's a bit like two open-topped sports cars speeding along in parallel, and someone jumping from one into the other. If that happens, you've been 'brain-jacked'. The risks of this happening have already been recognised.

Examples of possible attacks include altering stimulation settings so that patients with chronic pain are caused to be in even greater pain;

A sophisticated attacker could potentially even induce behavioural changes such as hyper sexuality or pathological gambling.

As regards hostile use of synthetic telepathy, I have heard several reports of the IRA and North American mafia using synthetic telepathy to make victims think they are going mad. There was a time when such 'symptoms' were regarded exclusively as an indicator of schizophrenia. Times have changed.

It remains to be established to what extent, if at all, this might reflect the increased use of synthetic telepathy for psychological warfare by terrorists.

Chapter Notes

INTRODUCTION

When people are microchipped, wouldn't they be aware of it? In some cases, yes, but microchips are getting smaller all the time. On 19 November 1999, BBC News Online Editor Dr David Whitehouse reported that scientists had produced the world's smallest transistor.

Microchipping people is nothing new. The US military are reported to be using micro-chips to enhance the performance of soldiers. According to the Daily Mail, 28 September 2015:

When it comes to eye cameras, the Pentagon has stated that the American military announced they were developing eye camera prostheses to help their soldiers in the field.

See: www.dailymail.co.uk/sciencetech/article-2187276/U-S-Army-Soldiers-able-to-run-Olympic-speed-wont-need-food-gene-technology.

On the internet, I found that there had been a lot of research on putting cameras in the eyes of insects and animals. I found that a word had been coined to describe living organisms that had been given embedded technologies – 'cyborgs'.

These developments have had health benefits, for example in helping blind and partially sighted people to see, and strengthening short-term memory in Parkinson's Disease sufferers. But in the hands of criminals and terrorists, electronic implants in people's heads have been used to create slaves, with no escape from their masters.

On use of microwaves and other devices to make people ill, see: www.adst.org/2013/09/microwaving-embassy-moscow-another-perspective

www.bbc.co.uk/news/world-us-canada-40883020